W9-AGT-952

two
wings
to
fly
away

penny mickelbury

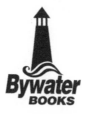

Bywater BOOKS

Ann Arbor
2019

Bywater Books

Copyright © 2019 Penny Micklebury

All rights reserved. No part of this book may be
reproduced, stored in a retrieval system, or transmitted
in any form or by any means, without prior permission
in writing from the publisher.

Print ISBN: 978-1-61294-149-3

Bywater Books First Edition: May 2019

Printed in the United States of America on acid-free paper.

Cover designer: Ann McMan, TreeHouse Studio

Bywater Books
PO Box 3671
Ann Arbor MI 48106-3671
www.bywaterbooks.com

This novel is a work of fiction. All characters and events
described by the author are fictitious. No resemblance
to real persons, dead or alive, is intended.

This book is dedicated to:

Eugenia Cooper-Newton.
What a marvelous friendship we've enjoyed Genie,
across years and miles.
And, like the TV bunny, we just keep going and going . . .

And also to:
Brave women everywhere.
Then and now—we stand on your shoulders.

CHAPTER ONE

"Slave catcher!"

The hissed word hung in the air, freezing Eugenia Oliver's insides colder than the damp November evening air chilled her skin. Though Eli's bare feet made no sound on the worn cobblestones and his two brief words were whispered, Genie's body reverberated as if a cannon had been fired next to her. She was headed home. She was almost there. Almost safe and warm. But she changed direction and walked toward Main Street. The fast, loud pounding of her heart and her suddenly dry mouth were her fear manifested. If a slave catcher really was prowling in the Quarter and Genie really was walking toward him instead of running away . . .

Dressed as Eugene Oliver as she often was, because even a Black man was safer than a Black woman alone, she moved with purpose toward the danger coming her way. The white man slowed his gait from a trot to a long-legged stride as he entered Thatcher Lane. Definitely looking for someone. His head swiveled from side to side. His eyes searched but found nothing but shuttered windows and barred doors. Genie was annoyed with herself. She should have heard the danger in the silence. It was supper time in Thatcher Lane. There should have been the clamor of children and women, the clatter of horses and wagons. There should have been the call of the lamplighter. Instead there was the silence of fear that only the presence of a white man could bring. And the anger. *That* was more dangerous than the fear.

Genie took a deep breath and caressed the derringer pistol in her pocket. She and the white man were close together now. She knew her neighbors could see her as clearly as the stranger. She also knew that inside half a dozen of the barred and shuttered houses were pistols and shotguns aimed at the white man. If he were foolish enough or arrogant enough to come alone into their Lane looking for runaway slaves, he would die foolish and arrogant. And then they all would die worse than that because even in Philadelphia, the killing of a white person was the most unforgivable of transgressions. They would die and their homes would be burned to ashes. Genie shivered, and November was not to blame.

This man, however, was no slave catcher. Genie was certain of that though she could not imagine who he was and certainly not what he wanted. Not in this area of Philadelphia, inhabited solely by Blacks, free and otherwise. The man removed his hat as Genie approached, nodded a greeting, and spoke before she could speak. "Good evening, sir."

Genie returned the greeting, adding a question. "Have you lost your way?"

"I've lost a boy I was chasing."

"Is the boy a thief?"

"Why, no, not that I'm aware . . . ah! If not a thief, why was I chasing him? A good question and I've a good answer."

The man spoke confidently. "He has information I need but he ran when I approached him. I chased him and saw him turn into this lane. Perhaps you saw him?" And the man described Eli as if he possessed an artist's etching of the boy.

Genie studied the stranger: His clothes were well made and of good quality, though not the clothes of a wealthy man. But confidence aside, he seemed too worldly to be naive enough to follow—to chase—a Black man into his own residential quarter, given the unrest of recent times, not to mention the encroaching darkness. "Do you know where you are, sir?"

"I am lost, to tell the truth . . ." He allowed his words to trail off as he looked very closely at the Black man to find the deeper meaning of his question. "I know I'm in the Black quarter if that's what you're asking."

"The boy you were chasing thinks you're a slave catcher."

"Good God!" Genie watched the surprise spread across the man's chiseled features, and then the revulsion, and finally the denial. "I am nothing of the sort! It is a heinous and cruel occupation, worthy of . . . I can think of no worthy punishment."

Genie could think of several worthy punishments but she dared not speak them. After all, the stranger was a white man, even if not a slave catcher. "Will you walk with me out to the main street, sir, so the lamplighter can begin his duties and the people resume theirs?" Genie turned and walked slowly out of the dark lane. She had turned her back to a white man. A stranger. She hoped he would follow. The stranger turned a scrutinizing gaze on his location. Houses lined both sides of the narrow street, and even in the swiftly falling dusk he could see they were well-tended, as were the tiny gardens that fronted them. He noticed slight movement at several curtained windows and the dark roundness of at least two long gun barrels aimed at him. Smoke rose from practically every chimney yet no lamp light was visible in any of the more than two dozen houses of various shapes and sizes that fronted the street. Dark within and without as the lamplighter stood silent and watchful—and fearful. And he himself was the cause—of the darkness and the fear. He hurried to catch up to Genie.

"Boston and New York have gas lights in the streets," he muttered, as much to have something to say as to cover the shame he felt at causing so much unnecessary discomfort.

"As does Philadelphia," Genie answered in a reasonable if subdued tone. "Just a bit west and south of here."

The stranger grunted acknowledgment of that truth and an understanding of the reason for it. He and Genie stood at the intersection of the lane and the main road where the already lit oil lamps were smoking and sputtering. They cast a golden glow on the carriages and carts, shops and stores of the wide avenue that ran perpendicular to Thatcher Lane. It was a mostly commercial avenue though there were a few houses, all of which appeared to be owned by a Colored person. Not only was this avenue unfamiliar to him, it was foreign to him. It was a fully functional commercial street and before this moment he had not known it existed. "I am Ezra MacKaye," he said, extending his hand. "I apologize to you and to your neighbors. I meant you no harm."

"Eugene Oliver is my name and your apology is accepted," Genie replied, returning the firm grip. "And if I can help you, Mr. MacKaye, talk to that boy for you, I will. Unless you intend to bring harm to him."

"And then you'll not help?"

"I will not."

They regarded each other. The issue of whether or not the boy in question was indeed a runaway slave hung like a vapor in the night air between them, but that no longer was Ezra's main concern. He kept his attention on the matter at hand: Eugene Oliver was not a tall man or a large one—he stood five foot seven or eight, was lithe and wiry, and his clothes hung loosely on him as if too large. Ezra thought perhaps they'd once belonged to a larger man and Eugene had received them as hand-me-downs, as was often the case for poor people no matter their color or gender. Ezra MacKaye towered over Eugene Oliver as if he were but a youth. He could no doubt overpower and subdue the smaller man if necessary—but he'd have his work cut out for him: Eugene Oliver held himself as if ready to spring, all his senses on alert. The white man, too, was alert, though he felt no need for a defensive posture. Finally, Ezra spoke. "I am a private enquiry agent, Mr. Oliver."

"Pinkerton's?" Genie asked, eyes widening with interest.

MacKaye's left eyebrow lifted slightly, as did the right corner of his mouth. "You know of Pinkerton's?"

"Everyone knows of Pinkerton's," Genie said.

"I was, when I lived in Chicago," MacKaye said. "I was sent here to do a job for Pinkerton's and I found that I preferred Philadelphia to Chicago. So, now I am a private agent."

Genie nodded but did not speak, and Ezra told his story: The son of one of Philadelphia's wealthy and powerful men had incurred a gambling debt he could not pay. The young man could not ask his father for money as it was not the first time he'd incurred such debt, so he stole several pieces of his mother's jewelry to pawn and blamed the maid. However, the maid had been in service to the young man's family for more years than he had been on earth. She also was deemed more trustworthy. Caught between his parents' wrath and his bookmaker's vengeance, the young man had scarpered. His parents wanted him—and the jewelry—returned, without involving the police. They hired Ezra for the job.

"The boy I chased into your lane—and I expect you know his name and where he lives—shines shoes and runs errands for the guests of the gambling parlor where the young man in question incurred his debt."

"That would be Dandy McDaniel's place at the end of Essex Street, near the water." Genie made it a statement and not a question. Ezra's eyes narrowed and he nodded. "And the young man in question would be Edward Cortlandt," Genie said, "son of Arthur, the banker."

Ezra erupted. "Confound it, man! How do you know that? This is a matter of utmost secrecy and delicacy! You can't just bandy that name about!"

"But I haven't bandied it about," Genie replied gravely. "I spoke it only to you and you already knew it."

Ezra calmed himself and met the Black man's steady gaze, as much of it as he could see beneath the bowler hat he wore low on his forehead. Ezra thought the man might be trying to hide his eyes. What he could see of them remained steady and focused on him. Eyes that Ezra felt would see inside him.

Philadelphia was home to many Blacks. More, Ezra had heard

it said, than anywhere outside the South. Some were former slaves while others were born free. More than a few, however, were, in fact, runaways, which would account for the reaction of the boy he was chasing. Was it possible that the boy was a runaway slave? *Of course, it was possible*, Ezra thought to himself, and he saw the sliver of eyes beneath the low-hanging bowler narrow. Eugene Oliver was watching him think.

Many of Philadelphia's Blacks were educated and a few of them were even wealthy, relatively speaking—the existence of the avenue where they stood and the lane that ran into it was proof of that—but Ezra had personal dealings only with Black servants: cooks, maids, shoe-shine boys, valets, livery attendants. Gene Oliver was proving to be a different experience. Here was a Black man who, even thinking that Ezra might have been a slave catcher, strode forward to meet him without a trace of fear. His right hand, though, was buried deep within his pocket. Now it was Ezra who felt a prickle of fear as a truth belatedly dawned: Oliver almost certainly had a weapon—a gun or a knife—and he would not hesitate to protect himself if necessary!

More and more lately, the Blacks were forced to protect themselves against impoverished and itinerant European immigrants, especially the Irish. They seemed to arrive in America with a hard hatred for the Blacks, as if the Colored people were responsible for the troubles in Ireland that had caused them to flee their homeland. They brought with them a determination to challenge the Blacks for a place in the established order. The passage six years previously of the Fugitive Slave Act seemed to legitimize their hatred of a people they didn't know and knew nothing about. Ezra, aware of how closely Oliver was watching him, extracted a narrow white card from his waistcoat pocket. "If the boy tells you anything that could be of use to me, Mr. Oliver, I'd appreciate it if you would let me know."

Genie accepted the card. "If young Master Cortlandt is still in Philadelphia, Mr. MacKaye, I will tell you where to find him." Ezra's stare told them how unlikely he found the Colored man's claim. Genie held the stare briefly before glancing down at the embossed card she held. "Do you know your way back to Flegler Street?" That query answered the question of whether Ezra's companion could read, and Genie gave directions before he could respond. "A pleasant evening to you, Mr. MacKaye." Genie touched her hat, nodded at Ezra, and turned toward Thatcher Lane and home. She walked slowly, listening for MacKaye's footsteps. After a brief hesitation she heard the white man's long-legged stride take him away, toward his own part of town. Genie inhaled deeply, with relief and to fill her lungs with enough air for the low, three-tone whistle that signaled all clear in the lane. She heard it picked up and carried until it sounded like a tune in harmony. She felt the fear she'd held since Eli's warning finally drain away. She ran her fingers over the raised letters of Ezra's card before putting it in her pocket, and she watched Thatcher Lane return to life. Doors and windows eased open a bit and cooking smells wafted out onto the night air. Genie's stomach rumbled. She was tired and hungry as well as cold, but before she could warm and feed herself she needed to talk to Eli.

Able to return to her true self, she walked slowly down the lane then abruptly turned sideways, flattened her shoulders, and sidled into a narrow space between two houses. She smiled at the thought of Ezra MacKaye, or any white man, looking for Eli here. Nobody who didn't live in the lane would or could know that behind the buildings on the east side of the street was an alley of smaller houses, some no more substantial than sheds and lean-tos, where the poorest Blacks—and the runaway slaves—lived. She stepped carefully into the Back Street and waited for her eyes to adjust. The meager glow of the street lamps did not penetrate this darkness, and those who lived here did not leave their doors and windows open except in the worst of summer's heat. She walked slowly, letting people see her in the darkness, letting them recognize her as one of them, letting them see that they were safe. She stopped in front of the shack that Eli shared with three other parentless boys but it was dark and felt empty.

She raised a hand to knock, then thought better of it. What could she say? *If you boys are runaways, go away before you jeopardize us all?* For it was not Eli's presence that constituted their jeopardy. The color of their skin and the fact of their existence was what jeopardized them all. She had no justification to accuse them.

Genie Oliver turned away from Eli's door and toward home, a mere four dozen steps back the other direction, to what probably was the most substantial structure in the Back Street: A real, if small, house with a brick foundation, a front porch, a chimney, and a peaked roof instead of a flat one. A swift but all-seeing glance into the surrounding darkness confirmed that no other person was present. Genie Oliver stepped up onto the porch, lifted the latch on the door, and stepped into the home where, with a relieved sigh, she returned to the self that didn't require the safety of camouflage. Miss Eugenia Oliver hastily removed the bowler that hung low on her head to obscure the woman's eyes of her face, and the scarf that contained the thick, heavy hair and gave the bowler its tight fit. She had watched Ezra MacKaye scrutinize her, had watched him think that she was small for a man, one who could easily be overcome in a fight. She also realized that while most women immediately saw through her disguise, no man ever had and probably never would. She quickly lit the wood that she'd laid in the fireplace that morning, and also in the stove. By the time she removed the layers of clothes she wore to give the appearance of more bulk than her slender body possessed, her little cottage would be warm, too.

Firelight illuminated most of the well-furnished room but Genie lit two kerosene lamps and the brightness permeated her spirit as well. She looked around and felt what she always felt when she surveyed her surroundings: No matter what happened in the outside world, in here she was clean and safe and comfortable and—free. No, Ezra MacKaye was not a slave catcher, but one day one of them would recognize her and she'd either have to kill him or be caught. True, Eugene Oliver was an effective disguise. People saw what they expected to see and Genie Oliver dressed

8

like a man, therefore he was a man. Besides, Eugenia Oliver did not exist until a young woman escaped bondage in Maryland and gave herself that name en route to freedom in Philadelphia. Now, wrapped tightly and warmly in a heavy robe, her feet snug within fur-lined animal skin slippers, Genie Oliver banished all thoughts of slavery and went into the kitchen, hoping that the stew was warm enough to eat and that the water in the coffee pot was hot enough to brew a strong cup of her favorite beverage.

She was returning the kerosene lantern to the mantel when a soft knock on the door almost caused her to drop it. She wrapped her hand around the derringer, transferred out of habit from street clothes to the pocket of the robe. She stood silently beside the door, listening. The whispered words she heard relaxed her and she opened the door. "Come in, William."

"I'm sorry to bother you, Eugenia," William Tillman said as he entered, appreciating as he always did the simple beauty of the small house.

"You're never a bother, William. Come in and warm yourself."

He thanked her and stood as close as was safe to the now roaring fire in the grate. The scent of her stew made his stomach rumble, and he knew that to delay her meal further would be rude. "You know how much we appreciate your bravery, Genie, but I do wish you wouldn't put yourself at risk that way."

She smiled at him. Using her name meant that he wasn't really angry though certainly he was concerned, as well he might be: What she'd done was dangerous, but not as dangerous as permitting a white man to wander their streets at will. Besides, William had been protecting her since her arrival in Philadelphia and she was used to it. "It is always my intention to be careful, William, as much as it is to help secure our safety." She still caressed the derringer in her pocket. Now she withdrew it and placed it on the mantel, and he laughed, then sobered as she recounted her conversation with Ezra MacKaye. He listened, waiting until she finished talking before asking a question that really was more of a statement.

"So there's no reason Mr. MacKaye should return here to Thatcher Lane."

"None." She held up his card. "I'll see him before he needs to think of Eli again."

"Are Eli and those other boys safe?"

"As safe as any of us are, William."

There being no adequate response to that, William Tillman stood and walked to the door, his body already tensing for the cold air he'd meet. "I'll send a message about our next meeting," he said, shaking her hand. "Please be careful and safe, Eugenia."

"You as well, William. And let Adelaide know I'll see her bright and early in the morning." She opened the door and he rushed out before too much cold air could rush in. She quickly closed the door and stood before the fire for a moment to banish the chill before serving her dinner. Their next meeting. Would it be sooner rather than later? There was no way to know or predict, which meant that they didn't know whether they would have days or mere hours to prepare for the arrival of Miss Harriet Tubman and the slaves she was delivering to freedom. They just had to be ready.

CHAPTER TWO

True to her word, Genie set out to work early the next morning. It was barely light, and she didn't know until she passed through the space between the Back Street and Thatcher Lane that Arthur would be there to meet her and walk her the short distance to work—half the distance up Thatcher Lane to the main street, turn right, fifth storefront on the north side of the street, the one with the red door. She was dressed as Miss Eugenia Oliver, a gentlewoman of Color. Her hand, deep within the pocket of her voluminous skirt, caressed the ever-present derringer. She was not afraid, not like last night. She was, however, wisely cautious, as always.

"Good morning, Arthur," she said cheerfully—and gratefully—when she saw him. He was the only person she trusted as much as she trusted William.

"'Morning, Miss Eugenia. How you today?" He touched his hat politely and offered his arm, which she took. Arthur was perhaps thirty years old and worked for William in his blacksmith shop. He walked with a pronounced limp, courtesy of a horse who had not been happy about being shoed, but anyone who equated Arthur's infirmity with weakness did so only once.

"Well enough, Arthur, thank you. And you?"

"Just the same, ma'am." Arthur was known to speak only to William and Adelaide Tillman, and to herself, and after his words of politeness she didn't expect any more. She appreciated his silence and was accustomed to walking in silence with him, so she was surprised, startled, almost, when he kept talking. "Mr. William tol' me about those boys live in that shack down from you. I got me two nephews, my sister's boys, don't have no place to live. They work carpentry and they good at it. Could fix that shack up real good."

Now Arthur was done talking, having uttered more words than she'd ever heard from him. Genie thought about what he'd said. Certainly, having repairs made to the little-more-than-a-hovel where Eli lived with two other boys would benefit them, and apparently Arthur's nephews as well, perhaps the entire street. But that would depend on the kind of men the nephews were, and Genie didn't feel she could ask Arthur.

She could, however, ask Adelaide, which she did almost immediately on arriving at the shop, but Adelaide didn't want to talk about Arthur's nephew. She wanted to talk about Genie's bold confrontation of Ezra MacKaye.

"Does anything frighten you, Genie Oliver?!"

"Many things!" Genie laughed when she spoke the words but it was the truth. "I just try not to show it." Or speak of it. Genie had been afraid most of the time for most of her life. It was only recently that some of the fear had dissipated and she felt it safe to relax. Then that fugitive slave law had been passed and not only were escaped slaves like herself endangered, but any Colored person could be grabbed up and sold South at the whim of a self-appointed slave catcher.

"So, you were afraid yesterday?"

"Terrified. But I was more afraid of what would have happened had he come too far into the lane and someone even more afraid than I had shot and killed him."

Adelaide's sharp intake of breath said that was a possibility she hadn't considered and that its implications truly were terrifying. Every house in Thatcher Lane would have been leveled, every occupant jailed. Or worse. No Colored person could kill a white one, no matter the reason, without dire consequences. Adelaide knew this. Not for the first time Genie wondered why William didn't talk more honestly with his wife. She was a very intelligent woman, and a very brave one: She knew of their Underground Railroad work and she not only supported it, but provided assistance whenever and however she could. She had to want more involvement, Genie thought, and the thought immediately evaporated as she thought how protective William was of her. He would be even more so of his wife.

"Arthur's nephews are good boys," Adelaide said. She explained how, at ages sixteen and seventeen, they had come to be in the care of their uncle: Their mother married a man who wanted to move the family to West Chester where he had a job working for the railroad. The boys did not want to leave Philadelphia so their mother allowed them to remain with their grandmother, who suddenly died. "She was the cook in a rooming house and lived there rent free. Since the boys can't cook—" With a wry smile and slight lifting of her narrow shoulders, she left the inference to achieve its logical conclusion.

"I don't think that place where Eli lives is the best place for Arthur's nephews but I think I might just know of a place," Genie said thoughtfully.

"Why not, Genie? It was William's idea."

Knowing better than to offer any comment critical of William, Genie said, "In another few days none of those boys will live in that place. It's not much more than a hovel, Adelaide, and it has no stove or fireplace, and not even the best carpenter can make a place livable without a stove to warm it in the winter. The boys will be sleeping where they work within the week."

"What's your idea, Genie?"

"You know Peter Blanding, the watch and clock repairman?"

Adelaide was nodding. Of course, she did—everyone knew Peter Blanding, if not by name then certainly by sight. He was over six feet tall with a shiny bald head and a snow-white beard that almost reached his waist. Genie saw the understanding dawn in her eyes. "Do you think he will, Genie?"

She was on her feet and wrapping her shawl around her shoulders. "I'm going to ask him right now." There was a room with a separate entrance at the rear of Blanding's shop where his son and daughter-in-law had lived until a month ago when the couple moved to New York to work for her father, who made watches and clocks for the wealthy instead of merely repairing them for the modest of means. Adelaide and every other merchant in their street knew this. What they didn't know, what only Genie, William and one other person knew, was that the cellar of Peter's store was a hiding place on the Underground Railroad. With Mrs. Tubman due to arrive with a new shipment in the very near future, having someone living in that room would be better than having it empty. No suspicion would be aroused by people entering and exiting the back door, especially if the people were Colored.

Blanding looked up when the bell above his door tinkled its greeting, and his face broke into its own wide grin of greeting when he saw Genie. He dropped his tools and hurried from behind his repair counter. "Eugenia Oliver!" he exclaimed. "To what do I owe such a visit?" He embraced her warmly and whispered into her ear, "Is anything amiss?"

"Everything is fine, Peter. I've heard nothing to the contrary," she whispered back. Where Mrs. Tubman was concerned, no news truly was good news. "You're looking well," she said aloud, stepping away from him. "I've heard that you take your supper with the widow Carpenter and I also hear that she is a very fine cook."

He blushed so furiously that Genie was afraid that his head would explode so she told him the reason for her visit to give him something else to think about. He readily agreed, even after wondering whether the boys were too young to be on their own, then reminding himself that he'd been on his own since about that same age. He took her through an all but invisible door at the rear of the shop and into the room behind it. It was partially furnished—the boys would need another bed, but being carpenters, that wouldn't be a problem. There was a cast iron stove with a stack of wood beside it, a built-in sink, and cabinets sufficient for clothes, personal items, and cooking and eating utensils. Genie unlocked and opened the door to the outside. It would be

14

perfect for Arthur's nephews. Instead of returning to her own shop to give Adelaide the news so she could tell William when he got home that night, and he, in turn, would tell Arthur the following day, Genie left Blanding and hurried to the blacksmith shop—hurried because chilly had become cold and because there were fewer people walking the route to the smithy. Fewer people meant greater danger.

Both William and Arthur were busy with customers when she entered and her arrival startled them. Arthur recovered first: She looked just as she had when he had left her several hours earlier, so no harm had come to her. Whatever business she had with William was not his concern unless William made it so. Arthur turned back to his customer. William, on the other hand, knew that Genie Oliver only visited his shop in the dead of night, disguised as a man, to discuss the safe passage of escaped slaves. She smiled brightly and nodded her head to indicate that there was no problem, and he returned his attention to his business. Only someone who knew him well would notice his agitation. She should not have surprised him like this!

"Good day, Mistress Oliver," he said, extending his hand to her a few moments later as his customer exited. "How are you?"

"All is well, Mr. Tillman," she replied, gripping his hand firmly and meeting his questioning gaze with an unwavering one.

"Adelaide?"

Genie could have kicked herself! She hadn't considered that her unusual arrival would cause her friend to be concerned for his wife. "Adelaide is fine, though no doubt worried that I've been away for so long," she said sheepishly, and quickly told him of the plan for Arthur's nephews. He gave her a wide, warm grin and hurried across the room to the forge to tell Arthur, who dropped the equine foot he was holding and hurried over to Genie faster than she would have imagined possible. He gave her a regal bow, thanked her profusely, said he'd see her in the morning, and returned to his work.

"That's a very fine idea, Genie, to put Arthur's nephews in that space. We can prepare the cellar without raising suspicion."

15

Genie nodded, then said, "I need to speak with Eli, William. He hasn't returned to the Back Street since he ran away from Ezra MacKaye and I need to ascertain whether he knows what Mr. MacKaye thinks he knows."

"We'll find him and send him to you," William said, adding that he'd drive her back to her shop in his mule trap. That way he could see for himself that his wife was well, Genie thought with an internal smile.

Ezra walked briskly, hands stuffed into his pockets and shoulders hunched against the cold, damp, grey dawn. He'd done considerable walking lately, from Montgomery Street all the way down to South Street, and across the city, from the Delaware River to the Schuylkill, looking for Edward Cortlandt. He'd learned that the back rooms of seedy bars and chop houses were not warm, welcoming places but ones that stank of grasping desperation. The men who frequented these places were not the kind of people he'd ever trust enough to do business with despite the fact that many of them were wealthy and prominent. They didn't even trust each other: Not one of Cortlandt's friends owned having seen him. In fact, to hear them tell it, they weren't really his friends, just men with whom he gambled, the difference between them being they were men who paid their gambling debts. On this dismal November morning, Ezra felt very much like a gambler himself. He was playing his final card: Checking the passenger manifests of the cargo ships for a man fitting Cortlandt's description. If he failed, he would lose the promised referral of his services by the senior Cortlandt to other wealthy Philadelphians. That dire possibility weighed heavily on him.

He kept his head down as he walked toward the docks but let his eyes wander, watching for Colored citizens. This was a new habit, one adopted since meeting Eugene Oliver five days earlier. What he saw were Black men and women everywhere, and not just servants, but carpenters and smithies and wheelwrights and hod carriers. They were part of the scenery, and Ezra chastised himself for his failure to notice before now. No wonder he couldn't find Edward Cortlandt; he couldn't even see people who weren't in hiding! He thought again, as he had so many times, of Gene Oliver's confident proclamation: *"If young Master Cortlandt is still in Philadelphia, I will tell you where to find him."* So sure of himself had he sounded that Ezra had wanted to believe him; had believed him, briefly. Then rational thinking had taken hold. How could a poor Black man find a wealthy white one who didn't want to be found in a city that lived and breathed catering to wealthy white men? Too unlikely for words.

"Help! Help me! Oh God please help me!"

The woman's screams followed by loud male commands to "Stop!" snapped Ezra from his musings and put him on alert. People were scattering, clearing a wide path for whatever trouble was manifesting. A horse bus clattered rapidly down the middle of the street, as if trying to get clear as well. Only Ezra did not change his direction, but he did stop walking, placing himself directly in the path of a running, screaming Colored girl. Close on her heels were two scruffy, scraggly white men.

"I ain't no runaway, honest to God I ain't!" The girl's terrified scream hurt Ezra's ears and sent a shiver down his back. He'd never before heard the sound of pure, raw terror.

"Move aside, mister. This ain't yer biz'ness."

He'd also never before personally encountered slave catchers. Until he met Eugene Oliver, he'd never even given them serious thought, beyond a passing knowledge of their existence. Now Ezra looked calmly and steadily at the two breathless men before him, looked into their eyes, one pair at a time, because their eyes were the best hint to the ages of the men as both were fully bearded with long, wild-looking hair protruding from beneath the wide brims of dusty hats. Their clothes were rough and dirty, their hobnail boots mud-caked. They looked and smelled as if they hadn't washed in weeks. Slave catching obviously wasn't a very prosperous enterprise. "This girl is a runaway?" he asked the one who had spoken and whom he judged to be the elder of the two.

"Like I said, this ain't yer biz'ness."

"No! I'm a free Colored person! I was born free!" the girl screamed from behind him. "I gave him my papers to prove it! He's got my papers! My name is Liz'beth and I work for Miz Read, me and my Ma, and Miz Read, she hires me out! I ain't no runaway! I'm free-born like my Ma!"

Ezra moved a step forward, trying to escape the shrill wailing of the girl who now held on to his coattails, but the slave catchers took his action as threatening.

"I'll shoot yer ass!" The younger man reached inside his coat as the words left his mouth, but the effects of the drink that was an obvious part of his existence slowed him, and Ezra grabbed the hand that held the pistol.

"I'll shoot you with your own gun," he said, forcing the man's hand to turn inward, toward his own chest, "if you don't let it go. I mean it."

"Help, Algie! Make him turn me loose."

"Give 'im the damn gun, Jack," the older man said, spitting a dark, ugly stream of tobacco from the side of his mouth without ever taking his eyes from Ezra. Because he was watching Ezra, he couldn't see how quickly and comically the gathered crowd moved away from the stream of nasty tobacco juice.

"Damn Quaker," Jack muttered, but he released the gun, and Ezra quickly cocked it and pointed it at Algie's chest.

"Do you have this girl's papers?"

"What the hell's the matter with you?" Algie snarled, his lips wet with tobacco juice. "Why you care what happens to a nigger slave girl?"

"How much will you get for her?" Ezra asked, and felt the terrified tug on the back of his coat. "When you steal people like this girl and sell them South, how much do you get? Because I'll pay you double. Right here and now. Give me the girl's papers and I'll pay you double what you'd earn selling her South."

"Twenty dollars!" Jack yelled, ignoring the warning look from Algie. "That's what we git! You give us forty and you can have her sorry Black ass!"

Ezra kept the gun leveled at Algie's chest and reached into his coat pocket.

"Why're you doin' this? You ain't no Quaker, you're a bleedin' Scotsman is what you are," Algie hissed, and spit again, this time directly at Ezra's feet.

"Do you want the forty dollars?"

Algie gave Ezra a look of cold hatred. This man, this slave catcher, would kill him given the chance. "Yeah," he finally said. "I want the forty dollars. And I want my gun back."

"Your gun?" Ezra asked He tried to sound amused though he was anything but. "This is a Navy Colt and there's only one way a degenerate like you could get a revolver like this: By stealing it."

"He were already dead, so I didn't steal nothin'," Algie said defensively.

Ezra's eyes scanned the crowd, then returned to Algie. "So. You steal from a dead sailor and you steal children. The only reason I don't shoot you myself is it would be a waste of good gunpowder." There was a muffled chuckle from the crowd as Ezra held out the money. Jack reached to grab it but Ezra pulled it back. "I want the girl's papers."

Algie, holding Ezra's calm, steady gaze with his hate-filled one, reached inside his coat and withdrew a rawhide pouch that was tethered to his waist. He tugged open the strings of the pouch, reached inside, and pulled out a square of folded paper.

"It's my papers!" The girl shrieked from behind Ezra. "It's my proof that I ain't no runaway!"

"Drop the paper on the ground and back up three steps. Both of you back up," Ezra said, waving the gun at Jack and Algie and realizing that he would, indeed, shoot them if necessary.

"Gimme my damn money," Algie hissed at him.

Ezra tossed the money at them, a collection of coins and bills. They scooped it up and painstakingly counted it. "Gimme back my damn gun," Algie demanded again.

Ezra pulled back the hammer on the gun with his thumb and the chamber rotated. The noise reverberated loudly and the two slave catchers turned and hurried away.

"I'll see you again and I'll remember you," Algie called out as he fled, and Ezra knew the threat to be real. "Nigger lover!" Algie called out, his parting shot.

The crowd that had formed to watch Ezra's confrontation with the slave catchers had not left with them, and not everyone in it was on his side against Algie and Jack. He also realized that the Colored girl still held on to him from behind. He reached around and drew her forward. "Get your papers," he said, pushing her forward. She resisted, and he felt the trembling of her thin shoulders. Then he looked down into her face. Whom he'd thought was a young woman was little more than a child, and she was terrified. Ezra bent forward, keeping a guarded eye on the crowd, trying to find the hostile elements, and picked up the folded square of paper. He offered it to her. Hesitating briefly, she extended a tiny hand, grabbed the paper, and held tightly on to it with one hand and to Ezra's coat with the other.

"Where do you live? Elizabeth, isn't it?"

"Liz'beth, yessir, and I work for Miz Read, me and my Ma do."

"Where?" Ezra asked again.

"Wherever she sends me," the girl answered.

"Where does Mrs. Read live?" Ezra asked. His patience was eroding. He had work to do. A Colored woman stepped from the crowd and walked toward him. She was dressed like all serving-class women, Colored or white, in a threadbare homespun cotton dress, apron and stockings, and heavy hobnail boots. Her only source of warmth was a thick woolen shawl, but the color was a dark, ugly gray.

"She prob'ly don't know her street name," the woman said. "Mistress Read got a boarding house on Apted Street, north yonder, by the river."

Ezra nodded. He knew Apted Street but had not known of a boarding house there. The Colored woman seemed to read his thoughts because she said, "Her folks passed away and left her with a big house, some servants, and no money. She rents out the rooms. And the servants." The woman touched the girl on her shoulder, then turned away. She joined two other Colored women and they hurried off to whatever work they were fortunate enough to have, and Ezra wondered if they all feared being stolen off the street and sold South. He was about to reach for his pocket watch when he realized he still held the Colt revolver. It really was a fine weapon, he saw, better than his own. He stuck it into the waistband of his pants, feeling suddenly self-conscious; but there was no need. The crowd had dispersed, leaving him and Elizabeth standing alone.

"Come, girl. You must get home and I must get to work." He started to walk and she trotted along beside him. Apted Street was perhaps a mile due north. He was calculating how long it would take to get there at the reduced speed required by having to adjust to the little girl's shorter legs, and then hurry back down to the docks, when the girl suddenly bolted. She was running as hard and fast as she had been when he first encountered her and at first he feared that Jack and Algie had returned. Then he saw two women running toward him, one white and one Colored, both holding out their arms toward the girl. They were still clinging to each other, the three of them, as Ezra approached.

"Whoever you are, sir, I thank you," said the white woman, a very pretty woman, sounding as if she'd just disembarked from a British schooner.

"Mrs. Read?" He knew he was correct, but he couldn't imagine how she could possibly know to be running toward him and the just-rescued Elizabeth.

"Abigail Read, at your service, sir," she replied with a slight curtsy. "This is Maggie Juniper. She is Elizabeth's mother."

Ezra looked at the Colored woman whose grip on the young girl seemed tight enough to break her arm. He looked into her eyes and into a potent mixture of pain and fear and hatred and anger and something he couldn't define. Helplessness? Hopelessness? He couldn't think of anything to say so he took out one of his cards and gave it to Abigail Read. Then he thought of something to say to Maggie. "Elizabeth is a very brave girl. And she runs faster than the wind."

21

Maggie looked down at her daughter, then up at Ezra. This time her gaze held nothing but pride. "I thank you, sir, and my swift girl thanks you." Her accent was as British as that of the white woman. Indeed, had he not been looking at them, he'd not have known that one of them was Black, turning another of his suppositions on its ear.

"How did you know to come for the child?"

For the first time the Read woman's features relaxed and she almost smiled. She was much more than merely pretty. "A friend of Maggie's witnessed your encounter with the . . . the hooligans and she ran to tell us. I don't know what I'd have done if . . ." She looked at the card in her hand for the first time, then looked back up at him. "Pinkerton's?"

Ezra tipped his hat and bowed to the women. "Formerly," he answered before bidding the women a good day and turning away. Then he quickly turned back. "Do you have any rooms available to let, Miss Read?" Not *Mrs.* He remembered that the woman had called her "Mistress" Read. He'd been considering a move from the rooming house where he had lived for some time but had made no move to seek new lodging. This seemed too good an opportunity to ignore. Apted Street, unlike Flegler Street where he currently lived, was completely and totally residential. When he finished work for the day he would have no worry that someone "wanting a private word" would come knocking at his door late at night.

"I have a ground floor suite of rooms with a private entrance available, Mr. MacKaye."

"May I visit this evening?"

When she readily agreed, he thanked her and hurried back the way he'd come. He was not looking forward to spending the day wandering the cold waterfront, trying to pry information out of people not inclined to talk to strangers. Seamen more often than not lived life on the edge and didn't begrudge another man that choice. So, even if the Cortlandt boy was stowed away on a ship, it was unlikely that any ship's mate would share that information with Ezra, even for a price. And no doubt, Edward Cortlandt would have paid more for the ship mate's silence.

Ezra called to mind the image of the man he was looking for, all the bits and pieces of information about his character and habits, and could not imagine him a stowaway on a working ship. He was a dilettante and the worst kind of snob. A man like Edward Cortlandt would do nothing to inconvenience himself, not even to avoid his father's wrath. So, if still in Philadelphia, he was not hiding on a ship; and if he'd left the city, it would not have been on a working boat. So where was the young fool? Now hungry as well as cold and weary, he boarded the first horse bus that would return him to the familiarity of Flegler Street—and give his sore feet a rest. Perhaps shaved, washed, fed and rested, he would have clarity of mind enough to imagine where Edward Cortlandt was hiding himself. But after taking care of himself he found that he wanted nothing more than to begin packing for the move to Apted Street, for even without having seen Miss Read's lodgings, he knew that was where he wanted to reside, especially after the street noise made it impossible for him to fall asleep after his bath and meal. Flegler Street was in the commercial district and he'd maintain his office here but he'd rest his body on Apted Street.

"I'm very sorry to be losing you, Mr. MacKaye," his landlady said when he shared his intentions.

"You'll not be totally rid of me, Mrs. McDougall," he said with a warm smile. He always enjoyed his encounters with her. She was as round as a biscuit, and her red-orange hair would no more remain braided and bound within its scarf than her five-year-old twin grandsons would remain quiet and obedient at the back of the house. Her green eyes always sparkled with merriment no matter the discussion.

"I've a single room on the second floor that you might like for your office."

"I hope I'm not causing you any inconvenience," he said.

"Not a bit of it," she said, waving away his concern with pudgy, bejeweled fingers. "I'll have no trouble letting your suite—" She stopped mid-sentence, her brow wrinkling. "Was there a problem of some kind, Mr. MacKaye?"

He hurried to reassure her. "Oh, no, Mrs. McDougall! At least not a problem with your hospitality. I just got tired of people knowing where to find me after hours."

Her face relaxed into a sympathetic smile. He paid what he owed, promised to have his belongings out by the end of the day, then went into the street to look for a trap to hire to make good on his promise. He also sent a note to Mistress Read saying he'd arrive that evening prepared to move in, enclosing enough money to convince her of his sincerity.

CHAPTER THREE

Genie and Adelaide were so busy in the shop the next morning that the arrival of Eli at the back door caught them both by surprise, startling them. They already were overwhelmed by the day's deliveries and were expecting no more. Adelaide went to the door and Genie heard the muffled conversation, then Adelaide returned with the message that Eli was there, as requested, and for a brief, confused moment, Genie didn't know what he wanted. Then she remembered and hurried to the back door.

"Hello, Eli. Thank you for coming."

"Yes, Ma'am, Miss Genie. Mr. William said you wanted to see me."

"Come in out of the cold, Eli," she said, beckoning to him, and she thought she'd have to grab his arm and drag him inside. "Come stand beside the stove and warm up." It was a very cold morning but Eli wore his usual cut-off pants held up with rope and a checked shirt, which at least had long sleeves. His feet, however, were bare. While Eli all but hugged the cast iron stove, Genie went to stand beside Adelaide and the pile of clothing they'd been sorting through. "See if you can find a pair of pants for him, please, and a shirt and jacket." Adelaide nodded, looking down at the boy's feet. There were no shoes of any kind in the donated pile.

"I wanted to ask you, Eli, if you remember what the man who chased you wanted to know—"

The boy's eyes got big and he backed up a step. "I ain't done no wrong, Miss Genie!"

"I know you haven't, Eli! That's not why you're here and you're not in any trouble. Honest! And the man who was chasing you apologized. He's not a slave catcher and he knows he was wrong to chase you." Genie was talking fast, watching Eli closely to be certain he understood and would not bolt. His breathing slowed, but he watched her warily.

"What do he want with me?"

"He's looking for the Cortlandt boy, the banker's son, and he thought you might know where to find him."

"He ain't the p'lice," Eli said forthrightly; he knew a policeman when he saw one.

"No, he's not. He's a . . . he's like a Pinkerton's. You know what they are, don't you?"

Eli nodded. "Ev'erbody know 'bout the Pinkertons."

"Do you know where the boy is?"

Eli nodded again but he didn't speak. His body stilled and Genie realized that he'd been shivering. For a brief moment she thought she should have secured Ed Blanding's back room for Eli, but it was indeed a fleeting thought for Eli would not have been able to pay for such a lodging, and he would have shared it with anyone who needed shelter. Genie could vouch for Eli but not for some of the boys he associated with. And even those she knew, she knew nothing about. "Will you tell Mr. MacKaye where the boy is, Eli?"

Eli was shivering again, this time not from the cold, and shaking his head back and forth, his face a stubborn mask. "I don't like talking to no white mens, Miss Genie."

She didn't need to tax her imagination to understand why: The boy had been a slave, and it required her entire imagination to envision how one so young could have planned and executed his own escape. He now worked the most menial jobs in the most disreputable establishments, servicing the men who frequented them, most probably because he had no skills other than farming. Of course he didn't like talking to white men. "If I go with you, will you tell Mr. MacKaye what you know?"

He considered this, then nodded. "If you stand with me I'll tell him."

"Thank you, Eli. When and where?"

He thought for a moment. She knew that he worked odd jobs all over town. "T'morrow in the evenin' time, back behind the big church on the square, the one with bells that ring the time. When they ring six times, Miss Genie."

Six o'clock tomorrow evening behind Christ Church. "I'll be there with Mr. MacKaye, Eli—wait!" she called out, for he had turned and was headed for the door. She looked over at Adelaide, who approached holding clothes out to Eli.

"These are for you, Eli," Adelaide said, offering a pair of heavy trousers, a woolen shirt, long underwear, and a thick scarf.

The boy looked at the items as if they might attack him.

"Take them, Eli," Genie said, "and go into the storeroom there and change." The two women walked away and left the boy to change into the clothes they'd thrust at him. They returned to their work and after several long minutes they heard the back door open and close. Genie went to the storeroom to find Eli's old clothes in a neat pile on the floor. Yes, they were little more than rags, but that wasn't why he'd left them: He had no place to store a second set of clothes. She locked the back door and walked slowly back to Adelaide after first depositing Eli's old clothes into the stove. "I hope we get some shoes that will fit him."

"If we do," Adelaide said, "I'll add a pair of William's socks."

For most of the year their shop—called Miss Adelaide's Dress and Hat Shop—did what was advertised: They made and repaired dresses and hats. Genie owned the business but it bore Adelaide's name because the Genie who had escaped slavery had been a well-regarded seamstress named Clara, and anyone looking for her runaway self would be looking for a seamstress. But since Adelaide was at least twenty years older, four inches shorter, and twenty pounds heavier than Clara the runaway slave, Miss Adelaide's was a safe hiding place. This time of year, however, as winter bore down, the two women used their skills to repair and refashion articles of clothing and material donated by churches and social organizations and given free to the poorest among them. Shoes and socks, however, always were in short supply because everyone, well-to-do and destitute alike, wore them until they were worn beyond the possibility of repair.

Because she was the more skilled seamstress, Genie undertook the most complicated tasks—making dresses or coats from the heavy draperies no longer welcome in a society drawing room, or fashioning garments of any kind from pillow coverings. Because nothing that was donated was thrown away, they always managed to create something useful for those who had nothing at all. By midday, Genie's fingers were bleeding and her eyes were burning. She got up from her sewing table, stretched her back, and changed from her Eugenia clothes into her Eugene clothes. At Adelaide's questioning look she explained that she was going to tell Ezra MacKaye when and where to meet Eli tomorrow night.

"Do you think he really knows where to find the Cortlandt youth?"

Genie nodded. "I do, otherwise he wouldn't subject himself to questioning by a white man." And wearing enough clothes to both keep her warm and give her bulk, she set out for Flegler Street, Ezra MacKaye's card and a note to him in one pocket, her hand caressing the ever-present derringer in the other. She walked swiftly; the afternoon was cold and no doubt it would turn bitter with darkness. The horse-drawn streetcar moved swiftly past on the iron rails in the middle of the street and for not the first time Genie felt strong, bitter resentment at the fact that Colored were forbidden to ride it. William kept telling her she needed to buy a horse and cart. Perhaps she would do that. How much time and effort she could save!

Flegler Street was busy and bustling as always—and loud! She didn't know how Ezra MacKaye could live here. She knew that she could not. Her quiet, dark, hidden Back Street was perfect for the peace of mind she required. She stopped in front of MacKaye's address and immediately was approached by a scruffy young man she recognized as one of Eli's housemates, though she didn't think she'd ever known his name.

"Can I help you with somethin', Miss Eugenie?" he asked in a whisper, standing very close to her. She couldn't think of his name; perhaps she'd never known it though he knew hers. He also knew who she was beneath her Eugene Oliver camouflage, and knew to respect it.

She withdrew the note and the card from her pocket. "Will you take this note to Mr. MacKaye—"

"He ain't there," the boy said before she could complete her request.

"Then give it to the landlady to give to him."

The boy was shaking his head. "He don't live there no more, Miss Eugenie."

Genie was speechless. This she had not expected. "Since when?"

"Yesterday. Me and Absalom helped him." He looked closely at Genie. "I know where he went, Miss Eugenie."

Genie almost laughed to herself. Of course, he did! Eli probably knew, too. "Can you tell me?" She needed to know his name.

"Reverend Richard Allen," he replied when she asked, and Genie almost choked. The boy hastened to explain: When he left slavery, he left it all behind, including the name he'd been given. Upon arriving in Philadelphia, he heard the name of the Reverend Richard Allen everywhere, including among the white people. He wasn't at all certain who Reverend Allen was or what he had accomplished but he knew that he was Colored and that was enough. Then he gave her a card—one of Ezra MacKaye's with the Flegler Street address on the front, and written on the back in a strong block hand: 765 APTED STREET. "That's where he went."

Genie was not familiar with Apted Street but wherever it was, she imagined a long, cold walk back the way she'd come would be required. She checked with Richard to confirm her suspicion, looked again at the card she held, thanked Reverend Richard Allen for his help, and offered him several coins in gratitude. He refused to accept them. "You earned it, Richard," Genie said. "Please take it." She held out her hand, the coins in her flat palm.

"Can I have me some warm clothes, Miss Eugenie?"

She scrutinized him as she'd not done before: His clothes were as threadbare as Eli's had been, the primary difference being that Richard had what appeared to be some kind of animal skin wrapped around his feet. "Of course. Go see Miss Adelaide—"

"Can we go now, Miss Eugenie, to get me some warm clothes?"

She shook her head. "I must get a message to Mr. MacKaye—"

He turned away from her and whistled loudly—three short, shrill bursts followed by two longer ones. Almost immediately a horse cart emerged from the narrow alley between MacKaye's building and the one next door. The driver wore a semblance of livery: A moth-eaten top hat perched on top of a too-large head, a coat several sizes too large for the narrow body, as if to offset the hat, gloves with no fingers, and a bright red scarf wrapped snugly around his neck. The cart stopped smoothly beside Genie and Richard. "This Absalom and he gon' take you to where Mr. MacKaye is on Apted Street."

Genie, suddenly aware that they were being observed, quickly clambered up into the cart, as much to prevent Richard forgetting that she was not Eugenia and trying to help her, as to get them moving. Three Colored men together in the street, even one as busy as Flegler, was dangerous. Sensing it, Richard quickly followed and told Absalom to "git up," but it was unnecessary— he had clicked the reins and the horse was moving quickly and steadily back toward their own part of town.

The wind had picked up and all three of them were freezing and shivering, and Genie knew how much worse it would have been had she been walking. She could and would stop first at the shop to get warm clothes for these boys, and when they walked in the door Adelaide took one look at them and hurried to the pile of men's clothing, beckoning the boys to follow her. In short order the boys were dressed and bundled but, unlike Eli, they kept their old clothing, adding the new garments on top.

"Miss?" Absalom spoke quietly, almost fearfully, and when both Genie and Adelaide looked at him he cringed.

"What is it, Absalom?" Genie asked gently.

"Can I have a blanket or something to put over top of me at night when I'm sleep in my cart?"

"You sleep in your cart all night?" Genie asked.

Absalom nodded—with some difficulty because he had two thick scarves wrapped around his neck. "Yes'm. The man I drive drinks and gambles all night—it's his cart—and I have to be ready to take him wherever he wants to go, which sometimes is all over Philadelphia, sometimes even out to Kensington or Southwark."

"And you remain in the cart?" Adelaide was appalled, and Genie was again reminded how narrow her friend's view could be, despite her inherent goodness. Adelaide was born a free woman and while she despised the horror that was slavery, she could only imagine it. No slave ever forgot how deeply it harmed. Genie had thought Absalom owned the horse cart. Now that she knew differently she had no trouble understanding how Absalom slept overnight in the cart without complaint. It was his job, and failure to follow orders could result in a beating—or in death— as easily in Philadelphia as in Georgia or the Carolinas or any slave state. So before Adelaide could question Absalom's behavior, Genie asked her about an especially ugly pair of parlor draperies they had on a shelf in the storeroom—so ugly that no woman, no matter how poor, would wear a dress or coat made from the material. However, it was heavy and would serve Absalom's needs perfectly.

The boy almost wept when Genie handed him the hideous purple, green, orange and yellow material, but she didn't think he saw the colors. He held it close to his body and it was the weight of the material that he responded to. "I thank you, truly I do."

"You're welcome, Absalom," Genie said.

"And it's wide enough to keep your employer warm, as well," Adelaide said.

Absalom shuddered as if the frigid wind had permeated the walls. "He can't know 'bout this, Miss. He'll think I stole it and he'll take it 'way from me and he'll beat me." And as if expecting the man to walk through the door, Absalom unwound the material from his body and folded it into a neat square. He touched the scarves at his neck. "I'll have to hide these, too. I'll put it all under the bench. He don't look under there."

"But doesn't he get cold?" Adelaide asked, and Absalom laughed and explained that his master had a "big bear rug" that he wrapped around himself, even covering his head when it snowed. And before Adelaide could speak again Genie headed for the door.

"I must get to Mr. MacKaye before it gets too dark."

"We gon' take you in the cart, Miss Eugenie," Absalom said with a courtly bow, and they left. It was a relatively short ride but Genie was grateful she didn't have to walk. When they reached Apted Street and Genie saw what was to her way of thinking a mansion that would have been right at home on the Main Line, she truly was surprised. It was a huge house, and a beautiful one, and it looked nothing like a rooming house. Nor did it want to, Genie thought as Absalom drove the cart past No. 765 and turned into a paved and well-tended alleyway that would have been right at home in Fairmount Park. She understood completely why Ezra MacKaye chose to leave Flegler Street for this. The cart stopped at a wooden fence and gate behind what she was certain was No. 765 and Genie climbed down.

"Is it locked?" she asked.

Both boys shook their heads, then Richard said, "It wasn't yesterday when we brought Mr. MacKaye's things."

Probably little need for locked gates here, Genie thought as she lifted the latch and entered a garden that even in winter was as magnificent as anything she'd seen in the South. She stood on the brick path admiring the space, elegant even with its fountains and ponds frozen, when she heard what sounded like a muffled scream. As she was convincing herself she couldn't have heard such a thing, she heard another. She all but ran down the path, pulled open the scullery door, and rushed inside. What she saw froze her: A tall, well-dressed man had all but ripped the bodice from the dress of a beautiful, black-haired woman almost as tall as he was, and she was almost purple-faced with anger.

"Charles! Stop! Stop it this instant!" She was screaming and pounding on his chest.

He, too, was purple with anger. "Abigail! Listen to reason!" he said in a growl. "Why won't you see reason?"

"I see you, Charles, and I don't like what I see!"

What neither of them saw was Genie enter the kitchen slowly and quietly. She wasn't certain what to do. Then she saw the body of a Colored woman on the floor, bleeding from her mouth and nose. No longer hesitant, Genie grabbed a skillet from the stove, came up behind Charles and hit him on the head as hard as she could. He whirled around, his fist raised to strike her. She hit him again on the side of the head and he crumpled and fell, blood gushing from the wound. She dropped the skillet and knelt down beside the woman on the floor to make certain she was breathing. Then she stood and faced Abigail, who was breathing heavily but was no longer purple. She held her bodice up with one hand and wiped tears from deep blue eyes with the other. The black hair had come loose from its pins and cascaded down her back. She looked from Genie to the woman on the floor.

"Is Maggie all right? Please help her! She tried to stop Charles from . . . hurting me and he hit her. Please, sir, make certain that she is all right."

Genie knelt down beside Maggie again and studied her face. She had been hit hard but she was stirring. So was Charles. Genie jumped to her feet and started for the door.

"Wait! Where are you going? Who are you? I must thank you—"

33

Genie was at the door, shaking her head. "I came to bring a message to Mr. MacKaye." She took the note from her pocket and dropped it on the table. "But I can't be here when this man gains his senses. He saw me—"

At that moment Charles groaned, sat up, saw Genie, and yelled, "Call the constabulary! That nigger hit me!"

Genie was out the door and down the garden walkway when the gate opened and Ezra MacKaye entered. His eyes widened in a mixture of shock and surprise, then narrowed in recognition. "Miss Eugenie indeed! You're not Eugene Oliver at all, by God!" He grabbed for her but she slapped his hand away.

"Your landlady has been . . . attacked. I hit the man who did it with a skillet. He saw me and wants to call the police to arrest the nigger who hit him. I must leave now. There's a note for you on the kitchen table." She pushed past him, ran to the cart and climbed in, not seeing that he had traversed the garden walkway in three long strides.

Ezra threw open the scullery door, strode into the kitchen, and stopped, staring.

Abby leapt to her feet, fear etched in her face. It eased when she saw who it was. "Mr. MacKaye," she whispered as she grabbed the ripped bodice of her dress and tried to hold it in place. Her eyes were on Maggie, who was struggling to sit up. Ezra hurried to help her up and into a chair at the table.

"Where's the man who did this?"

The front door slammed shut and Ezra realized that cold air penetrated the kitchen despite the fire in the stove, then Charles Gresham strode in on a wave of anger. He stopped short at the sight of Ezra. "Who the hell are you?" he growled.

Ezra grabbed him by the lapels of his coat and yanked him forward, lifting him slightly. "I'm not a man who needs to harm women to prove his worth."

"The Constabulary are coming and I'll have them take you with the nigger!"

Ezra hit him hard on the side of the face, in the exact place Genie had hit him with the skillet, and he went down. Telling the women not to change anything—especially their appearance—before the police arrived, Ezra bolted, running as fast as his long legs would carry him. He had to reach Genie and the boys before they were seen by the law. He turned left out of the alleyway and into the main street, looking both ways. He spied them headed toward the river. He started to give chase but thought better of it as he recalled what had happened the last time he chased a Colored person. He didn't think he'd be mistaken for a slave catcher this day, but he didn't want to call attention to the horse cart slowly making its way with the other street traffic. A cart that carried three Colored people. He let loose a long, shrill whistle and Genie turned toward the sound as somehow, he knew she would. She saw him and he dropped his right hand down low beside his leg, palm down. She nodded briefly and turned around and almost immediately the cart halted, but not one of them turned to look at him. Who in the world was Eugene/Eugenia Oliver?! And could he hire him/her to be a private inquiry agent? Hire all of them, for they sat still as statues in the cart, not once drawing attention to themselves by turning to look his way.

He casually approached the cart and told them what had happened.

"How did he summon the police so quickly?" Genie exclaimed.

"He had a carriage waiting and sent the driver," Ezra answered.

"That nice brougham that was in front of the house when we passed by," Absalom said. As a driver he had noticed the carriage when the others did not.

"How close is the police station?" Ezra asked. He didn't know this part of town; he'd have to learn, and quickly.

"Close," Richard replied nervously, looking east.

"You boys go the other way, then," Ezra said, "but slowly, you understand? Not like you're running away from something." And when they nodded their understanding he said to Genie, "You must come with me, Mistress Oliver—"

"Why? That man will say that I struck him and I'll be arrested!"

Ezra smiled widely. "He will say that a Colored man struck him, but you're not a man, are you? The police will learn that

Mistress Read has two Colored women in her employ and no Colored men and that it was one of the women who struck him with the cook pot, which is why he regained consciousness so quickly. If a man had swung a cast iron skillet at his head he'd still be flat on his back. Or dead. Furthermore, I intend to focus their attention on the brutal attack on Mistress Read that made it necessary for one of the women to strike him." He paused briefly to be certain the three of them understood and accepted his plan, then offered Genie his hand.

"Stand aside, Mr. MacKaye. Eugene Oliver requires no assistance." And she proved it by jumping agilely down. She thanked Absalom and Richard for their assistance. "I'll see you both tomorrow. Please be safe."

"But Miss Eugenie—"

She saw and heard their worry. "I'll be quite all right. Won't I, Mr. MacKaye?"

"No harm will come to her, I promise you," he said.

Neither of them responded. They had no faith in the promises of white men. Absalom clicked the reins and the cart moved slowly forward. Genie and Ezra turned in unison and moved quickly back to Abigail Read's house, entering again through the gate at the back garden, into the scullery, where Ezra told her to wait. Then he hurried in and whispered to Abby, who in turn whispered to Maggie, and the two of them quickly approached her. Maggie took one look at Genie and her face wanted to break into a wide smile, but Charles Gresham had made that painfully impossible so instead she gently touched Genie's face.

"I don't understand how anyone could look at your face, look into your eyes, and believe you to be a man," Maggie said to the beautiful young woman standing before her.

"But almost no one looks and fewer still see," Genie replied, removing the hat and scarf and releasing her hair.

Abigail Read gasped and Ezra MacKaye stared. She was beautiful! Ezra didn't know how he could have believed her to be a man, the masculine clothing notwithstanding. He turned and hurried back into the kitchen just in time to see Charles struggling to his feet. Ezra pushed him back down and threatened to hit him again if he moved. He didn't, but Ezra sat where he could watch him.

Deep within the scullery, invisible to the men, Genie shivered in a woolen shift as Maggie Juniper hurriedly pulled a dress of heavy material over her head and guided her arms through the sleeves. It warmed her immediately and fit her almost perfectly. She guessed that it had belonged to Abigail Read since it was of a style no longer in fashion and it was in a storage cabinet in the scullery. It was a day dress, not an evening gown, but the fabric was rich and expensive. Oh what she could do with a dress like this in her shop! Because they wouldn't need to be as elegant as Abigail Read's, she could fashion three garments from this much material. She gathered it in her hands, weighing and feeling its value. She had made dresses like this for the women in the house where she served but she'd never worn anything so luxurious. She was forbidden to try on any garment belonging to white women. She closed her eyes to the memory. She opened them and looked into the deep blue eyes of Mistress Read, who had been observing her with an expression that she couldn't read. Whatever it was though, Genie found that she couldn't hold the gaze because it made her insides churn, so she looked at Maggie Juniper, who was looking back at her. Then Maggie looked at Abigail Read, then back to Genie, who was working to make eye contact with Abby. Maggie watched them watch each other and nodded her head as if in agreement with some words that hadn't been spoken. Then everyone in the room jumped at the sound of pounding on the front door.

Ezra MacKaye jumped to his feet and pulled Charles Gresham to his. He sent Abigail Read to answer the door and called for Maggie to come into the kitchen where he whispered to her until Abby returned, two uniformed policemen trailing in her wake.

"A nigger struck me and I demand his arrest!" Charles wailed.

The policemen looked at Maggie, at her bloody, swollen face. They looked at Abby, still holding her ripped bodice with one

37

hand. Finally, they looked at Ezra expectantly, and he answered the unasked questions.

"I am Ezra MacKaye and I rent a suite of rooms from Mistress Abigail Read. She was attacked by this man—it is my belief that he tried to have his way with her—and her maid tried to prevent that . . . that . . . bestiality. You can see what he did to her—"

"Lies! All lies!" Charles thundered.

"Then what happened to that good lady's dress and her maid's face?" The ranking officer finally spoke.

"Look at my head! Look at my face!" Charles pointed to his bloody wounds. "Arrest the nigger who did this to me!"

The policeman looked at Maggie. "Did you hit this man?"

"No, sir. I did not."

"It was a man, you fool, not a stupid serving girl! It was a man who came up behind me—"

"Come out here, Genie!" Ezra called out, and she emerged slowly, timidly from the scullery. She had added an apron to the dress and wrapped her head in material she'd found in the cabinet. She had rolled the sleeves of the dress up above her elbows and counted on the fact that the policemen would see only a Colored servant woman and take no notice of the quality of the dress the servant was wearing. She kept her head and her eyes lowered. As much as she might wish it she could not forget the rules of slavery.

"What is your name, girl?"

"Eugenia Oliver, sir."

"Do you know who hit this man?"

"I did, sir," Genie answered, still looking at the floor.

"That's a lie!" Charles thundered. "A man hit me, I tell you!"

The smile deep inside Genie gave strength to the long-banished slave girl. "I hit him with that skillet," she said, addressing the floor. "Two times I hit him: once on the back of the head and then again, on the side—" she touched her temple "—when he turned around. He was mad and I didn't want him to hit me like he hit Mrs. Maggie so I hit him again, harder this time, and he fell down."

"Is this girl telling the truth, Mistress Read?" the Chief Constable asked Abby.

"Yes, sir, she is."

"That's a lie!" Charles roared.

"You shut your mouth!" the policeman roared back. Then, to Genie: "Why did you hit him? You know better than to hit a white man, don't you?"

Genie raised her eyes for a quick glance at Abby to find deep blue eyes staring at her. She quickly lowered hers again. "Yes, sir. But he was . . . hurting . . . Miss Abigail. I was in the scullery and I heard her cry and I looked out. I was looking for Mrs. Maggie but I didn't see her. I saw him, the one I hit, tearing Miss Abigail's dress off her. I came out and saw Mrs. Maggie on the floor. I saw the skillet. I heard Miss Abigail crying. I hit him."

"Now I'd like to suggest, Officer, that you take this man away and lay against him the charges of—"

"I don't need your assistance to perform my job," the policeman snapped at Ezra. To Charles he said, "If you would please accompany me to the Magistrate, sir."

Charles looked at the man wide-eyed and open-mouthed. He didn't speak or move. All eyes were on him, including those of Genie and Abby who had forced their eyes from each other to observe Charles being taken away, wanting him to be taken away as quickly as possible. True to his nature, however, Charles was not cooperating. He slapped the policeman's hand from his arm. "You would do well to remember who pays your salary," he snarled at him.

The thin line that was the policeman's mouth gave what might have been a smile. "I never forget that it is the Honorable James William Laughton to whom I am indebted," he said, and while his mouth didn't move his eyes glinted in satisfaction as all the color drained from Charles's face. The places where Genie and Ezra struck him stood out in stark relief.

Charles fell into one of the chairs. Not only was Jimmy Laughton his arch enemy, but Charles owed him a lot of money, a debt he could repay if Abigail weren't so damned intractable!

If she'd just marry him as he'd asked, her considerable net worth would offset his own negligible one. But no! She'd rather run a boarding house than make a home for him and entertain Philadelphia's powerful and wealthy. There was a time when every young society girl in the city would have jumped at the chance to marry Charles Gresham!

"You'll stand up now, Mr. Gresham, and behave yourself, or I'll hit you as well. We'll exit the front door and take your pretty brougham to the lockup." The constable inclined his head to Abby, ignored the rest of them, and push-pulled Charles to the front door. No one bothered with the niceties of showing them out.

As befitting the mistress of the house, Abby recovered her wits first. "Thank you, Mr. MacKaye and Mistress Oliver." She took a deep breath and forced herself to meet Genie's eyes. "What you did required great courage, even if . . . if you'd been a man."

"Man or woman, Mistress Oliver has more courage than most I've seen," Ezra said, recalling his first encounter with Genie.

"And for the second time your own courage has benefited us, Mr. MacKaye," Abby said, "and we are most grateful."

Ezra bowed, then turned to Maggie. "Do you require a doctor, Mrs. Juniper?"

Maggie Juniper's left eye was swollen shut and her face was heavily bruised. She stood up slowly, swayed, steadied herself, and managed a small smile, which caused her to wince in pain. Abby rushed to her side and, before Maggie could reply, said she would send for her doctor.

"And who will you send?" Ezra asked with a smile.

"I must be leaving for home," Genie said quickly. "If you will tell me where your doctor is located and give me the proper letter to him, I will deliver it."

Ezra gave her a withering look. "It is practically dark. You can't go home now, Mistress Oliver."

"Not dressed like this I can't," Genie replied, and they all knew that she intended to return to her Eugene guise. And since she wasn't seeking their permission, she turned from them and went into the scullery where she began the transformation.

"You are welcome to remain here for the night, Mistress Oliver," Abby called out to her, and Genie felt the odd stirring in the pit of her stomach. Apparently, the woman's voice as well as the deep blue eyes affected her thusly.

"Thank you for your kindness, Mistress Read, but I must leave," Genie called out.

"Have you a husband, children, waiting for you?" Abby asked.

"An empty house and a neglected business," Genie replied, "but my absence overnight would cause worry among my friends."

"Even dressed like a man," Maggie said quietly, "she'll have a long, cold walk to her home." She knew where the Colored part of town was, and after a brief moment of thought, both Ezra and Abby realized how far Genie would have to walk to reach home.

"I'll leave with her and if we go to Main Street I'll be able to find a cart to hire—to transport Mistress Oliver and to deliver the note to your doctor," Ezra said.

Maggie shifted her weight from one foot to the other and, finding that she could balance herself, declared that she had no need for the doctor, and that what everyone needed was a good meal which she'd have ready in a matter of moments. "And yes," she called out to Genie, "you must have a meal before going out into the cold and I'll brook no argument from you."

Genie was smiling when she emerged as Eugene from the scullery. Abby gasped and grabbed the ripped bodice of her dress, causing both Genie and Maggie to laugh out loud. "You're safe with me, Mistress Read, I promise!" Genie said, and Abby blushed a deep scarlet and turned away. She took pins from her hair and fashioned a temporary fix for her bodice and they all sat at the kitchen table and ate a thick vegetable stew with thick wedges of corn meal bread.

"What is your business, Mistress Oliver, if I may ask?" Maggie asked.

"I work at Miss Adelaide's Dress and Hat Shop on—"

"I know it!" Maggie exclaimed before Genie could say where it was. "I bought a dress and a shawl there."

41

"I hope you found them satisfactory," Genie replied, and Maggie extolled the virtues of the garments purchased from Miss Adelaide's, reminding Abby that she, too, liked them. When she ran out of words, Ezra asked, "How is Elizabeth? Is she working today?"

A range of emotions washed over Maggie's face, finally settling on a brave smile. "She goes to school now, Mr. MacKaye, and she lives with a family during the week so she's not out alone. I do miss her but I know she's safe, and she's being schooled."

"Please give her my regards," Ezra said.

"I will, Mr. MacKaye. She'll be pleased. She speaks of you often."

Ezra stood. "Mistress . . . Mister Oliver, we should take our leave."

Genie stood and bowed slightly to Maggie and Abby. "Thanks to your soup I'll be warm on the journey home."

"Supper will be served at seven o'clock, Mr. MacKaye," Abby said.

"I'll be here," Ezra said.

"I'm very pleased to have met you both," Genie said to Maggie and Abby, and exited the scullery door, followed closely by Ezra MacKaye.

"What a remarkable woman," Abby said in an almost whisper, still watching the space where Genie had been.

"Indeed, she is," Maggie said, watching Abby.

"And an unlikely companion for Mr. MacKaye, don't you think?"

"I think she's quite beautiful," Maggie replied. "Don't you?"

Genie and Ezra hurried down the alleyway behind Apted Street toward Main Street. The warmth provided by the hearty soup they'd just eaten evaporated within seconds as it was bitterly cold and they were walking toward the river, into the wind. They spied a horse cart almost immediately and Ezra sprinted for it, relieved to see that the bundled-up driver was a Colored man. He had nodded politely at Ezra but he leaned over and peered closely at Genie when she approached.

"Miss Eugenie? Is that you?" the driver asked.

"It is. Good evening to you."

"Is you goin' home?"

"I am. Are you available for hire?"

"Yes, ma'am. Climb in."

Genie climbed in as quickly and easily as if she had springs in her legs. Ezra reached into his pocket to pay the driver but he shook his head—he didn't need to be paid to drive Miss Eugenie home. But when she insisted that he accept the payment, he did so with a tip of his hat to Ezra.

"Thank you, Mr. MacKaye, and I'll see you tomorrow evening," Genie said in parting.

Ezra frowned. "For what purpose?"

"Didn't you see the note I left for you? It's why I was at Mistress Read's residence," she said impatiently.

Ezra touched his pockets and withdrew her note from an inside one. "I haven't read it," he said.

"Then I suggest you do so," she replied as the driver clicked the reins and the cart moved away.

Ezra did, squinting at the note in the gaslight. *It'll be dark as pitch behind that church at night*, he thought. And teeth-chattering cold. He didn't need to go because he'd lost the chance to earn Cortlandt's bonus payment, but he would go because he had no way to tell them that he wouldn't be there. It didn't occur to him that they'd have what he wanted to know.

CHAPTER FOUR

Arthur was there waiting when Genie emerged from the narrow space between the Back Street and Thatcher Lane, and his warm smile confirmed that she'd been right to return home the previous night. She could not, however, free her memory of Abby Read's invitation to spend the night. Genie had not been an overnight guest in another's home since the earliest days of her escape to freedom. The memory was crystal clear: She was alone and terrified, in Philadelphia because Blacks could be free here. But how? Where? Mrs. Carrie Tillman had answered those questions—and many more. These were her thoughts when she realized that Arthur was watching her, waiting. Had he spoken?

"So them boys, they gon' be there waitin' for you when you get there, Miss Eugenie. I hope you ain't mad 'cause I told 'em to go there 'stead of bein' in me and Mr. William's way. We got work to do."

He sounded so contrite that Genie almost laughed. She just wished she knew what he was talking about. "I can't imagine what you could do to make me angry with you, Arthur," she said. "I can't imagine being angry with you."

He accepted her praise with a slight bow and continued his unprecedented monologue. "They was just so worried 'bout you! I told 'em you can take care of yourself but they said it was the white man they didn't trust and I can't fault 'em for that. I don't trust no white men, neither."

Now Genie thought she understood: Absalom and Reverend Richard Allen were coming to the shop to make certain that Ezra had kept his word and seen her safely home last night. "You did just right, Arthur. Thank you."

He was relieved. Then he looked worried. "You was out late at night with a white man? Which white man is that, Miss Eugenia, and do Mr. William know him?"

Now Genie did laugh, and yes, she told him, William knew who the man was though he hadn't yet met him. "May I ask a favor of you, Arthur?"

"You know you can, Miss Eugenia."

"Will you please tell William that I think he's right, that I do need a horse cart?"

Arthur's wide grin showed all of his teeth. "He certainly will like hearing that! He worries 'bout you."

Genie knew that her friends worried for her safety and that bothered her. She took great care to keep herself out of harm's way. In the current climate, however, being cautious was no guarantee of safety. And she could not free her mind of the sight of Abby Read—a wealthy white woman—attacked in her own home by a wealthy white man. If Abby Read wasn't safe within her home, how could she, Genie Oliver, expect to be safe out in the street at all hours of the day and night, derringer notwithstanding? *Abby Read.* She wished she hadn't brought Abby Read into her mind. She didn't know why thoughts of the woman unnerved her.

"Miss Eugenia?" Arthur had spoken and she hadn't heard him. Again.

"I apologize, Arthur. What did you say?"

"Should I tell Mr. William to have a horse cart ready for you to see this evenin'?"

She shook her head. "No, Arthur. I've an appointment this evening. Will you take me in the morning?"

He agreed, grudgingly and unhappily, and she entered her shop to satisfy Absalom Jones and Reverend Richard Allen that she had arrived safely home the previous night and to thank them for their concern. When they left Adelaide marveled at their names. Genie, who understood completely, explained it to her: The two boys had managed to escape slavery and make their way to Philadelphia, anxious to leave every vestige of their previous life behind, including their names. And to discover that in Philadelphia two names known to everyone, Black and white, were Absalom Jones and Reverend Richard Allen! Famous Colored men. Of course they'd want to claim those names for themselves.

"So that those searching for runaway slaves would not suspect them?" Adelaide asked skeptically. "Even a stupid slave catcher would know those two names. And why didn't Eli take a new name?"

Genie cared deeply for Adelaide but sometimes, like now, explaining how slavery affected the mind and the spirit felt much too taxing. She thought she knew why Eli would keep his name: Because his mother had given him that name and it might be all he had left of her. And for too many other reasons to count. As for Absalom and Richard, Genie could easily imagine that their previous names had been bestowed by slave owners, many of whom chose Greek or Latin names for their slaves, often to mock what they considered heathen names of a heathen people. So certainly they would not have wanted to keep Tiberius or Agamemnon as their names in their new, free world. Yes, those names would not only mark them as slaves, but they would also have reminded them of a hated past. Unfortunately, their newly chosen names could betray them as well. "Richard thinks their chosen names may have the opposite effect," Genie said, hoping that Adelaide understood, wishing that she knew someone who would, could, understand.

Abby Read and Maggie Juniper served breakfast to their guests—five men who politely and appreciatively ate the heaping servings of eggs, bacon, sausages, potatoes and biscuits, and drank coffee by the pot—no tea drinkers here. All five had their white linen napkins tucked into their shirt fronts to protect their business suits against spills, and all five read newspapers. Only Ezra MacKaye engaged the women in conversation, inquiring about their health, especially Maggie, and whispering to Abby that Charles Gresham was in more trouble than he had money to buy his way out of.

"Does that mean he'll not be back to bother me?" Abby whispered.

Ezra scowled. "He knows that I live here. He won't return."

Both women wanted to inquire after Eugenia Oliver but neither thought such a query appropriate, though for different reasons. If Maggie had been privy to Genie's thoughts she'd have assured her that she understood, and she did. Not only had she immediately known that Genie was a woman dressed in men's clothing, she'd recognized her for the slave that she'd once been: because of the kitchen cloth she'd wrapped around her head, the disused bed sheet she'd wrapped around herself as a makeshift apron, the bare feet that peeked from beneath the skirts, and the lowered eyes that never met those of the white men in authority. She recognized and understood these behaviors because she'd been taught to recognize them by her husband, Jack Juniper, himself an escaped slave who spent his life at sea, not because he wished to be away from his wife and daughter but because he wished to remain free. He would be home in two months, perhaps to remain for twice that long. She wondered if Jack and Eugenia would feel comfortable enough with each other to be friends. She certainly intended to attempt friendship with this woman that Abby found so "unlikely." Abby was pouring more coffee for Ezra MacKaye when Maggie saw that she leaned in close and said something, and given the length of his reply, Maggie thought she'd probably asked about Genie Oliver.

"I did," Abby acknowledged when the men were gone to their employment and they were alone in the kitchen. "I was concerned that she'd have to walk home alone but Mr. MacKaye spied a horse cart with a Colored driver—and one who knew Mistress Oliver—so he was confident that she arrived safely home. I was much relieved to hear it."

"As am I," Maggie replied, wondering how Genie Oliver was known by a horse cart driver, one of the many things she wondered about the woman. At the top of the list was the electricity that passed between Genie and Abby when they met. Maggie had known Abby Read since they were children and while she easily understood the rejection of Charles Gresham—he was a swine—there were other suitors whom Abby had rejected and Maggie did not understand the reason: intelligent, charming, handsome, wealthy young men, all rejected by Abby for reasons that she could not fully explain. Now, after witnessing what passed between Genie and Abby, Maggie thought that perhaps she did understand, though she most certainly could not explain it.

"Do you find her unusual, Maggie?"

"I find her . . . interesting," Maggie replied.

"Why do you think she wears men's clothes?"

Ah! "Many women disguise themselves to buy a measure of safety if they must be out alone," Maggie said, and added, "especially Colored women." Most women sought to travel with friends or relatives so as not to be alone but when company was not available and walking to and from work was the only means of getting there, a disguise provided some protection from the unwanted, and potentially dangerous, attention of men, both Colored and white.

After a moment Abby said, "Let's visit the dress shop where she works. I'd like to see it."

"And I'd like to see it again," Maggie replied.

Genie and Adelaide would not have welcomed two additional visitors to the shop that day. From the moment they unlocked the front door there had been a steady stream of patrons seeking warm clothes in preparation for the winter that was getting closer with each passing day. It was the end of November, and snow flurries swirled in the sky almost every day. The women were grateful that the pace of donations kept up with the need for warm clothes, and for the first time, shoes were among the donated items. Genie thought immediately of Eli and Richard and Absalom and the other boys who tied rags on their feet or went barefoot in the ice and snow, and she put the largest shoes aside for them—years of working and walking barefoot resulted in very wide feet.

"You know, you have your own small army," Adelaide said to Genie when they finally were alone and able to eat a bite.

"Army?" Genie was puzzled and confused.

"Those boys, those parentless, homeless boys, like the ones who were here this morning and wouldn't leave until they saw you safe. They would do anything for you. I know you feed them, Genie—we all know—even though you believe it to be a secret. And you clothe them and talk to them and give them the kind of information they need to be safe and—"

Genie lifted her hand to silence her friend. Her relationship to those boys was not a discussion she could or would have with someone who didn't understand being alone and afraid. Genie helped those boys because she could, because if she didn't, perhaps no one else would, and certainly the boys never would ask for help. She inhaled deeply and recalled her own early days in this city and knew that she, too, could have been barefoot and homeless. She was not, because she had stolen money from her master who was dead by her hand. She found her way to Philadelphia because she could read. Her mistress had seen to her education. Certainly, that was a gift but not one given out of kindness. Genie would forever hear the woman's voice proclaiming that she'd *rather be dead than live in a house with an ignorant Black heathen. She'll learn how to read or I'll beat the Black off of her.* And she survived and thrived because of Carrie Tillman's goodness. "I do what I can and what I must, Adelaide. No more, no less."

"You're a good woman, Genie Oliver, and a good friend."

"Thank you, Adelaide. I pray that you always think so." She stood up with a grimace at the pile of clothes that still surrounded her. "I must go. We'll begin again tomorrow." She went to the back to change her clothes and added a second scarf when Adelaide called out that it was snowing again. Then she grabbed a pair of shoes and socks for Eli and rushed out, hoping that she would arrive at the meeting place behind Christ Church before Ezra MacKaye so that Eli would have time to put on the shoes and socks.

Ezra was a quarter of an hour early. He knew where the church was, as did most residents of Philadelphia City, but he'd never been inside. Seen at close proximity for the first time on a cold, blustery late November night, the massive stone structure seemed to loom out of the darkness like an island in the sea. Light surrounded and bathed it and made it seem to exude warmth and comfort. Ezra was impressed that stone could feel anything but cold and forbidding, and he wondered if it was a trick of lighting. People were entering as if it were a Sunday morning instead of a Thursday evening, and he realized that the Evensong was about to begin.

He huddled within his coat, wrapped his scarf tighter, and made his way to the building's rear, hoping that the sense of warmth carried over to the back side though even if it did, he thought as he turned the corner, the light would not.

"Ben Franklin and Thomas Jefferson and Betsy Ross all said their prayers here at one time," he heard from the darkness. Genie Oliver's voice, confident and reassuring, put him at ease, though she did not make herself more than a shadow until Ezra was all the way behind the church and fully concealed by the darkness. "Thank you for coming, Mr. MacKaye."

Genie emerged fully from the shadows in her disguise, and though it was what Ezra expected, he still found himself slightly disoriented by the sight. This was, he knew, quite a beautiful woman but he could not find her beneath the layers of male clothing. "I am pleased to see you again, though I thought I'd be early. I suppose I should have known better," he said dryly.

Her mouth twitched in what may have been a suppressed smile though it was too dark to be certain. She had arrived early, correctly guessing that Eli would, too. She wanted to give him his shoes and socks and time to put them on before their meeting. The boy was momentarily speechless, then, by turns, disbelieving and excited. He dropped to the ground, dressed his feet, then stood and paced about for several seconds, his arms extended sideways as if for balance. Then he performed a brief march, halting it quickly as Ezra arrived and molding himself to the church wall, invisible in the darkness.

"I do wish I had better news for you."

"But your note said you had the information I wanted! I took that to mean that you know where to find young Cortlandt!" he exclaimed, adding sourly that anyway the information may have come too late to benefit him.

Ignoring that, Genie said, "I do know where he is. I also know that he's being held for ransom."

"The devil he is!" Ezra couldn't contain his anger and frustration any longer. "Where is he and how much do they want?"

"It's not money they want," Genie said quietly, and waited for Ezra to calm himself before she answered. "They want assurances from his father regarding the placement of new stops along the railroad line."

"But Arthur Cortlandt is a banker!" Ezra exclaimed, anger returning.

"Who just bought a railroad," Genie replied with calm reasoning.

Ezra stood breathing for a moment, thinking about what he had just heard, recalling the recent debate about expanding railroad service from Philadelphia to Pittsburgh, Harrisburg, and New York. Before he could pose a question, though, Genie Oliver said, "Best let Eli tell you all about it," and Eli stepped forward, nothing more than a shadow in motion. "You remember Eli, Mr. MacKaye." It was not a question.

"Good evening, Eli."

"'Evenin', suh."

"I'm sorry I frightened you the other day and after the events of recent days, I'll be a hundred years old before I ever chase another Colored person. I hope you will forgive me."

Eli didn't say anything but Ezra heard him expel breath. The boy was not entirely certain that he could trust Miss Eugenie's claim that he should trust the white man. Eli inhaled deeply several times and began to talk. The story he told was of wealthy, older men from New York and Chicago who lured young Cortlandt into their poker game. They let him first win a little, then lose a little, win a bit more, then lose more and more, until he had no hope of ever breaking even. Then they had their leverage. It took a while for young Edward to understand that the men didn't want money from him. He drank to excess and even when sober he was not a quick thinker. Even after he stole his mother's jewelry, worth much more than the small fortune he'd gambled away, and the men refused to accept it as payment, he still didn't fully understand their intentions. Until the morning they'd snatched him out of the back alley behind the house on Poplar Street where he'd been renting a room and took him to a private railway car down by the docks, where they forced him to write the ransom demand to his father.

Ezra was silent for a long moment. "There's a question I must ask, Eli, and I don't wish to be insulting. But how do you know all this? Were you present at these poker games, at the abduction?"

"Yippie tol' me."

"Who?"

Genie interceded. "The New York man is Dutch. Van-Something his name is. Eli can't pronounce it. His servant is an old man, born on an upstate New York plantation. His name is Dutch, too, and Eli said it sounds something like Yippie."

"But why would these men carry out such a scheme in the presence of witnesses?" Ezra found it too much to believe.

"That's a question you can answer better than I can, Mr. MacKaye: Why do your people treat us as if we're invisible, blind and deaf? But the easy answer in this case is that the New York Dutchman doesn't know his loyal old slave speaks and understands English."

Ezra heard the dry irony in Genie Oliver's voice and he thought he heard Eli stifle a snort. He was already wondering whether to snatch Edward Cortlandt from the train car before it was moved, or tell old man Cortlandt of the ransom demand first. He reached into his pocket and withdrew several coins. "I'm very grateful for your assistance, Eli," he said, knowing that to offer money to Genie Oliver would be an insult.

Even though their eyes had adjusted to the deep darkness they still were just shadows to each other, but the sound of the money was distinctive. "You don't have t' give me no money. I'm just doin' a favor for Miss Eugenie."

"Take the money, Eli," Genie said softly, and the boy slowly stretched his hand forward, prepared to snatch it back if necessary, if the man was trying to trick him. He leaned forward and watched as Ezra counted five half-dollar pieces into his hand; then he held his hand close to his face to better see what was there. Then he looked from the white man whom he still didn't trust to the Black woman whom he did trust, his expression a question. "You earned the money, Eli. I thank you and Mr. MacKaye thanks you. Your information is very helpful."

Eli nodded and touched his cap, whispered his thanks, then turned and swiftly vanished into the darkness, his feet making a shuffling, scraping sound. Ezra remembered that the boy was barefoot when he last saw him and he thought it likely that Eugenia Oliver was responsible for the shoes, though he really had no basis for the thought.

"Miss Eugenie?" The question came from the dark and from closer than Ezra would have guessed, and it unnerved him. He thought that Eli had disappeared into the night. "Wit' some a' this money, can I buy me some more warm clothes and some food?"

"Go see Miss Adelaide, Eli. Tell her I said to come. Go to the back door. Knock two times, wait, then knock one time."

There was no further sound from the cold darkness. Eli was gone. Genie and Ezra moved closer together so that their conversation was no more than whispers.

"This information is reliable?" Ezra asked.

"It is."

"Do you know where that rail car is going?"

"I do," Genie replied with more gravity than Ezra so far had heard in her voice, "and that is a matter of great concern." She inhaled deeply, expelled the breath, and continued. "It will go to an unused spur on the Reading line."

"It's deserted, isolated?" Ezra asked, calculating how many men he would need to hire to surround and take the train and free Edward Cortlandt.

"It is. Which is why it is a stop on the Underground Railroad."

The air around them stilled as Genie Oliver revealed information about herself that only two other human beings knew. Ezra MacKaye knew that his response to that knowledge would forever put him on One Side or The Other, would make his actions of recent days and weeks pale in comparison. Rescuing a girl from the clutches of renegade slave catchers was one thing. Abetting the escape of slaves was quite another. "What are you thinking, Genie?"

"That we must stop the train and take young Cortlandt before it reaches the depot."

Ezra posed his next question carefully. "Is it not possible to wait for the train at the depot and then . . . "

"A shipment is scheduled to arrive there in two nights' time and there is no way to stop it." Genie paused a moment to give her words time to find meaning in the man's mind. "Two families from Maryland, going on to Albany, New York." Genie paused again. "Mrs. Tubman will be bringing them."

"Great God Almighty!" Ezra exclaimed.

"There are those who think she is."

"So, we must stop a moving train and rescue a hostage without being arrested or killed," Ezra mused.

"Or blow it up where it sits," Genie said.

54

"Edward Cortlandt would be killed," Ezra said in a tight voice. "Better than Mrs. Tubman being caught," Genie said in so cold a tone that Ezra shivered, and the November night air was not to blame. He wondered, not for the first time, who Eugenia Oliver really was.

"There must be a way for us both to achieve our goals."

"Does that mean you don't intend to report the imminent arrival of Mrs. Tubman? The bounty on her head is considerable."

"I told Abigail Read and Maggie Juniper when I first met them that I was not a slave catcher, that I despised all like them and the work they did, and now I will tell you the same thing: Slavery is an abomination and should be ended. I will do nothing to perpetuate the practice."

"Good," Genie said, silently praying that this man would not betray her trust in him. "Then yes, I do have an idea for the rescue of young Cortlandt. But first I think you should tell his papa the situation, tell him you have matters under control, and get money from him. Enough to purchase chloroform and the services of six strong men."

The silence that met Genie's idea told her that Ezra MacKaye was rendered speechless—with anger or amazement, she wasn't certain which—so she hastened to explain that she would arrange for a break in the track that would derail the train. The two men guarding Edward Cortlandt would have to exit the car, in the pitch darkness, to investigate. They would be subdued and rendered unconscious with the chloroform, allowing for the rescue of young Cortlandt. Ezra then could deliver all three to Cortlandt Senior, collect his payment, and be hailed a hero. And Mrs. Tubman could deliver her shipment in peace—and in secrecy.

More silence, and since Genie had nothing more to say she could only wait. Finally, Ezra spoke, asking two questions: Was Genie certain there would be but two guards with Edward, and where would the break in the track occur? Genie had both answers and she felt more than heard Ezra's acceptance. Then, there was another query: The cost of the chloroform?

55

"I . . . don't know . . . exactly . . ." she said warily.

Ezra understood immediately, having made more than a few similar, questionable arrangements himself: She very well could be paying more for a few men's silence than for the drug itself. "Fortunately, Mr. Cortlandt lives nearby. Will you wait here for me?"

"No, Mr. MacKaye. I am cold and hungry and I want to go home. I will meet you in the morning after I have completed the purchase of a horse cart—you say where and when."

Ezra gave a dry chuckle. "A very wise purchase, Miss Oliver."

Genie's chuckle was even drier. "I'm glad you approve, Mr. MacKaye."

"I maintained my office on Flegler Street—"

She interrupted him with an apology and the opinion that she might well not be a welcome visitor there, either as Eugene or Genie, adding that it also might not be wise for them to be seen together. She suggested instead her shop, adding that he could enter unseen from the rear if he preferred, though, she said, few, if any, would pay him notice if he entered through the front door. He grunted and asked for the address, which she gave him. "What time?" he asked.

"I arrive at nine o'clock and have no plans to leave," she replied, and after sending regards to Miss Read and Mrs. Juniper, she wished him a good evening and left him in the darkness behind the massive church. Alone, he realized that he was cold to the bone and lightly covered with a snow that he hadn't realized was falling. He pulled his scarf tighter around his neck, pulled his hat further down on his head, and hurried out to the street where he ran to catch the first horse bus he saw, not caring where it was going. He'd plot his destination when he warmed up. For now, he wanted to think quietly about his conversation with Eugenia Oliver, about all that was implied as well as what had been said. And he wondered whether he'd have an opportunity to meet Harriet Tubman.

✳ ✳ ✳

56

If he had posed that question to Genie she would have responded, Certainly not! She herself had never met the woman called the Moses of her people, and she didn't know anyone who had, not even William. The people in direct communication with Mrs. Tubman did not know the people who made the arrangements for her arrival. It was their job—Genie and Willian—to prepare the place and have it ready in two days' time. The travelers would arrive when they arrived. Genie and William would be told only that they had arrived safely—or not—and the latter had never occurred.

Genie huddled deeply into her coat and prepared for the long, frigid walk home when she heard her name whispered. She whirled around to find Eli standing beside a horse cart driven by Arthur! She clambered up into the wagon and gratefully wrapped herself in the blanket Eli offered while he wrapped himself in another. She greeted Arthur warmly and knew from his smile that the cart was hers, which made her even more grateful at not having to walk home. She felt almost warm despite the light snow that still fell. Assuming that the men hadn't had time to eat, she asked Arthur to drive them to The Joseph Family Dining Room. "I am buying us dinner!" she exclaimed, and even the horse seemed to understand because she picked up her pace before Arthur could click the reins. "The horse! Can the horse wait outside while we eat? It won't be too cold?" Genie exclaimed, and both Arthur and Eli laughed, and she finally joined in.

Joe Joseph spied them when they walked in the door and he rushed over. "Genie Oliver! How wonderful to see you! Why have you been away so long?" he exclaimed, hugging her warmly.

Genie wondered the same thing as she surveyed the room full of people who seemed to sparkle in the firelight—candles glowed and flickered throughout the cozy room and large logs crackled in the hearth. The aroma of roasting meats and simmering vegetables and baking bread added to the sense of warmth and welcome. So often—perhaps too often—Genie rushed home at the end of her day to be alone, to eat the meal she had prepared for herself, to take stock of her activities—and to be grateful. She believed herself to be safer when alone. She took notice of the diners as Joe led them to a table: People she knew, liked, respected. If asked she would say that she had friends but the truth was that she spent no time with them unless there was a reason, and being with them because they were friends was not a reason. At least not one that she used with any regularity.

She saw Adelaide and William at a nearby table and detoured to greet them, people she considered good and dear friends and with whom she almost never shared a meal. As surprised as they were to see her inside a restaurant, they were even more glad. They hugged her warmly and asked Joe to make room at their table for her, Arthur and Eli, and while that was happening Genie whispered to William that Ezra MacKaye would be at the dress shop the following morning. William's curt nod meant that he would be, too.

And he was, well before Ezra arrived, giving Genie the opportunity to explain the circumstances that caused her to enlist his help. Before she could finish, William was shaking his head. The deep frown of concern that was tinged with fear spoke more loudly than his calm, reasoned words: "I do not think it wise to involve this man in our affairs."

"He's already involved, William, because of the Cortlandt boy."

"Another reason not to like this situation: Cortlandt's bank supports pro-slavery causes."

"And if MacKaye returns his son he'll be indebted to him."

While William weighed this thought, Genie told him of Ezra MacKaye's actions two days earlier inside Abby Read's house, and she followed that with a recitation of his rescue of Maggie Juniper's daughter from the slave catchers. He gave a resigned sigh and, taking Genie's shoulders in his strong hands, looked deeply into her eyes. She knew what he was looking for and she held his gaze, unblinking and unwavering. "You will have Arthur with you every step of the way," he finally said.

Genie's face showed her surprise, but it was brief. Then she laughed and gave her friend a quick hug. She should have known that Arthur was more than a smithy in William's blacksmith shop. A mere smithy would not be sent to walk Genie to work every day, nor would he live in a beam-and-stone cottage adjacent to the stables where, she knew, several strong, fast horses were lodged. And she suddenly realized that she had witnessed Arthur working on long guns at the forge. Of course, he was no *mere* smithy. And as if he were privy to her thoughts William said, "We are in possession of several new weapons, which Arthur will go deep into the forest to learn to shoot. You will accompany him, Genie, please, and become proficient in the use of these weapons."

"Of course," she said, recognizing that she had been given a look deep inside the steps taken to protect and safeguard Mrs. Tubman. "Perhaps Arthur can also teach me how to drive my cart and care for my horse, and you can tell me how much I owe you?"

He was about to respond when the bell announced the opening of the front door. They heard Adelaide's light voice and a deep male one, and they emerged from the back room to greet Ezra MacKaye. The two men shook hands as Genie introduced them.

"The charming Miss Adelaide would be your wife, Mr. Tillman?"

"Yes, Mr. MacKaye, I'm happy to say." Then with a smile of apology, he begged Adelaide's forgiveness and led Genie and Ezra into the back room where he wasted no time confronting Ezra. "Eugenia makes a convincing argument for trusting you, Mr. MacKaye, but I am not yet convinced."

"I can only promise you, Mr. Tillman, swear to you, that I will do nothing to harm you or . . . those close to you, and I can only hope that you will accept my word," Ezra replied.

"Your actions of recent days and weeks suggest that your word can be trusted," William responded, scrutinizing the man, "and Eugenia's opinion is a weighty one. Still. Lives depend on what we do and how well we do it. A mistake—"

He didn't complete the thought and he didn't need to.

"We're asking and expecting a lot of you, Ezra," Genie said.

59

Ezra gave a wry chuckle and agreed that indeed they were, but he graciously acknowledged that if the plan succeeded both sides got what they wanted. Nobody lost. "But I remain concerned that the plan has so many moving parts and pieces—"

"Easily remedied, Mr. MacKaye," Genie said curtly.

"As you've made clear, Miss Oliver," Ezra replied with equal chill.

William studied them, then reviewed in his mind the plan that Genie had outlined to him, and he quickly understood that the simplest, most direct option would be the elimination of the Cortlandt boy, which they could have done with Ezra MacKaye none the wiser—and he knew it. "We have no time to waste," William said. "Genie, you'll begin your lessons with Arthur immediately."

She nodded and wondered only briefly where they would go to shoot weapons without being heard and thought probably at the same location she would practice driving a horse cart without attracting notice: On the estate of one of the wealthy abolitionists who supported their cause. She could shoot the derringer. Could she shoot a revolver? If necessary, she thought.

"He won't balk," she heard Ezra say. "As much as he despises his son's behavior, he loves his son and wants his safe return. If he has received the ransom note he will know that the boy is in grave danger. He will pay what I ask."

"Then we will meet again at first light in the morning to—" William hesitated briefly and smiled at Ezra, "—to put all those moving parts and pieces in order. At the stables. Genie will show you where, Mr. MacKaye."

Ezra nodded his assent even as he wondered what lessons Genie was to begin with Arthur, and who Arthur was.

CHAPTER FIVE

Maggie Juniper locked the scullery door behind the two hired servant girls who cleaned the kitchen after breakfast and dinner—the two meals served daily in the Read House. The two young women were part of a full staff that had been employed by Abby's parents. Abby, however, did not want servants living in her house so she had dismissed the entire staff. She also wanted to foster the belief that she took in boarders because she needed the money. She laughed internally at the lie. She was an extremely wealthy young woman who refused to give a man access to her fortune. Advice her mother had given, and which she heeded. She herself was in the front hall supervising the two servant girls who came daily to clean the guest rooms and the public areas of the mansion. Aside from the paying guests, however, only Abby and Maggie lived in the house full time. Maggie did the cooking but not the cleaning; she was not a maid. She was and always had been a companion for Abigail. The fact that all the available rooms were let meant that Abby could keep the furniture and floors gleaming, the linens starched, the silver polished, the crystal of the chandeliers glittering like diamonds without having to touch her own money. She looked all around her. It was indeed a beautiful house, beautifully furnished. Her mother, wealthy in her own right, had had excellent taste. Charles was right: Abby and her house were worth a fortune. And that didn't take into account the jewels he knew nothing about. Would never know anything about.

Maggie put a covered plate of the evening's meal and a pot of coffee on the stove for Ezra MacKaye. He'd sent a messenger with a note of apology explaining that the press of business would cause him to miss supper. Maggie was willing to wager that the business did not include dinner. And because she liked Ezra MacKaye, she did for him what she would not have done for another guest: She made certain that he would have a meal whenever he returned.

Arthur Cortlandt careened about the library of his mansion like a wounded beast. He bellowed like one, too. And, in truth, he was wounded: If pride and ego could bleed, the floor would have been soaked. "I demand that you tell me how you knew Edward had been taken even before I knew! You will tell me!" he bellowed. Again.

"I cannot, sir, I am sorry—"

"I paid you to find my son!"

"And I have found him, Mr. Cortlandt."

"But you won't tell me where he is."

"No, sir. I cannot. What I can do is rescue him—"

"What I can do is pay the damned ransom and rescue him myself!"

"Have you been asked for money?" Ezra posed the question calmly, softly almost, and Cortlandt stopped careening about.

"Not yet, but I expect that they—whoever they are—now that they have my attention, they'll say how much they want."

"It is not money they want, sir," Ezra said in an almost whisper.

"Everyone wants money!" Cortlandt replied in a bellow.

"The men who kidnapped your son do not want money, Mr. Cortlandt, which is why they asked to meet with you in person. If they wanted money they would have asked for money and not for a meeting."

Cortlandt finally stopped careening and bellowing and looked at Ezra as if seeing him for the first time. "How do you know they asked to meet with me in person? Who are they then, and what do they want, Mr. MacKaye?"

"They want to be the ones to decide where the trains on your new railroad line will stop," Ezra answered.

Cortlandt's eyes narrowed to slits, and his lips flattened into a straight line as the businessman overtook the father. "The hell you say," he snarled. "Who do they think they are to make such demands of me!"

"Have they harmed him?" Emily Cortlandt asked, and both men whirled around to face her. They hadn't heard her enter.

"I don't think so," Ezra replied. "In fact, it is in their best interests to see that no harm comes to him."

"What do you need Arthur to do?" she asked, and Ezra explained that he had a plan (mentally apologizing to Genie!) to rescue Arthur from his captors without violence, but he would need to hire men and horses and wagons—and he would need to purchase chloroform.

"Why such an elaborate plan?" Arthur queried, snarling now instead of bellowing.

"The men who have your son are not bankers or businessmen, Mrs. Cortlandt. They're thugs, hoodlums, violent men. I want to avoid shooting." Ezra looked at and spoke to Mrs. Cortlandt, the real power behind the throne.

"I thought you said they were businessmen!" Arthur accused. "Make up your mind, man!"

"The men who arranged the kidnapping are businessmen, Mr. Cortlandt, which is how they know that you just bought a railroad, but the men they hired to carry out the kidnapping and hold Edward until they get what they want—they're not good men."

"Yet you want me to hand my railroad over to them!"

Ezra shook his head. "I want you to meet with them, listen to them—remembering that you don't know what they want until they tell you—then convince them that you can't make such a decision on the spur of the moment. Tell them you'll need a few hours to confer with your partners. As businessmen they'll understand that, and that will give me time to secure your son's release."

"Why can't I just tell them I know what they've done and demand my son's return?"

"Because you'll jeopardize your son's life and my associates' as well," Ezra said, patience waning.

"I don't give a damn for your associates!" Cortlandt was back to thundering.

"You should, Mr. Cortlandt, because I can't secure your son's freedom without them." Ezra's tone was icy and he didn't care if Arthur Cortlandt didn't like it. He was tired of Arthur Cortlandt.

"Give him what he asks, Arthur," Emily said, and left them as quietly as she had arrived.

Arthur Cortlandt wore his wealth around his waist and on his face: Both reflected his appreciation of good food and drink and his frequent indulgence of them. Emily Cortlandt wore her wealth on her body: Her gown and jewels were fit for royalty—as was her carriage and behavior. Her voice was soft and pleasant, her manner gracious, but she fully expected that her husband would do what she told him to do. He sighed deeply, a deflated balloon. "Even after all the hurt and heartache he has caused her, she just wants him back." He sighed again. "As do I." He opened his desk, withdrew a check, and wrote it for twice the amount Ezra was prepared to ask for. He knew that he'd not have time to get to the bank before his meeting with William Tillman, but he decided that even in the darkness before first light the vision of Arthur Cortlandt's check would be proof that they could afford to put their plan in motion, and would be as well received as if it were the actual money it represented. He was proved correct.

"Good work and well done, Mr. MacKaye!" Tillman said, clasping Ezra's hand. He was the last to arrive, and the warm greeting and hot coffee he received helped to mitigate the frigid temperature outside. Four other people were present: Genie, William, and two men unknown to him. William introduced a wiry but very muscular, bearded man as Arthur, who nodded at him but did not offer to shake his hand. The other man was not introduced, and Ezra wondered only briefly at what appeared to be a serious lapse by William Tillman until he considered what he knew of Tillman: He was not the kind of man given to lapses in good behavior and Ezra knew instinctively that he probably never would see the stranger again. Or that his name would be recognized and it therefore would be dangerous for Ezra to know it—dangerous for both of them. Ezra suddenly was struck by the gravity of this undertaking—and the danger. He studied the three faces before him: William Tillman was not merely a blacksmith, nor Arthur merely a laborer, and whoever the third man was he could not be named. And Genie Oliver certainly was more than a pretty young woman who worked in a dress shop. In fact, she spent so little time there that she probably owned the place, and he smiled inside himself at the thought, amusement that quickly dimmed as he realized that he almost certainly was correct.

"Now that Ezra has secured the funding we require, Genie will finalize the plan," Tillman said in his quiet way, and all eyes moved from Tillman to Ezra to Genie, where they remained as she spoke.

Ezra was surprised but pleased to learn that the railroad car where Edward Cortlandt was being held had been under constant observation by two sets of watchers, day and night. They were secluded in the woods across from the tracks where the rail car was parked, providing an excellent view of the car. Before he could ask, Genie reported that young Cortlandt was alive if not especially well late last night. "Apparently the young man drinks large amounts of spirits and then expels it all after several hours, something his captors would rather he did outside in the woods instead of in the closed confines of the rail car." She hesitated a moment before continuing. "From the description of his behavior it is possible that he is also being drugged."

"What description?" Ezra exclaimed. "Does he appear injured?"

Genie shook her head and explained that young Edward was extremely unsteady on his feet and had to be practically carried into the woods to vomit. According to the watchers, he appeared more dazed than inebriated. "He doesn't seem to know where he is or what he's doing, is how it was explained, and this from a man who works in a saloon and is well acquainted with the behavior of drunken men," she said.

Ezra, wondering whether Eli was one of the watchers, thought this answered the question.

"We must extract that boy immediately!" the unnamed man said with quiet urgency.

"We're almost ready," William said, looking at Genie, and she nodded.

"If that boy is being given drugs, I doubt that a physician is administering them. That means that a couple of barely literate hooligans are dispensing alcohol and probably laudanum, which is a deadly combination." The unnamed man spoke again. He now sounded more angry than urgent, and Ezra wondered why.

Genie's breath seemed to catch in her throat and she briefly closed her eyes. When she opened them everyone was watching her. Recovering her breath, she said, "Since we pledged to rescue the young man we will move tonight, late, when they all are slowed and dimmed by drink. However, there are two potential problems: Though there are two men in the rail car guarding young Cortlandt, a third man arrives daily with provisions. He is on horseback and does not remain overnight, but he adheres to no schedule so we should be prepared to deal with him as well. The more serious concern is that both kidnappers are armed. It is our wish and our intention to subdue them with the chloroform. If, however, it becomes necessary, we will fight fire with fire." She paused and looked directly at Ezra. "It will fall to you to move immediately and quickly to apprehend the boy."

He nodded, then said, "If I may ask: Who owns that rail car, why is it empty, and can it be moved?"

"Good questions all," the unnamed man responded. "Yes, it can be moved and it will be moved as soon as it is emptied of its current occupants. And I suppose the most accurate answer is that it belongs to no one: It was abandoned by a company recently bankrupt and subsequently absorbed by one Arthur Cortlandt. So, I suppose that technically and legally it belongs to him, though I doubt he is aware of its existence."

"Do the men who orchestrated Edward's kidnapping know that his father 'technically' owns that rail car?" Ezra asked.

The unnamed man gave a smile that did not reach his eyes. "Almost certainly," he replied, but if he planned to elaborate, the words were lost at the sound of the stable door opening. At the same moment revolvers appeared in the hands of Arthur and Genie and were aimed at the door. Eli rushed in, breathless, filthy, and stinking like a swamp.

"They movin' the train car!" he said in a choked whisper. "By noontime today!"

For a stunned moment no one could speak as they took in Eli's words and their potential impact on what was already a daring and dangerous plan.

"Which direction?" the nameless man demanded.

"To the junction, the man who brings the food said," Eli replied with a hint of confusion. He didn't know what a junction was but he did know this: "And he was still there when I left to come tell y'all. Him and three horses." Three horses, not four. There was no horse for Edward Cortlandt, so either they planned to release him . . . or he wouldn't need one.

Normal breathing returned. They all knew what a junction was even if Eli didn't, and more crucially, where it was: in the busy and always occupied rail yard near the docks. William Tillman said grimly: "We go now. Immediately."

"Are we ready?" The unnamed man asked.

"I obtained all the necessary provisions on my promise to pay," William said. He looked at Ezra. "If you will kindly leave Mr. Cortlandt's check here with me?"

Ezra withdrew the check from his pocket and gave it to Tillman. "I fully expect to return," he said quietly.

"And I fully expect that you will, Mr. MacKaye," William replied and placed the check in the pocket that held his gold watch.

Genie touched the unnamed man's arm and told him that if the messenger and his horse were still at the rail car, it was his duty to do "whatever is necessary" to make sure the horseback rider was not a problem for them. Then she looked at Arthur and smiled and asked if he had the "end of the world" ready for the inhabitants of the rail car. Arthur returned the smile and promised that "they'll come runnin' outta there like the devil his own self is after 'em!"

Then Genie looked at Ezra. "Whenever and however Edward Cortlandt emerges from that rail car, he is your responsibility. You'll have chloroform to subdue him—everyone will have chloroform, as our objective is to empty that car and move it to a location of our choosing without any loss of life. If possible. However, the only life that we are committed to preserving is that of young Cortlandt."

Ezra knew that he was looking at and listening to Eugenia Oliver but he could barely believe it. True, she was dressed in her Eugene clothes and the butt end of a revolver was visible in the waistband of her pants, but he had just heard her order the deaths of at least three men in a flat, cold voice that he did not recognize. Then, in a completely different tone, she said, "We do not know how many Mrs. Tubman is bringing to freedom this time, or how many of them are women and children. We have heard that there is a bounty on her head though we do not know if this is true. But true or not, we will do all in our power to ensure that that rail car is empty and parked where she expects it to be when she arrives. That is what is expected of us and that is what we will provide."

"Then with God as our guide, let us go," Tillman said. "Everyone saddle a horse. Eli, you take a fresh one and lead the way." Then he gave the boy a scrutinizing look. "After you eat a few biscuits and bacon," he said, and muttered under his breath, "Not much point in a bath, I don't imagine."

If Eli heard the bath comment he paid it no notice; he was too focused on biscuits and bacon. Arthur removed the saddle from the horse Eli had ridden in on and placed it on a fresh mount, and he gave each rider a bag of provisions which contained food for those who were waiting in the woods for them. The horses were superior—some of the best Ezra had ever seen—and he was certain that some of Arthur Cortlandt's money was paying for them, as well as for the chloroform they all possessed and which

Ezra hoped they would use to subdue their quarry instead of the alternative. They exited the stable through the back and into a dirty, litter-strewn alley. The stench of the nearby docks rose up to greet them as strong as if it were the middle of summer instead of close on winter. The early hour and the dismal location meant the five people on horseback were not noticed because only the most drunken derelicts were found here, and those few who weren't drunken derelicts had no interest in the lives of others. Eli led them slowly to the railroad tracks adjacent to the docks where there were more people, but working people, too busy to notice or care who was riding by so early in the morning. They rode slowly, single file, beside the tracks until they reached the wood, then Eli spurred his horse to a gallop. They followed a well-worn path beside the tracks, deeper into the wood, when Eli stopped suddenly and dismounted. He put his finger to his lips and motioned them all to the ground. Then he knelt and touched the tracks and looked at Genie. She followed suit, and the look of horror on her face told them all what was happening though they all touched the tracks and felt the vibration: The rail car was moving. Slowly, but it was moving.

Unnamed Man ran forward without a word and before anyone could stop him, so they waited in silence for his return. Ezra, standing beside Genie, leaned down and whispered to her, "Who is he?"

She hesitated only briefly before whispering the answer: "Job Mayes."

Ezra couldn't prevent his surprised intake of breath. He would have wagered a small fortune that Job Mayes was a mythical figure created by enslaved Blacks to give themselves hope, for no ordinary man could have done the things attributed to this man: A runaway slave who had killed half a dozen people in retaliation for the sale of his wife and children, and half a dozen more during his escape from the Virginia plantation where he was enslaved and en route to his freedom. There was a bounty of several thousand dollars on his head but there was no image of him. No one knew what he looked like, and if asked to describe him, Ezra could give no better description than a thin, dark-skinned Colored man with short hair. Who ran like the wind. No wonder he had successfully escaped. And suddenly he was back with them, having made no sound. They gathered around him.

"Two men on horseback are pulling the car with leather straps attached to the hitch. Moving very slowly."

"How many?" Genie asked.

"The two pulling the car and two riding behind but I could not see inside the car. Three of our men are following behind on foot, in the woods, and the other two are bringing the cart," Mayes said.

Genie thought deeply for only a few seconds. "Throw fire-cracker sticks to the front and back of the car at the same time. Take the riders when the horses throw them. Eli, go behind and help our men make certain no one escapes from the car." To Mayes she said, "You and Arthur take the two in the front. Ezra, watch the rail car and take Cortlandt. And as we see, best to be prepared for surprises. Move. Now." And this time Genie led them along the tracks into the wood, Mayes close behind, whispering directions.

They stopped and dismounted at Genie's raised hand. Arthur unpacked small packages of fire sticks and tin boxes of matches and gave them to Mayes and Eli who ran forward, followed by everyone else except Arthur, who secured their horses so they wouldn't bolt at the sound of the exploding fire sticks. He would bring their horses forward when the noise abated, which didn't happen for quite a few minutes after the explosions. Yelling, screaming, shouting, cursing—and the screeches of birds startled by so much human noise so early on such a cold morning—filled the air, followed by two gunshots. Those galvanized Ezra, who grabbed his horse and galloped forward, his own gun in his hand. He could not get this close and lose Edward Cortlandt!

"There's that damn nigger lover! Pull him down off'n that horse!"

Ezra saw and heard them a moment too late. Algie and Jack were upon him before he could aim and fire the pistol he'd taken

70

from them weeks earlier. Jack grabbed his arm and simultaneously kicked his already nervous horse and Ezra went flying. His arm was snatched out of its joint. He hit the ground on the same shoulder, and the pain was so intense he could only lie there writhing.

"Not such a big shot now, are you, boyo?" Algie snarled, delivering two hard kicks to his right side before spitting at him. Ezra found he wasn't too wounded to evade the filth but rolling over cost him dearly. That regret vanished quickly as Jack galloped back. Dismounting before the horse halted, he ran toward Ezra, aiming a kick toward his groin. Ezra drew his knees into his chest and, reaching with his good arm, grabbed Jack's foot and used the man's own forward motion to lift and throw him. Because he was drunk Jack had no hope of keeping his balance. He hit the ground hard. His head hit something even harder. Both Ezra and Algie heard the crack.

"Jack! Jack, boy!" Algie called out as he ran toward the immobile Jack. "Get up from there! We got to go meet Tom so we can grab that old mammy and collect the bounty on her head!" But Jack didn't move so Algie stomped over to Ezra and delivered two hard kicks to the kidneys. "You bastard," he yelled as he aimed another kick. But he was drunk, too, and instead of another kidney shot, this kick landed on Ezra's right buttock. Hard. The pain shot through his entire body.

Ezra groaned and Algie gave a satisfied grunt. He came around to face Ezra and leaned over him. The weak early morning sunlight showed the clearly etched hatred in the man's puffy face, along with the dirt. "You got my pistol on you?" he snarled as he forced Ezra's knees down and his coat open. He gut-kicked him twice then grabbed the weapon and cracked Ezra across the face with it. Blood spurted and Ezra lost consciousness.

Then there was another crack and Algie dropped to the ground on his knees. His eyes closed as if he were praying. Another crack and he fell sideways, unconscious.

"Mr. MacKaye, you got to get up, suh." At the sound of the voice in his ear, Ezra forced himself up to semi-consciousness.

71

Eli. The boy was almost as filthy as Algie. But not quite, and Algie smelled much worse. "I don't think I can, Eli. I don't think I can move at all."

"Where 'bouts is you hurt?"

"Feels like everywhere, but for sure my left arm is no good." So, Eli grabbed his right hand and elbow and pulled him up, but his entire right side hurt. The gash on his face ran a river of blood and the pain made him dizzy again. He held on to Eli until he felt steady. Then he recalled what Algie had said about collecting the bounty on a mammy's head and his knees buckled. Eli steadied him again. "I've got to get to Genie." Then, another thought: "And young Cortlandt! Did you see him, Eli?"

"Yes, suh. That's where Miss Eugenie went—after him. One of them kidnappers grabbed the boy up on his horse and rode off with him. Miss Eugenie and Mr. Job, they followed. Seemed like they knowed all about what we was doin'."

"They know everything, Eli: They know about Mrs. Tubman, too."

Eli started and jerked Ezra so hard he cried out. "I'm sorry, Mr. MacKaye but we got to go catch up with them! Can you ride?"

"If you help me up, Eli, I think I can stay up," Ezra said, without real conviction, and with Eli's help he mounted the horse. He had to force words from a mouth clenched tight to stifle groans. "Tie those two up Eli, please," he said, gesturing toward Jack and Algie. "Tight, so they can't get free, and hide them so they won't be found for a good while. And get my pistol!" He tried to turn his horse to follow Genie but he needed his one good arm to hold on, so he had to wait for Eli to finish binding Jack and Algie and mount his own horse, then take the reins to Ezra's horse and lead them forward. Since every equine step sent pain cascading through his body it was a good thing that Genie and Mayes had not got too far ahead. The two kidnappers had Edward Cortlandt on the ground and were wrestling with him, trying to punch him into submission while the young man cursed them with all his drugged and drunken strength. They hadn't seen Genie and Mays approach. Genie fired a shot into the air and the kidnappers jumped to their feet, whirled around, and met two pistols aimed directly at them.

"Lie down on the ground, face in the dirt," Mayes commanded, and when they obeyed Genie chloroformed them, then bound them both hand and foot. Then she turned to young Cortlandt but before she could speak he snarled at her.

"Who in blazes are you?"

"Hired by your father to bring you home," Genie said.

"Liar. My father hired an ex-Pinkerton Scotsman named MacKaye to bring me home. You're not ex-Pinkerton and you're certainly not a Scotsman."

"Right on both counts," Genie said.

Cortlandt's eyes narrowed. "I've heard about niggers like you. Free-born and educated. But I tell you this: Touch me and I'll see you hang." *And I've heard that you were much like your father*, Genie thought, as she uncapped the chloroform and poured some into a cloth. Cortlandt knew what was coming and he cursed and wriggled but he was already impaired. Genie had the cloth over his nose and mouth and seconds later the young man was limp. And blessedly quiet. Genie dragged him toward the wagon. One of her men jumped down off his horse and helped deposit him in the wagon with his captors.

"Somebody's comin,'" one of Genie's men hissed, and it sounded like a shout. "Two riders on horseback."

Genie drew her pistol and aimed it toward the approaching riders as Mayes dropped to the ground behind the wagon, pistol in hand, ready to ambush if necessary. "It's your white man and the boy." The whisper was directly into Genie's ear, and she jumped a foot. The soft chuckle and pat on the back told her she wasn't the only one on edge.

Eli led Ezra's horse into the clearing and every Colored man gasped at the sight of him. He all but fell off his horse into their arms, and they led him to the back of the wagon and helped him up. The three bodies already there made for a crowd, but Ezra was too glad to be able to recline to care.

"What happened?" Genie asked, and Ezra told her, including the rescue by Eli.

"I owe that boy my life. And maybe I'm not the only one."

"What does that mean?" Genie asked.

Ezra whimpered in pain as he lifted himself upright and pulled Genie in close with his good arm. "They know about . . . they said they were after collecting a bounty on a mammy's head. And if they know, perhaps others do, too."

Genie said nothing for several seconds. Then she beckoned to Mayes and whispered with him for several seconds, after which he grabbed Ezra's horse and galloped off. Genie returned to the wagon where four men now lay—three of them drugged unconscious and one wishing that he were. Ezra watched her closely through the one eye that still functioned properly. "I've done my job," she said wearily. "There are others whose job it is to worry if and how we are compromised. Come, let's get you and these fellows back to town." She peered closely at him. "And you to a doctor."

But she first held a whispered conversation with four of her men—they were to clean the rail car and move it back up the tracks to its original position, and they galloped away immediately. Then she called Eli in close.

"You did a fine job this morning, Eli, and I'm very proud of you and very grateful to you." He responded like the boy he was instead of like the man he'd been forced to become: He ducked his head and mumbled something Genie couldn't hear but which she fully understood. "And I have more work for you, Eli, if you will accept it."

"Yes, Miss Eugenie, anything you want."

"Mr. MacKaye is very badly injured and he will need much care. Will you act as his manservant until he heals?"

Eli looked at her as if she'd asked him to walk on his hands. "You want me to live in that house with him?"

Genie nodded. "You'll be safe, Eli, Mrs. Juniper will see to that. You remember who she is?"

Eli nodded. He thought that Maggie Juniper reminded him

of his mother, or what he thought he remembered of his mother, but that was mostly wishful thinking because, in truth, he remembered nothing. The miles and years between him and his mother dimmed her image in his memory. He wasn't even sure of her name. "I'll do my best, Miss Eugenie."

"That I know for certain, Eli," she said, and told him to go immediately to William or Adelaide—whomever he could find—and get himself cleaned up for service in a great house. "Tell them to cut your hair and get you new clothes and shoes."

Eli's eyes grew large and shone with excitement, all traces of fear gone. "Then what do I do, Miss Eugenie?"

"Meet me at the scullery door at Mistress Read's. I'm going now with Mr. MacKaye to deliver the Cortlandt boy to his father and to hope that the man will send for a doctor." Genie gave the boy a quick, fierce hug. "Go now, Eli—but carefully!" The woods would shelter him for a while but then he'd have to take the road by the docks. It was a short run to William's smithy shop from there but Eli could not run. Dare not run and call unwelcome attention to himself. She knew that he knew how to be careful. She had to trust that he would.

Genie was climbing up to the wagon bench when Ezra called to her. "Is there more chloroform?"

She returned to the rear of the wagon, bottle in one hand, handkerchief in the other. "Not too much."

"Why not?" Ezra groaned.

"You must be awake to meet Mr. Cortlandt."

Ezra groaned again, then inhaled deeply as Genie's kerchief covered his nose and mouth. He'd be grateful for any length of time inured to the pain that wracked his body. And it was good that he was numb because Genie pushed the wagon harder and faster than she ever would have before. She wanted to get off this road. If the police caught her—caught Eugene Oliver, a Colored man, with four unconscious white men in his wagon, three of them bound, she'd be hung before sundown . . . or worse: She'd be sold South. And if the hooligans who beat Ezra knew about

Mrs. Tubman's presence in Philadelphia that coming night, Ezra was right in thinking others might know, too, which would surely put coppers, constables and the sheriff on the road. She clicked the reins and the wagon's speed increased. Her horseback-riding companions easily kept pace.

Genie stopped when the docks came into view. The place was teeming with activity and commerce. She looked into the back of the wagon and all four men were stirring. "Where are you meeting Cortlandt?" she asked Ezra.

"At the end of Essex Street."

Genie rolled forward a few feet and immediately spied the rich man's brougham, as out of place at the docks as the man himself. "I see him. Sit up now, so he sees you." She rolled the wagon forward several feet more, then halted when an armed man emerged from the back of the carriage. "Mr. MacKaye is here with a delivery for Mr. Cortlandt!" Genie called out in her strongest Eugene voice, and the armed man and his two companions froze in place.

"Are you there, Ezra?"

"Yes, sir," MacKaye replied, and stumbled as he tried to ease himself from the wagon with only one hand for support.

"Where's my son?"

"Right here, along with his kidnappers."

At those words, Arthur Cortlandt strode from the safety of his carriage toward Genie Oliver's rickety wagon, and he drew back at what he saw. "Why is my son bound like a steer?"

"Because, sir, he preferred to be touched by the hands of his captors than those of his rescuers," Ezra replied, looking from one to the other of the silent Black men in Genie Oliver's employ, both of whom still sat astride their horses. "And because, thanks to your son's kidnappers, I was in no condition to do the job myself."

Cortlandt directed his man to lift a lantern toward Ezra and he cringed at what he saw. "I'm sorry you have had to endure that kind of treatment. I'll make certain they pay," he said, nodding toward the still-bound kidnappers.

Ezra was deciding how much detail to give his employer about his son's captivity when galloping hooves claimed their attention. The three Black men employed by Genie jumped to the ground as one and, as if magnetized, moved toward each other and into the shadows. Each had his hand on his weapon.

A lone horseman rode up, pulled to a stop, dismounted, and nodded at Cortlandt as he touched his hat. "One dead man at that unused train stop, sir, and that's all that's there. Place is so clean you could hold Sunday service in it."

Like all of Cortlandt's men, this one was tall, muscular, clean shaven, and well dressed, and he had at least two visible weapons. Ezra figured on two more: a derringer and a knife. "What kind of man was he?" Ezra asked, and saw the glint of appreciation in the other man's eyes. "A ne'er-do-well. Even dead he stank of bad whiskey, and it had been weeks rather than days since he'd visited with soap and water."

Ezra risked another question: "Was he there alone?"

The man nodded, then shrugged. "No honor among thieves, I suppose." He pointed to the back of the wagon. "When those two wake up maybe they can explain how he got dead." Then he shrugged again and looked at his boss. "I'll tell the sheriff when we hand over those two, Mr. Cortlandt. Let the law figure it out."

But Ezra didn't think the kidnappers would know the dead man. He believed the man was the Tom that he heard Algie refer to, and that he died waiting for Jack and Algie. If the three of them had been at that depot together . . . "I've paid for enough of Mr. Oliver's time this day," Ezra said to Cortlandt. He didn't want to think any more about the danger they had just escaped. Immediately the rich man's employees removed the three inert figures from the back of Genie's wagon, first unbinding Edward and gently placing him in the front of his father's carriage, and then handling the two kidnappers like bags of flour or sugar, throwing them, still bound, over the backs of waiting horses. Then Cortlandt did something no one expected: He gave each of the Black men a silver dollar and thanked them for their help.

They acknowledged his generosity, and Genie's companions mounted their horses and rode away.

Ezra, intent on a private word with Genie, moved toward her too quickly and the pain knocked him down. Genie hurried to help him up. "Tell Eli … untie 'em … move 'em to the light," he whispered before several pairs of hands hoisted him to his feet and toward the brougham.

"Eli's busy getting cleaned up to meet you at home," Genie whispered back. "Tell them to take you home," she said.

"I'm taking you to my doctor first," Cortlandt announced, and Ezra didn't argue. "I'll tell him what you've accomplished tonight. He's a brilliant doctor and a shameless gossip. You'll have more business than you can handle by the time you heal, MacKaye."

Ezra forced his mind to ordered thinking. No one would doubt Arthur Cortlandt if he said his son's kidnappers gave his rescuer a beating, especially after they saw Ezra, and the police readily would believe that the dead man at the isolated depot was up to no good and paid the price. When the police discovered Jack and Algie and found them unable to account for their time, they'd be connected to the botched kidnapping on Arthur Cortlandt's say-so. He was giving in to unconsciousness when another thought presented itself: All the business his firm could handle, Arthur Cortlandt had said! Himself and a Black man who really was a woman and a runaway slave! When it wouldn't hurt he'd have himself a long laugh at that thought.

When they arrived, Montague Wright didn't look like a gossip, he looked like a riverboat gambler, but Ezra didn't care. By the time they arrived at the doctor's office, the ride in Cortlandt's upholstered brougham being only slightly more comfortable than the one on horseback or in the back of the wagon, Ezra wanted only to be relieved of the pain coursing through his body. The doctor saw to that immediately, which was a good thing because Ezra could not have endured what transpired next. And he surely would not have called it healing.

* * *

The servant girl who answered the knock at the scullery door shrieked in terror at the sight of the disheveled and dirty Colored man, which brought Abby and Maggie running. Only slightly surprised at Genie's presence, they quickly sent the girl to attend to her duties upstairs and invited Genie in. Without asking whether she was hungry or thirsty, Maggie put the kettle on and laid a place at the table. Genie hadn't realized that she was hungry or thirsty or tired until she sat down and contemplated eating. Whatever was put in front of her she'd welcome, and the cheese and pickle sandwich on fresh baked bread and the hot tea with plentiful honey relaxed and soothed her almost to the point of somnolence.

"I apologize for arriving so unexpectedly," Genie said, rousing herself.

"Are you all right?" Abby asked, looking at her closely. Too closely, Genie thought. It's as if she sees through me . . .

"I've come with information and a request for your indulgence. Ezra MacKaye has been seriously injured—"

The two women exclaimed and were talking simultaneously, asking what happened and what they could do to help. Genie didn't think it was sufficient to tell them that he'd been rescuing a kidnap victim; they deserved more and better. But the truth? "He was helping to thwart a plan to capture Mrs. Tubman and a . . . package she soon will deliver."

Abby went white as chalk and Maggie choked on a sharp intake of breath. Genie pounded on her back to restart her breathing. She told them that he was badly beaten, that he currently was being tended to at the surgery of Arthur Cortlandt's doctor, and that he most likely would require constant attention when he arrived home later in the day. "I've taken the liberty of enlisting Eli's services. I hope that I have not overstepped too widely and presumed too greatly on your kindness."

Abby reached across the table and took her hand. She held it tightly in both of hers but she did not speak, leaving Maggie to reply for them. "Both you and Mr. MacKaye have become important to us, Genie. I'll never be able to repay him for saving my Elizabeth, and now that he's saved Mrs. Tubman as well—"

Abby, still holding Genie's hand, found her voice. "Eli is welcome here," she began, then frowned slightly. "Was he injured as well?"

Genie shook her head. "He probably saved Ezra's life," she said, and if that wasn't the truth, it was close enough to it.

"Where is he now?" Maggie asked.

"Getting himself cleaned up. He should be here soon. And he will make himself available to help you as you may need him," Genie said, suddenly wondering why Abby hadn't hired a manservant since all of her lodgers were men.

Abby released Genie's hand and stood up. "Mr. MacKaye no doubt will require extra sheets and towels and blankets."

"And more coal for the grates in his rooms," Maggie said, standing as well.

Genie raised her suddenly cold hand to halt their exit. "Perhaps Eli could do those things when he arrives, so that he can know where to locate what he will need?"

Abby nodded acquiescence and sat back down though she did not, much to Genie's dismay, reclaim her hand. Maggie poured more tea and put more cheese and bread on her plate and Genie thanked her.

Both servant girls appeared then, buttoning their overcoats and tying their scarves over their heads, all the while casting wary glances at Genie. Abby paid them and hurried them through the kitchen, into the scullery, and out the door.

"Eli is a good boy but he has no experience in a house like this," Genie said to Maggie.

"I will take good care of him and give him all the help he needs," the older woman said.

"Thank you, Maggie."

"You don't need to thank me, Genie," Maggie replied, her voice filled with enough warmth to ward off the frigid air coming in through the scullery door, and she thought that while Eli may have had no experience working in a manor house, Genie

80

Oliver—or whatever her name was—most certainly did. And Maggie suddenly was struck by another realization: Something about Genie reminded her very strongly of her seafaring husband, Jack, who didn't stay away from his wife and daughter for months at a time because he wanted to but because, as a runaway slave, it was the safe thing to do. And just as Jack Juniper was the name he'd chosen for himself in freedom, Maggie believed that Eugenia Oliver was a chosen name as well.

Abby re-entered the kitchen followed closely by Eli. Genie almost didn't recognize him. His hair was cut almost to the scalp, his face was shaved clean, and he removed a scarf and overcoat to reveal a starched white shirt and trousers held neatly in place with a pair of suspenders almost the same color as the pants.

"Miss Eugenie, Miss Maggie," he greeted them, trying to keep his face from cracking into a grin of pride.

"Why don't I show you to your room first, Eli, then Mr. MacKaye's suite of rooms?" Abby said.

Eli looked stunned. "My room? I got a room? My own room?"

Abby nodded and led him down the long hallway to the stairs leading up to the servants' quarters where, Genie thought, he'd be the only resident, for she knew that Maggie and her daughter occupied a suite of rooms in the family wing of the mansion. "When Ezra is back to health," Genie said to Maggie, "you all may have to find work for Eli."

Maggie smiled and nodded. "I think Master Eli will be a good fit in this house."

CHAPTER SIX

Ezra MacKaye looked worse than any of them could have imagined, and if he could have spoken he'd have told them that he felt worse than that. But he didn't speak for almost three days. He was almost always asleep. When he woke Eli fed him beef broth and warm milk with honey and brandy, as ordered by the doctor. When he was conscious enough to feel the excruciating pain he was in, Maggie gave him three droppers of laudanum in a glass of water, which returned him deeply to sleep. The doctor himself had brought Ezra home to be certain that he would be properly cared for, and he pronounced himself thoroughly satisfied. When Eli acknowledged that he could not read and Maggie said that she could, Dr. Wright gave her the laudanum bottle and the dropper and made her promise—swear—that she would administer the prescribed amount, no more and no less. "This man took an awful beating. His body bears bruises that only I and the servant boy Eli will ever see. Should ever see. I'm glad the man doesn't have a wife to see what he has endured."

Eli slept in the room with Ezra in case the man should wake and need him, but he paid frequent visits to his room upstairs because he could. He liked knowing that it was there, that his clothes were in the drawers, his shoes in the closet, his razor on the shelf. In fact, he just liked knowing that he had clothes and shoes and a razor and a room to keep them in.

Every time Ezra had a dose of laudanum Eli presented himself to Abby or Maggie to see if they needed his help because he could be certain that the patient would sleep deeply for several hours, especially if he'd also had warm milk with brandy. Eli didn't want the servant girls to clean Ezra's rooms but Abby insisted, and she remained and watched them though she sent Eli away. He made the girls nervous with the malevolent glares he bestowed on them. He didn't want anyone else doing anything for Ezra. Except perhaps Maggie. Or Abby. Or Genie.

On the fourth day Ezra remained awake for several hours before declaring the need for laudanum. On the fifth day he stood up but found himself unable to walk. He could, however, hold a pen, and he sent a note to his Flegler Street landlady asking that she send any mail with Eli, telling her that he'd been in an accident and that he'd see her when he had recovered. On the sixth day Ezra walked, ever so stiffly, from the bedroom to the sitting room, where he spent the better part of the day dozing in front of the fireplace. On the seventh day, a Sunday, he joined the other members of the house at the table for the midday meal though he did not have permission to eat anything but soup, mashed potatoes, and bread pudding. He fell asleep at the table and when Eli woke him Ezra found that he could not stand, even with assistance. So, Eli and the other men lifted Ezra in his chair and carried him to his bedroom where, again under Eli's direction, the men lifted Ezra from the chair, being careful not to jar his still tightly wrapped left arm and shoulder.

"Oh, hellfire and damnation!" Ezra exclaimed when finally laid on his bed.

Maggie, who had followed with the laudanum bottle and dropper, quickly placed the requisite number of drops in the glass of water Eli kept beside the bed for that purpose and Ezra drank it down, then lay still to wait for it to work its magic. "Any moment now, Mr. MacKaye," Maggie said, knowing by now what he was thinking and feeling, and hoping that she was right. In keeping with the doctor's orders, as of today Ezra now was getting only three drops of the drug once a day instead of as needed.

"I'm sorry to be so much trouble," Ezra said, his words already beginning to slur. "Especially to you, Eli . . ." And he was asleep. Eli covered him and added more coals to the grate as Maggie led the other men from the room, thanking them for their help.

"We heard that he'd been in an accident of some kind but we had no idea that he was so badly injured," said Cornelius Eubanks, a traveling salesman and the first and longest resident of Abby's rooming house.

"Accident!" scoffed Lyle Butler, the newest and least liked resident. "That man took a beating, a good one! And from what I hear of him, he probably deserved it."

The other men looked at Butler but did not respond, and they all quickly walked away, all but Butler retiring to the warmth and comfort of their rooms. It was a bitterly cold night and snow was falling, but Butler dressed himself for the weather and, without a word of goodnight to the others, left the house by the front door. Maggie wanted to lock it behind him—his past behavior suggested that it would be well past curfew when he returned—but technically the front door was unlocked until ten o'clock when residents then used a side entrance, which, unknown to them, alerted both Abby and Maggie that someone had entered. Fortunately—and thankfully—Lyle Butler was the only person to enter after hours and Maggie couldn't imagine where he could go this Sunday night and remain past ten. Even the most disreputable establishments would be closed tonight, and even the most unkind horse cart drivers would shelter their animals tonight: The cold and snow were bad enough but a raging, howling arctic wind cut to the bone.

Eli put another blanket on Ezra, a few more coals on the fire, and made himself comfortable on the armchair and ottoman. There were no heat grates in the rooms in the servants' quarters in the Read mansion, for which Abby profusely apologized several times. What Eli wanted to tell her was a room in a house, even without a grate, would be warmer than any place he'd ever slept before, but he kept the thought to himself and marveled at his good fortune. How lucky he was to have Eugenia Oliver in his life. His only concern at the moment was whether he'd be able to get Ezra to his appointment with Dr. Wright tomorrow.

Genie Oliver's biggest concern at the moment was how to leave Adelaide and William without offending them. She had gratefully accepted their invitation to spend Sunday afternoon with them and two other friends, Peter Blanding and Catherine Carpenter. Genie did not socialize often or easily and she pledged to change that aspect of herself, especially since meeting Abby. However, Adelaide and William were friends of long standing and she felt she owed it to them to at least try to be sociable. She had begun after the mission, the day following Eli's transformation.

"I could hardly believe my eyes!" Genie, back to her normal routine, exclaimed. "Was that really Eli?" She and Adelaide were having lunch with William and Arthur in the blacksmith shop, where it was warm.

"We did a good job if I do say so myself," William beamed, then amended, "though most of the credit goes to Arthur," after the ironmonger loudly cleared his throat.

"I could benefit from such a transformation," Genie mused, "though, and no disrespect intended, not at your hands," she said waving her hand at Arthur and William, rendering them speechless with embarrassment. They all but ran from the room, which caused Adelaide to collapse into spasm of giggles. It was infectious, and soon both women were giggling like schoolgirls. "I meant what I said," Genie said trying to stifle a laugh, "on both counts."

Adelaide was laughing so hard she could barely breathe. Genie had never witnessed such mirth in this woman that she spent almost all of her days with, and she enjoyed it. "I'd be pleased to transform you, Eugenia," Adelaide finally managed to say. "And I don't think we need worry about William and Arthur. In fact, they'll likely not reappear for hours." She was still enjoying the men's embarrassment. "Shall we begin with a trimming of your hair?"

Genie put both hands to her head and snatched them quickly

away as if they were burned. "Oh yes, Adelaide, please!" She had not given much thought to her appearance, especially since she more often than not disguised herself as a man, a practice that would not be so necessary now that she had a horse cart, she thought happily. And since she would be seeing more of Abigail Read—a thought she tried very hard to keep at bay.

Adelaide asked Genie to help her lift a heavy cauldron of water to the stove to heat, then led her into the storage closet at the rear of the blacksmith shop and closed the door. She lit a lantern that was sitting on a shelf, and even in dim light Genie could immediately see that the contents of the closet had nothing to do with blacksmithing. She wondered if Adelaide understood the importance of what was on the shelves and realized even more fully than she ever had that Adelaide was not kept in the dark about her husband's other profession, that the woman knew everything she needed to know and acknowledged nothing—for her own safety as well as that of her husband. She pointed to a narrow bench and Genie sat while Adelaide withdrew a pair of shears from her smock pocket.

"Relax," she said, and gave Genie a gentle pat on the shoulder. "I won't make you look like Eli," and they both giggled again. Adelaide was swift and sure with the shears, and thick hair dropped to the floor. "There will be more than enough left to braid," she said as Genie stole quick, worried looks at the floor.

Genie touched her head again when Adelaide signaled that she was finished, and smiled at what she felt even though she could not imagine herself with less hair. While Adelaide swept the floor, Genie undressed herself and suddenly felt the closet's cold. She shivered as Adelaide opened the door. "Wait here for one moment. I'll return quickly," she said, which she did, with the information that the men were pouring the hot water into the tank. "You will warm up instantly," she said.

Armed with soap and a thick cloth Genie more than warmed, she luxuriated. She washed herself from head to toe until the water was gone. The shower was an enclosed room at the back of the blacksmith shop that usually held warmth from the forge, but not on a day as bitterly cold as this one. Genie was shivering again until Adelaide appeared with a thick blanket and led her to a chair next to the stove, which she had stoked. Genie sat with a grateful sigh. "I can't thank you enough, Adelaide. I feel like a new woman."

Adelaide stifled a smile and allowed that she looked like one as well. "Perhaps a bit less transformed than Eli but most presentable," she pronounced.

"I can't put those clothes back on!" Genie exclaimed.

"You most certainly cannot, since they're fueling that fire," Adelaide said with a nod to the stove. Genie had been so focused on cleansing herself that she'd given no thought to what she'd wear afterward. Adelaide, however, had, and she produced an armload of clothes for Genie to choose from: donations that were being stored here because there was no room for them in their shop. Genie was looking through the bundle of clothes when a look of horror crossed her face. Before she could speak, however, Adelaide dropped two leather pouches into her lap, and Genie grabbed them up with relief and gratitude. The small one, which she wore around her neck, contained objects from her barely remembered mother and grandmother. The larger one, a two-inch-by-three-inch square, she wore around her waist and it contained money and valuable documents. This one she opened and withdrew several coins.

"Will this pay for my new wardrobe—and for Eli's?" she asked with a genteel pat to her newly cut hair.

Adelaide accepted the coins with a smile that she thought hid what she was thinking: that Eugenia Oliver more than paid her way in the world, every day. She had, just three days ago, risked her life for her people; she fed and clothed and found work for boys whom no one else cared about. And it was Genie who solicited the donations of clothes and food that they were able to give away to those most in need.

"If I am able to pay my own way, Adelaide, then I should do that," Genie said as she dressed herself. She looked lovely, and she looked down at herself, pleased with the effect, which surprised Adelaide. Genie had never cared about her appearance.

"Are you hungry, Adelaide? I have stew and fresh baked bread on the stove. Will William mind?"

"William will be glad to be rid of me for a while, and I of him!" And they bundled themselves for the ride to Genie's in her horse cart, an experience she delighted in. Why had she ever believed that she didn't need it, or, worse, that she didn't deserve it? She drove the long way home—down the main street and through the alley—so that she could park the cart in front of her house and then Adelaide could take it, pick up William, and take them both home.

Genie quickly lit lanterns and both fires, for even though she'd left coals banked in the stove the small cottage was frigid, which didn't prevent Adelaide from walking in circles, exclaiming at its beauty.

"Have you not been here before, Adelaide?"

"You know that I have not, Genie Oliver!" she replied, recrimination barely disguised in her voice. Genie could but accept it for she knew that not only did she routinely reject Adelaide's invitations to dine with them, she had never invited them into her home, preferring her solitude to anyone's presence.

"Then I apologize, Adelaide. Please sit down and make yourself comfortable while I see to food. Would you like coffee or tea? Or perhaps some warm mead?"

"Eugenia! You have mead?" Adelaide exclaimed, shocked as well as pleased.

Genie laughed. "I do. I make it myself so it is not very strong. In fact, it is more sweet than strong."

"Then I'd love some!"

And they ate stew and bread and drank mead and laughed and talked until Adelaide declared that she'd been away for too long and should return for William. She thanked Genie for her hospitality, her earlier pique forgotten, and Genie let her know that as her friend she always was welcome in her home, and Adelaide reciprocated though it wasn't necessary: Genie had refused more invitations to Adelaide and William's home than she had accepted.

And now here she sat three days later having accepted a dinner invitation. She was full and sleepy and trying to think of a graceful way to leave their home without offending them. She knew that both William and Adelaide would be hurt if she left now. Peter Blanding and Catherine Carpenter, now formally engaged to be married, were still present also. The five of them had attended service at the First AME Church earlier and then returned to the Tillmans for Sunday dinner. And a feast it was! Now seated before a roaring fire, relaxed and full, Genie let the conversation swirl around her. She didn't try to participate; it required all of her energy to keep her eyes open. Then she realized that all the other eyes were on her, which meant that something had been said that required her response.

"Well—" she began, not knowing how she'd extricate herself from this predicament, when William saved her.

"Reverend Richard Allen and Absalom Jordan have been bringing regular reports from Eli—"

"Every time you say those names!" Blanding exclaimed, and William raised his hand to stop him: He knew what was coming.

"What they tell us," Adelaide said, "is that Mr. MacKaye remains bedridden and therefore Genie can't see him, but Eli will send for her as soon as he is able to receive her."

This was news to Genie but it made sense as she considered it. It would be most unseemly for her to visit Ezra MacKaye in his bedroom, even dressed as Eugene, and it would have been useless in any case as long as he remained unconscious.

"We all will visit him when it is possible," William said, looking steadily at Genie. "You will advise us when that is possible."

"Of course," she replied, and at that moment a fierce gust of wind rattled the windowpanes and blew down the chimney, scattering ashes out of the grate. William quickly swept them up and added another log to the fire while Adelaide drew the draperies tighter at the window and her shawl tighter around her shoulders.

Peter Blanding stood. "We should thank you for a most wonderful repast, Adelaide, and take our leave so that we all may be warm at our hearths."

And just that quickly Genie was free to leave. She resisted all efforts and offers to walk her the short distance to her home, insisting correctly that she could—and would—run more quickly than she could be walked. And she was correct. The blowing snow at her back pushed her forward. She turned sideways and flattened herself to squeeze into the narrow space between two houses that took her to the Back Street, and while the wind was less fierce here it was just as cold. In a few steps she was at her door and quickly inside. She whispered a prayer of gratitude that Eli was safe and warm inside Abby Read's house, and she hoped that Reverend Richard Allen, Absalom Jones, and the other boys were equally protected from the weather this night.

The morning brought a bright blue sky and an end to the wild, snowy wind. The temperature, however, remained dangerously cold and the snow that had fallen overnight was a sheet of ice. Eli, who gave no thought to attempting to get Ezra to the doctor, got him ready for breakfast instead. They were all seated, Eubanks had said grace, and Maggie and Abby were putting the serving plates on the table when Lyle Butler made his drunken, noisy entrance, almost tearing the front door off its hinges when he stumbled into it. He crashed to the floor and lay there in a drunken stupor. Abby was so shocked she almost dumped a plate of sausages on Mr. Eubanks's head. She looked in speechless horror at Butler sprawled in the middle of the foyer.

The commotion brought the normally reticent Josiah Jones to his feet. "I say sir! You simply mustn't behave this way!"

"And I say sit down you stupid old goat!" Butler slurred at him, managing to sit almost upright.

"You will leave this house immediately," Abby said, having recovered, and angry now that the shock had worn off, "and you will not return. You are no longer welcome in this house."

"Not until I've had my breakfast," Butler slurred, "and not until the end of the month. I'm paid up until then." He had managed to stand but was weaving back and forth as if on a small boat on rough seas.

90

Using his right arm for leverage Ezra pushed up to his feet. No longer bent by pain and drugs he stretched to his full height and glared at Butler, a much smaller man who, even drunk, should have been intimidated by the sight. He was not.

"Or what, nigger lover?"

Ezra withdrew the revolver that he now kept in his waistband. "Or I'll shoot you and you'll owe Mistress Read for a new rug. An expensive one, I daresay."

Butler sobered quickly. "But my things? And where will I go?"

"Back to the docks where you belong!" thundered Josiah Jones, startling everyone. He filled his plate and started to eat.

"See the landlady at 965 Flegler Street," Ezra said. "That's where I'll have your things sent. Now leave here."

Butler turned and stumbled to the door and exited much more quietly than he had entered, leaving behind, however, his stench. Abby waved her hand back and forth before her face. "I wish the wind were still blowing," she said. "We could leave the door open for a few moments and that smell would be gone, though it would be cold."

"I think I can help," Eubanks said, withdrawing his pipe and tobacco pouch. "If you don't mind?" he asked Abby and his table mates, and when no one objected he filled the pipe bowl and lit the tobacco and then walked over to where Butler had stood and drew on the pipe. Then he went to the front door, drawing in and expelling smoke as he went, then to the fireplace and sprinkled some of the tobacco leaves onto the fire. Soon there was no trace left of Lyle Butler—other than the bad memory of the man.

After breakfast two of the cleaning women were sent to empty Butler's room of all of his belongings and to report to Abby on the room's condition: Filthy and smelly they reported, but otherwise undamaged. "But we'll have to double boil them sheets to get 'em cleaned white again, Mistress Read," they said.

Abby nodded, thanked them, and told them to place Mr. Butler's belongings at the front door. She went to inform Ezra and wondered whether she could ask him why he would send a ne'er-do-well like Butler to his former landlady. She found the door to his sitting room open and her hand was raised to knock when she heard a muttered 'hellfire and damnation.' She backed up a step, prepared to leave, when she heard her name called.

"Come in, please, Abby," Ezra called out, "before Eli kills me! I used to think the boy liked me but now I'm not so sure."

Abby entered the room to find Ezra up and walking, Eli close behind him, urging him forward, arms outstretched to catch him if he faltered, which he did not. "Well done, both of you," Abby exclaimed. Eli beamed, Ezra growled.

"The boy is trying to kill me, I tell you!"

Abby smiled broadly. "Most impressive, Mr. MacKaye, considering that you could barely breathe when they brought you here ten days ago, to say nothing of walk. In fact, I wondered whether you'd be able to walk again, so dire was your predicament."

Ezra sobered immediately and turned to face Eli. He shook the boy's hand. "He has been a godsend, no doubt about it, as has Genie Oliver for sending him to me, and you and Maggie for helping me heal." He walked over to Abby and extended a hand to her. "You have my gratitude, Mistress Read."

"You're welcome," Abby said, shaking his hand, "but you did the hard work."

Ezra wanted to say that it was Eli who had done the hard work—refusing to let him die—but he'd embarrassed the boy enough for one day. He would never, though, forget the boy's whispered incantations: *You cain't die, Mr. MacKaye, I ain't gon' let you die. You hear me? Don't you die! I ain't gon' let you die!* Not if he lived to be 100. Day and night the boy had sat by his bed . . .

"Butler is gone and his belongings are at the front door," Abby said.

"Eli, will you hail a cart to deliver Mr. Butler's things to Flegler Street? Tell the driver to collect his payment from Mr. Butler or he may drive away and keep whatever is in the bags."

Eli nodded and hurried away. He didn't need Ezra to tell him to hire a cart with a white driver who could legitimately drive off if he wasn't paid, something a Colored driver could not do. The first Colored driver he saw he sent to Miss Adelaide's Dress

Shop to tell Miss Eugenie to come visit Mr. MacKaye "at her convenience," and he paid the driver from his own pocket, still amazed at the changes in his circumstances: He had coins in his pocket and words in his mouth and his own room in a big house. He hurried back to find Ezra at his desk writing notes that Eli would be asked to post later that day, though one he would want to be personally delivered to Mr. Cortlandt at his bank. While Ezra was busy at his desk Eli went looking for Maggie. He liked helping her and she liked having his help—and his presence. They didn't discuss their pasts but she knew from his still jumpy behavior and the haunted look in his eyes that his past had been brutal and horrible. He made quick work of cleaning the ashes from the fireplaces and grates and replenishing the coal scuttles and firewood in the main rooms where fires burned constantly in cold weather, even in the rooms that were not in use, though those were smaller fires. "In the evening, just before the men come in from work, add more logs so it's warm," Maggie told him. He volunteered the information that he had never lived or worked in a manor house and he welcomed whatever she shared about how such houses worked. When she asked if he wanted to remain after Mr. MacKaye no longer needed his constant attention, he dipped his head once.

"Yes'm, Miss Maggie," he whispered. "Please ma'am."

The mid-afternoon ringing of the front door bell surprised them all. Abby went to answer it and the bell she rang brought both Maggie and Eli to the front of the house: Dr. Montague Wright and his assistant had arrived to tend to their patient. "We came to you because we didn't think you could get to us," he said in his too-loud voice. Eli hurried to get Ezra ready while Maggie took the men's coats and boots and offered tea or coffee.

"Coffee," Wright answered for both of them, "which we'll take in the drawing room once we've seen to the patient," and he turned toward Ezra's suite, remembering precisely where it was. Abby returned to the kitchen to make coffee and cut cake while Maggie went to add logs to all the fires.

"You can leave now, boy," Wright said, waving his hand dismissively at Eli, his eyes taking in everything about Ezra. "You look quite well, Mr. MacKaye," the doctor said loudly, as if they weren't in the same room.

"Thanks to Eli," Ezra replied coldly, "whom I'd like to remain in case you leave orders that he will need to help me carry out." Wright looked from Eli to Ezra and shrugged. "As you wish. Let me see you walk," he demanded, and Ezra stood and walked.

"Good. Now let's see those bruises—though you walk as if they've quite healed." Wright studied Ezra's lower limbs, touching here and there, nodding and muttering to himself. "Remarkable, really. Never seen wounds heal like this."

Ezra would not tell him that Eli massaged oil and ointment supplied by Arthur into the bruises, and he would have cried out so great was the pain had Maggie not first administered laudanum. This was when he could have the drug as needed, and he needed it during Eli's massages. Horse liniment was what Arthur sent, and horse liniment was what cured him. "I have practically no pain," Ezra said, "and very little stiffness, as you can see."

Wright nodded. "Now, let's remove the binding from that shoulder," he said, directing his assistant to hold Ezra upright while he unwrapped the cloth. Ezra was breathing deeply, expecting more pain than he actually felt. Eli had rubbed some of the liniment into his damaged arm and shoulder as well, though not as often or as intensely, and Ezra didn't know how effective it had been. "Stand now, Mr. MacKaye, and let that arm fall away from your body. Just endure the pain if you can." Ezra closed his eyes while the assistant took hold of his arm and gently moved it away from his body, away from the position molded to his chest and side where it had lain for ten days. It hung weekly and limply though not very painfully. "All right, good. Now let's lay you down on your belly while we make certain that shoulder has remained where it belongs," Wright brayed.

Ezra heard Eli's intake of breath and felt him move slightly. He shook his head, signaling the boy to be still no matter what Wright did, knowing he would obey no matter how difficult. So even when Ezra cried out as the shoulder was manipulated in its socket, Eli did not move. Ezra continued to breathe deeply. Wright sat him up and touched all over his shoulder and down the arm, nodding and humming and muttering to his assistant. "We're going to wrap you up again, Mr. MacKaye, though not as tightly. There is still more healing to do, and binding the shoulder will guarantee that it remains in its proper place. I'll see you in my office in one week's time." He strode from the room, the assistant on his heels, without a backward glance. "A good doctor but an awful man," Ezra muttered. Eli silently agreed, thinking that MacKaye had no idea how awful, for Eli was certain that the doctor was a man of the plantation.

Abby sat in the drawing room with Dr. Wright and his assistant, whom he had never named, a silver urn of coffee and a tray of cakes and sandwiches at their disposal. Because Montague Wright didn't require any voice but his own to have a conversation, Abby and the assistant sat and listened to him talk, his flow of words interrupted only when his mouth was occupied with food and drink.

Eli re-dressed Ezra and hurried to the kitchen to ask Maggie for warm milk and brandy when the gentle tap on the scullery door announced Genie's arrival. They both were overjoyed to see her. She and Maggie exchanged warm hugs and Eli hung back shyly until Genie grabbed him for his own hug. He had started to tell her of Dr. Wright's visit and Ezra's recovery when the doctor's loud voice boomed out and Genie froze. Then she began to shake.

"Montague Wright. Ezra's doctor is Montague Wright. He's from a Maryland slave-holding family. No wonder he and Arthur Cortlandt are friends," she said and sat down hard in one of the chairs. She could have fallen off had Eli not caught her, and both he and Maggie were thinking, *Not just any Maryland slave-holding family but the one that owned her.* That awful, loud voice, Genie thought as she recovered and reclaimed herself. The brother of her mistress. What was he doing in Philadelphia? He must not see her! She made a shaky though unsuccessful effort to stand up.

"Where are you going, Genie?" Maggie asked.

"I must leave! He can't see me!"

"And he won't if you remain here in the kitchen. But if you go out into the street—"

Genie collapsed in on herself. She had really allowed herself to believe that she was a free woman, that her past was well behind her. How foolish!

"Take Mr. MacKaye his warm milk, please, Eli," Maggie said, giving him a tall, napkin-wrapped glass.

Eli took the glass but his eyes remained on Genie. If someone were to test his loyalty, Eugenia Oliver would win. He hurried away, intending to give Ezra his warm milk and hurry back to the kitchen where he could keep an eye on Genie, but Ezra took one look at him and demanded to know what was wrong. Eli told him, and Ezra sprang to his feet as if totally free of pain. He was out of the bedroom and into the sitting room before Eli could stop him.

"Mr. MacKaye, no! If you go running out there, Mistress Abigail will know something is wrong and so will that doctor, and he cain't never see Miss Eugenie, Mr. MacKaye! Not never!"

Ezra stopped. Reluctantly. Eli was right and he knew it, but if Genie was in trouble—there was nothing he could do about it. He took the warm milk from Eli and drank it down, welcoming the brandy's burn and waiting for it to relax him. He knew, though, that as long as Montague Wright was holding forth in the drawing room he could not relax. What must Genie be feeling, having to listen to the man! For that matter, how was Abby enduring him?

"So, you prefer Philadelphia to Baltimore?" Abby asked her guest when she could insert a word into his monologue though she was long past caring what he thought or felt about anything. What an insufferable—she didn't know what to call him!

"In some respects, yes, I do. We didn't live in Baltimore proper—we were out in the countryside—so life was slower and quite a bit more genteel. But I certainly earn a better living in the city! Nothing in the countryside but farmers and ignorant nigger slaves who have no money to pay for medical care."

96

Perhaps because you don't pay them any money, Abby was on the verge of saying when Wright prattled on. "And speaking of earning, I have an apprentice starting with me in a day or so and wonder if you have a room to let?"

Abby was momentarily taken aback. While she'd be grateful to have Lyle Butler's room let so quickly, she didn't want anyone in her house or at her table with the manners of Montague Wright. "I do have a room that has just come available and should be ready to let in several days. I'd be delighted to meet your apprentice—"

Wright bristled. "Why should you need to meet him? I've told you that he is my apprentice. That should be sufficient enough recommendation as to his character."

Abby bristled right back. "The room is available because the occupant, who came highly recommended, was a drunken boor. Had I met him first I most likely would have had some insight into his character, thanks to his perpetually red nose and its veins."

Wright, who was rendered momentarily—and uncharacteristically—speechless, saw Eli pass in the hallway with an empty glass on a silver tray but he gave a servant's movements no importance. He should have.

Eli all but ran into the kitchen, all but threw the tray to the table, and literally ran through the scullery door into the alleyway. A startled Maggie looked after him. "What on earth—where is he going in such a hurry?"

"I think I might know," Genie said quietly, her trembling momentarily stilled as she got up and looked toward the scullery.

Eli, oblivious to the cold, ran through the alleyway to the street and stopped beside the brougham belonging to Dr. Wright, startling the top-hatted Black man in the driver's seat, who looked almost fearfully at Eli.

"My name is Eli and I work for Mistress Read and Mr. MacKaye. Is you a free man, suh?"

The brougham driver blinked. He'd never been called "sir" before.

97

"Is you a free man?!" Eli demanded, and the driver shook his head. "Slave?" Eli asked, and the man nodded. "How many more in your house?" Eli asked, and the question demanded that the man speak.

"My wife and my daughter," he whispered.

"Do you want to be free, suh?" Eli asked, and the man nodded. "What is your name? And your wife and daughter?"

"I'm Robert, my wife is Josephine, my girl is Mary," the man answered, still whispering. Then, in panic, he added, "Dr. Wright said if he hears any talk of freedom he'll sell 'em down south!"

"Not if Mr. MacKaye gets you outta there first," Eli said, and ran back the way he'd come, returning to the kitchen in time to hear Montague Wright exiting through the front door and Ezra and Abby speaking quietly as they came toward the kitchen. Then he heard Abby exclaim, heard her feet running to the kitchen. She ran to Genie and grabbed her, holding her in a tight embrace, which Genie quickly and gratefully returned. Both women wept silently but only Genie could hear Abby's whispered, "I am so very sorry!" Ezra, Maggie and Eli watched silently for a few moments, then Ezra cleared his throat.

"I'm sorry to interrupt but Abby, please tell them what you told me."

Abby wiped her eyes and turned to look at the people she considered her family, but she kept one arm tightly around Genie as she spoke. "But given what I've just learned about Montague Wright and who—and what—he is, I believe that the servant man the apprentice wants to bring with him is a slave," and she almost choked on the word and buried her face in Genie's shoulder.

"You prob'ly right, Mistress Abby," Eli said, and shared his conversation with Robert.

"You said I'd do what?!" Ezra exclaimed. "I can do no such thing, Eli, and you should not have said that I could!"

"But you saved Maggie's little girl," Eli said, "and you helped Miz Tubman bring some people to freedom—"

"I saved a boy I'd been hired to find, and with your help, Eli—"

"What we did—all of us—helped Miz Tubman, and you know that's the truth, Mr. MacKaye."

Ezra nodded. "You're right, Eli, but that doesn't mean I can go into a man's house and take his property—"

"Ezra!" Genie and Abby exclaimed simultaneously.

"Do you believe that human beings can be property, Mr. MacKaye?" Maggie asked. "Like a horse or a plow?"

Ezra, miserable, shook his head. "Of course not—"

"That's how slaves are treated, Ezra," Genie said. She was shaking again and Abby tightened her grip. "Bought and sold, chained and whipped, sometimes barely fed and sometimes not fed at all, poorly clothed in winter . . ." She couldn't talk anymore because the long-suppressed memories had come rushing back to mind, overtaking the words.

"I will find out what I can do," Ezra said, "and I will do whatever I can."

"There are women's abolitionist organizations," Abby said. "My mother belonged to one until my father forbade it. I wish I had joined. I should have joined! I should know more and I should do more! I will do more!" Genie held her while she wept.

"How will you find out if you can do anything, Mr. MacKaye?" Maggie asked.

"I know many lawyers and policemen and constables—" he began.

"And the women's groups will know, too," Abby added, then looked worried. "Can we possibly learn anything before Wright's apprentice shows up with his servant? I want to reject him because Wright recommended him but I'd like more reason."

"I just hope it's not too late," Maggie said.

"What does that mean, Miss Maggie?" Eli asked for all of them. Too late for what?

Maggie began to busy herself, as if dinner preparations would help her think. "Ever since that fugitive slave law was passed in 1850 things have been different. More . . . dangerous . . . and it gets worse every day. In little ways right now, but the big ways will come. I can feel it."

Genie nodded. "It's the reason I finally got the horse cart. Even dressed as a man I felt too exposed, too vulnerable. Even if I could outrun one slave catcher or one hooligan, even if I could shoot one, I could not outrun anyone on horseback."

"Shoot someone!" Abby exclaimed. "You would . . . you could shoot someone?"

When Genie didn't respond Eli added, "Mr. William and Arthur both was happy you got that cart, Miss Eugenie. And Mistress Abby, you and Miss Maggie need one, too. Y'all don't need to be out like you is," he pronounced, sounding more like a man than a boy, causing Ezra to cough into his hand to cover a smile.

"I have a brougham," Abby said.

"You do!" Ezra exclaimed. "Where is it?"

"In the carriage house. I haven't used it since my parents died. I got rid of the horse—"

"Eli, can you have Arthur come look at it? See what shape it's in? If it needs wheels? Straps? And if William has a horse we can purchase?"

"We!" Abby exclaimed. "Now you see here, Ezra MacKaye!"

"The boy is right, Abby: You and Maggie should have the protection of a carriage when you're out. I'll pay for it—"

"I don't need you to pay for it!" she huffed, the tears of just a few moments ago forgotten. "I can take care of myself!"

"Of course, you can," Ezra said soothingly. "But would you allow me to hire and pay the driver? And would you, on occasion, allow me to use your brougham?"

Abby's eyes narrowed and she scrutinized Ezra's much too innocent visage. She was being had. She knew it, she just couldn't prove it. "Why can't Eli drive it?"

"Eli, can you drive a brougham?" Ezra asked him

"What's a broom, Mr. MacKaye?" he asked, his brow wrinkled in serious thought, and everyone laughed, including Eli himself.

"We need to prepare the evening meal," Maggie said with a smile and a hug for Eli. "The gentlemen will arrive soon. Eli, will you see to it that the drawing room is clean and that all the fires are ready to be lit?"

He ran from the kitchen and the adults, smiling and happy, now that he was back to being more boy than man. Abby gave Ezra a steady look. "Why can't Eli drive us?"

"Because your driver must be able to protect you if necessary. A white woman traveling with a Black woman, either of you traveling alone? Maggie's right: Things are changing, though I don't know from what to what. But I never will forget the sight and sound of little Elizabeth running from those thugs and not a single person, in a street filled with people, came to her aid— not a man nor a woman, not a Black person nor a white one. She was a child and no one helped!" Ezra sat heavily at the table, supporting himself on his right elbow and seeming to try to hold his left arm closer to his body.

Genie spoke for the first time in a few minutes. "I'm going to get Eli to help you back to bed," she told Ezra.

"I don't want to go to bed!"

"Then to your sitting room, perhaps a nap in front of the fire before dinner?"

"I don't want a nap," he snapped, "and I can take myself wherever I need to go!" He stood too quickly and swayed, and the three women reached out to steady him.

"Of course, you can," Genie said. "May I join you for a few moments?" Then she looked suddenly at Abby. "If that's all right with you? I don't want to do anything to tarnish your reputation."

Abby blushed, thinking that Genie sitting with Ezra MacKaye in his sitting room was not how she'd like Genie Oliver to tarnish her reputation. "As long you're back in the kitchen when the men arrive."

Genie followed Ezra to his suite having taken full notice of Abby's blush, and understanding the reason for it. "You certainly look much better than when I last saw you," she told Ezra when he sat and wrapped himself in a blanket. She lit the coals in the grate, fanned them, and watched the fire catch. She fanned it more and felt the warmth spread toward them.

"I feel much better," he replied. "Wright's a decent enough doctor though Eli and Arthur might be better." He told her about the horse liniment and she laughed so hard she almost choked. "I might be able to pull the brougham myself," he said, and she was still laughing when Eli came in. Ezra shared the joke and Eli laughed, too, and demonstrated how Ezra would look pulling a brougham with one arm. He added more coal to the fire and left them still laughing.

"Thank you for taking such good care of him, Ezra."

"It's the other way around, Genie. Thank you for sending him to me. I don't know what I'd have done without him."

"Between you and Abby—and Maggie!—he now has a place to call home and people to call family."

"When I first saw him and chased him . . . he had reason to fear me and to run." It wasn't a question and didn't need answering. "And you really thought I was a man." She shook her head. "Maggie said men never really see women. She knew right away that I wasn't a man but she didn't betray me."

"I think that women are better than men," Ezra said, sounding just a little bit puzzled by his pronouncement.

"I think I agree with you," Genie said.

"And next to you, Abby Read is about as good as a woman gets."

Genie turned a scrutinizing gaze on him, looking for his meaning, and when she found it she stood up. "I'll go now, and I'll visit Arthur. When would you like him to look at Abby's brougham?"

"As soon as he's able."

"I'll tell him," she said, leaving him. Then she turned back. "Have you heard from Cortlandt? How's his son?"

He gave a grim chuckle. "He sent a note by Wright, along with another check. Seems that junior was treated even worse than we thought and that our timely intervention truly did save his miserable life."

Genie was smiling when she left him, smiling when she walked into the kitchen and saw Abby, a smile that grew wider when it was returned. Maggie fabricated a reason to leave them alone for a moment. Genie went into the scullery and Abby followed,

102

giving them time for another close embrace. Genie told her that she was sending Arthur as soon as he could come—possibly even tomorrow, knowing Arthur. "And will I see you tomorrow?" Abby asked.

"I must go to work some time!" Genie exclaimed.

Oh how I wish you didn't, Abby thought. *How I wish you could remain here with me.* But she kept those thoughts to herself and nodded as Genie said that she most likely would bring Arthur tomorrow. And then Genie was gone . . . and just as quickly back.

"Maggie, may I please have a carrot for my horse friend?"

Maggie gave her two carrots and a hug, and Genie left thinking that Eli wasn't the only one to find a family. Nor was he the only one who would spend the remainder of that day contemplating all that had occurred. Two of them had similar thoughts: Ezra and Abby both pledged to end their ignorance about the circumstances confronting Colored citizens, not only in Philadelphia but in all of America. It struck Ezra that he had recently read (though he didn't recall where) that there was widespread objection to making them citizens. They weren't citizens? Then what were they? Certainly not property, as had been made abundantly clear to him. The thought troubled him deeply, as it did Abby. She had come from England with her parents ten years earlier, a wealthy white woman with no need to concern herself with the plight of Black Americans any more than she had with Black Englishmen and women. Maggie, an indentured servant in Abby's parents' home, had come to Philadelphia with the family in the same role. When the elder Reads died suddenly, Abby, who considered Maggie her friend, asked her to remain as a paid employee—and friend—not as a servant. And though Maggie was ten years older the two women felt more like sisters to each other than anything else, a relationship that did not change when Maggie met and married Jack Juniper, a seaman who worked the ships that regularly sailed between Liverpool, England, and Philadelphia. Abby thought it romantic that Maggie and Jack were connected by their two countries. What Maggie had never told Abby, had never told anyone, was that Jack was a runaway

103

slave from Maryland who believed seafaring to be safer than working on land. Maggie also kept to herself the thought, and the fear, that as long as her husband could never truly be free, neither could she. Or their daughter, no matter the circumstances of their birth.

Genie and Eli, both runaway slaves, always lived with the same hollow fear inside: that one day they'd be found out or, worse, caught. Hearing Montague Wright's voice so close was the same as hearing the voice of her owner, Matilda Wright Will. Montague was her brother and had visited her home often. Genie heard—endured—the loud, braying, self-centered voice several times a week for years. She had allowed herself to believe that freedom meant she'd never hear it again. If he saw her he would know her and he'd return her to Matilda. Or worse, keep her as a slave in his own house! The thought chilled and terrified Genie. She must make certain that in the future Eli was able to transport Ezra to Montague's office so the man would never have to return to Abby's house. The man, or his apprentice.

CHAPTER SEVEN

After weeks of foreboding and threatening, heavy snow came to Philadelphia, and with it, the strong, bitter wind returned. Six or seven inches by dawn and it continued, heavy and thick. The wind blew it into drifts that made roads and walkways all but impassable. Cornelius Eubanks, the traveling salesman, was on a trip. Josiah Jones and Henry Carson watched the weather from the living-room windows before, during and after breakfast. Mr. Carson, saying he had work that demanded his attention, decided to take his chances and walk. He packed a bag with extra clothes and shoes and set out with a cheery "Good day, all!" Mr. Jones, older than Mr. Carson by quite a few years, decided to spend the day in his room reading. He asked if his coal grate could be kept stoked and Abby promised to have Eli check it at regular intervals. She also told him there would be food on the sideboard at midday for which he thanked her profusely, understanding that she was not obligated to provide but two meals daily.

Abby, Maggie and Eli ate their breakfast and then cleaned the kitchen afterwards. Eli, without being asked, said that he would clean Mr. Carson's room since no one expected that the servant girls would come in this weather even though they lived nearby. Both the snow and the wind had increased in intensity over the last hour. It was almost impossible to see across the street so a two-block walk would have been difficult if not dangerous.

"I doubt that we should expect Arthur with the horse today," Abby said, though she had been looking forward to his arrival with some excitement. He had appeared with Genie the day following the initial discussion of Abby's carriage to inspect it and he declared that it was "good enough to be used." He replaced the leather straps and harness and both benches—the driver's outside and passengers' inside. And he hired Absalom and Reverend Richard Allen to clean the carriage and the carriage house, as well as the living quarters above, for Ezra, true to his word, had hired a driver. The only thing missing was the horse. And the driver.

"And before you ask, Abby, I do expect that Donald Bruce will arrive today if he was able to get to Philadelphia, and he'd have sent a telegram if he couldn't." An almost healthy Ezra MacKaye was the only one of them who seemed to pay no attention to the ever-worsening weather.

"How?" Maggie asked. "Even if his train arrived on time it's a long walk from the station to here."

"He's a Pinkerton's," Ezra replied, as if that answered the question for the others as it did for him.

"Well, Montague Wright certainly is no Pinkerton's man and I'll not be disappointed if he and his apprentice fail to arrive today," Abby said.

"Maybe they'll get buried in a snow drift and not be found until spring," Ezra said.

Maggie attempted, not quite successfully, to disguise a laugh as a cough but Eli didn't even attempt subterfuge: He laughed outright, imagining the loud, braying-like-a-jackass doctor and his apprentice, frozen inside a snowbank for months to come.

Though they walked as briskly as the falling and drifting snow permitted, Genie and Arthur felt frozen solid by the time they reached the dress shop. Their heads touching, they had tried to talk over the howling wind. Arthur apologized for not being able to deliver Abby's horse today. Genie assured him that Abby wouldn't expect him given the weather. He thanked her for the chance to earn some money by making the necessary repairs to Abby's carriage, and to be able to hire Absalom and Richard to help with the repairs and the cleaning of the long-neglected carriage house. "Ever since Eli got that job them boys been wantin' a real job, too."

"I will do whatever I can for them, Arthur," Genie said, not adding that she almost had a commitment from Joe Joseph to hire one of them to work in his restaurant.

"I know you will, Miss Eugenie, and those boys they know it, too."

Arthur declined the offer to come inside the dress shop to warm up before continuing on to the blacksmith shop. "No point to get warm and dry only to get cold and wet again," he said.

Genie stood as close to the wood stove as possible to strip and re-dress. Adelaide, who had arrived only moments earlier, was still hanging her wet clothes in the storage closet. Genie joined her there and they left the door open so that the room would warm.

"We don't have to wonder if it's really December," Adelaide exclaimed with a shiver.

"Indeed, we don't!" Genie agreed, thinking and hoping that the rough weather would keep Montague Wright away from Abby—but she had no way of knowing.

"We should be able to get lots of work done today," Adelaide said. "There won't be many people out shopping."

"I hope so," Genie said, "because you know what it will be like when this storm blows itself out."

Adelaide nodded. The worse the weather, the more in demand the clothes they made available. "But it may be a while. William said a man from the docks was in over the weekend and he said this was a bad storm that would last a few days. Some boats have been blown off course, and a few that were due to dock here in Philadelphia in the next few weeks will have to go farther south to dock."

"Will it keep snowing like this, do you think? If it does, Adelaide, we won't be able to get to work either!"

107

The storm raged for another seventy-two hours and as Genie predicted neither woman was able to get to work.

As Ezra predicted, Donald Bruce arrived as expected, though barely because, as he told it, "a dumb Irishman found it amusin' to give me wrong directions to this house. Fortunately for me a Black man saw me fall head first into a huge pile of snow, nothin' but my feet visible to the world. He grabbed both feet and pulled me out, God bless him, otherwise—" And he closed his eyes as he contemplated the otherwise.

The two Scotsmen were delighted to see each other again, and Bruce pronounced himself more than delighted to meet Mistress Abigail, Mistress Maggie, and Master Eli. He was, he said several times, very happy to be away from Chicago and Pinkerton's.

"You didn't like Pinkerton's?" Eli asked, baffled. He'd heard wonderful things about Pinkerton's!

"I didn't like some of the people we found ourselves working for," he answered with a scowl. Then he brightened as he looked at the faces before him. "But I will like working for the people in this house. I'm sure of it."

He hopped from foot to foot with excitement when Eli showed him the carriage house and his living quarters upstairs— a sight that made Eli laugh because while Ezra and Donald were roughly the same height, Donald was at least fifty pounds heavier, most of that weight carried in his belly. He did a complete inspection of the carriage and scrutinized the new leather seats and straps. He ran his large hands over the wheels, at first gently, and then tugging and pulling them until he declared himself satisfied. Taking one more turn about his new surroundings, he followed Eli through the snow back to the main house where the three additional days of weather-mandated confinement allowed him time to get to know his new employers. And to learn the real reason his friend had summoned him.

"I work for a man who owns a bank and a railroad—" Ezra began before Donald gave a hoot of laughter.

"Of course, you do, laddie! And lots of people hate his too-rich guts!" Then he sobered. "Is that what happened to you?"

Ezra nodded and told him as much of the story as he could, including Eli's rescue of him, but leaving out all references to Mrs. Tubman. "But they knew too much about him, Donnie, and he professes not to know how that's possible and he's concerned."

"As well he should be, especially with a son like that! Is the boy to blame?"

Ezra shook his head. "He's too stupid and self-centered for long-range planning."

"So, I'm not to drive and protect the ladies of this house?" Donnie said, sounding so forlorn that Ezra laughed.

"Indeed, you are, but they won't need your services every day—for shopping and Abby's women's anti-slavery group meetings, and Maggie's trips to visit her daughter. And when you and I are away Eli will be here, which is why I want you to teach him to fight."

"I'd be delighted! And to shoot as well, of course?"

"A man can't have too many shooting teachers—"

"He's already got one?"

"Indeed, he has," Ezra said, and paused. Then, "Wait until you meet her."

Before Genie opened her eyes, she knew the snow had stopped but even if it hadn't, she was going outside today. A fourth day of confinement was too much to contemplate, especially in her small house. Perhaps in Abby's mansion . . . No! She would not allow thoughts of Abby. She couldn't . . . and yet she couldn't stop them: Abby holding her tightly, weeping as if she carried all the blame for slavery and the people who practiced it, apologizing to Genie for what she had suffered. No, she could not think of Abby, for what could those thoughts be? How wonderful it would be to hold and be held by Abigail Read forever? No, not a thought she could have.

"Silly!" she chided herself as she leapt out of bed. "Ridiculous!" she chastised as she threw herself into what she hoped would be enough clothes to keep her warm. "Useless," she said glumly as she cautiously opened her front door, expecting a mound of snow to drift in. Instead her front porch and walkway were clear and she heard cheery voices coming from Thatcher Lane. She hurried to the narrow space that she could squeeze through to access the lane and saw a dozen people working to make the street passable. She obviously wasn't the only one who welcomed the chance to escape from indoor confinement. She exchanged greetings with several people and offered to help, an offer that not only was refused but was met with looks and expressions of gratitude to her, as if she'd done them a favor rather than the other way around. And she knew, even without the words being spoken, what the gratitude was for. Which meant that her work with the Underground Railroad had come to an end, which she regretted. However, what she regretted most was that somebody had made her participation widely known. She would need to speak with William about this, though he probably already knew. She hoped he was home.

"Is something wrong?" Adelaide exclaimed when she saw the snow-covered Genie at her kitchen door.

"I couldn't bear to remain inside another day!" Genie exclaimed, knocking snow from her feet as she stepped inside and closed the door. "I won't come in any further so you won't have to clean up behind me." She lifted her head and sniffed the air like a hunting dog. "You've kept boredom at bay by baking."

"Guilty as charged!" Adelaide acknowledged. "Would you like cake, pie or bread pudding?"

"Ooooh! Bread pudding, please," Genie said, "and I'll eat it standing right here while you tell me where William is."

"He and Arthur and the boys are earning a small fortune clearing streets and hauling people and things out of snowbanks," she replied while serving Genie a bowl of bread pudding—which she practically inhaled, it was so good.

"He's not cleaning your lane?" Genie asked

Adelaide shook her head. "The residents began clearing our lane at first light—me included!" she said proudly, before adding that her body now ached every time she moved. Then she added that William was not allowed to help because he'd "done so much for everybody already." She frowned when she said it, and Genie knew that she understood the meaning.

"Is William very angry?"

"Furious! But quietly so. You know how he is."

Genie did know. "Then perhaps I should go help William and Arthur because all I feel right now is lazy."

"Have you forgotten how you felt after your most recent . . . escapade?"

Actually, she had forgotten. After she had seen Ezra's condition her scrapes and soreness seemed of no consequence. "I'd rather have something to do than nothing to do, Adelaide," Genie said lightly, "even if there's a price to pay. However, if you'd teach me how to make that bread pudding . . ."

Adelaide laughed and hugged her. "If you stop by on your way home I'll give you some to take with you."

"William won't mind?"

Adelaide gave a most unladylike snort. "He's still working his way through a butter cake and a sweet potato pie."

Genie felt the cold almost immediately when she left the warmth of Adelaide's kitchen. Even though the wind had abated the temperature seemed not to have risen noticeably. When she got out to the main street she saw that it, too, was clear, and she heard the clang of a horse bus nearby. She also saw that she wasn't the only bundled figure moving about. Apparently three days of confinement was more than enough for lots of people. She walked briskly toward the blacksmith shop and was surprised to see, coming toward her, her horse cart! Before she could speak the horse came directly to her and practically knocked her over with a strong head butt, the one that was a request—a demand—for a carrot or an apple. Genie laughed and stroked the animal's face. Then she dug around in her pockets hoping to locate a treat.

"Aha!" she exclaimed, unearthing half a carrot which the horse inhaled the way Genie just moments ago had inhaled Adelaide's bread pudding.

"You spoiling that horse!" Arthur yelled from the driver's seat.

"Of course, I am," Genie said reasonably as she walked toward him. "Good day, Arthur."

"Good day, Miss Eugenie," he replied touching his head, which wore a scarf and a hat. "Why you out in the cold?"

"I couldn't stand being inside any longer. I understand that you and William and the boys have been busy."

He nodded. "But I was on my way to find you, to see if you thought it would be all right to take Miss Abigail her horse."

Genie's heart and stomach lurched simultaneously. "I think that's an excellent idea," she said, and climbed into the cart.

Arthur drove to the back of the stables and told Genie that he was going to get Abby's horse, which he would ride, leaving her to drive the cart. She jumped down and hurried inside to speak with William in the few moments she had before they needed to leave. He was surprised to see her, though pleased, and he knew immediately that she had been too restless to remain inside. "You'd no doubt be out if the snow was still falling like rain."

"You know me too well, William. And apparently someone knows us both too well."

He scowled. "Mr. Still is none too pleased."

"We are of no further value to him," Genie said sadly.

"Not in terms of helping people to freedom," he replied, "but there is other work to be done. We are not totally useless."

"Do you know who is responsible for the . . . transgression?"

William's lips tightened in anger but he did not respond; he would not, she knew, but he didn't need to. She had her own thoughts on the matter. "Will you and Arthur take Miss Read her horse?" he asked.

"If you think the roads are passable."

"For the horse, certainly. For your cart? Probably. If not, you can ride the horse and leave the cart."

"Then we'll go," she said, turning away. She stopped walking but did not turn to face him. "Job Mayes."

There was absolute silence in the space between them. Then William said, "He has been dealt with."

Genie left him, more than a little shaken by what she heard in his voice. If Mayes had been dealt with as harshly as he deserved to be . . . well . . . she was just as happy not knowing. He had risked the lives of several people, Mrs. Tubman included. But why? She found that she didn't want to know that, either.

Arthur was atop a very sturdy-looking dark brown gelding that Genie had not seen before, and he held out to Genie a bag that he clearly wanted her to take before she climbed into the cart. She looked inside and grinned widely: apples and carrots that humans would not salivate over but which horses would. She thanked him, reached into the bag and chose a carrot for the gelding which he grabbed almost before Genie could get her hand safely away, and then picked an apple for her own sweet horse who was much more genteel in her retrieval of the fruit. Genie clambered up into the cart, took the reins, and followed Arthur toward Abby's. It was slow going but not impossible as the road had been cleared, especially in the middle near the horse bus tracks. But everywhere the snow had been moved from the middle of the road to the side, making drifts six and seven feet tall in some places. With there being no sign of moderating temperatures, these snow mounds would soon become ice mounds, and dangerous.

Eli heard and saw their arrival in the lane behind the house, and he immediately sounded an alarm that brought everybody at a run, the adults as excited as he was. Donald greeted the horse as if he were a long-lost friend. Abby pronounced him beautiful and promptly named him Gerald after her father. Maggie allowed as he resembled her father a bit, which sent Abby into a fit of boisterous laughter. Ezra took Arthur aside for a discussion that would have angered Abby had she heard it, but Arthur promised that she never would know what they discussed, or that Ezra paid him and William in addition to what Abby already had paid. "We most likely will be needing your services often in the future, sometimes on short notice." Arthur gave a curt nod and a firm handshake that meant Ezra could have whatever he wanted whenever he wanted it. Genie watched the scene unfold with a happier heart than she'd had in a very long time. Donald led Gerald into the carriage house to hitch him up and told everyone to prepare to go for a ride.

Abby rushed over and grabbed her hand. "Come for a ride, Genie!"

Genie gave her a quick hug but demurred. "You and Maggie and Eli should take the first ride since this is, after all, the carriage for this residence. Perhaps Ezra should join you as well."

Ezra was shaking his head. "The ladies and gentleman of the house should get the first ride. But first you'll have to dress for it." And suddenly they were all shivering—they'd run from the house in their excitement without coats, hats, scarves, or boots—and as a unit they all turned and ran back inside.

"Miss Eugenie, you wanting to stay here for a while?" Arthur asked.

She nodded. "I think so, Arthur, so you go ahead. I think I might be able to persuade Donald to bring me home," she said with a smile and an inquiring glance at Ezra.

"Of course," he said, "or more likely Abby will want you to stay overnight so you and she and Maggie can sit up all night talking and laughing."

Genie's heart skipped a beat and a breath caught in her chest. She couldn't look at Ezra so she made small talk with Arthur instead. Then Donald drove the carriage out and what a sight that was! Gerald even seemed to prance a bit. Donald had polished the old coach to a shine. The new leathers shone, too. Ezra whistled his approval and Gerald danced a bit more. Then Abby, Maggie and Eli came running out of the house and stopped and stared, speechless. Donald jumped down and opened the door for Maggie and Abby. "You'll ride up top with me, young Eli, if that's to your liking," Donald said and Eli's smile was so wide it almost split his face as he climbed up next to Donald and imitated the Scotsman's regal posture. Maggie and Abby waved from inside the carriage at Ezra and Genie, no longer able to ignore the cold. Thanks to the forward-thinking Donald, both he and Eli had heavy blankets to cover them from waist to toe while Abby and Maggie were covered from top to toe.

"How have we managed without the carriage, Maggie?"

"How have we managed without Ezra and Donald?" was Maggie's reply as Donald drove the carriage sedately away.

Genie and Ezra hurried inside, hung their coats on the racks in the scullery, and rushed to stand near the fireplace. Ezra put in more logs and set the water on the hob to boil. Then he took the teapot from the cabinet.

"What wonders you've worked, Ezra," Genie said to him as she noticed how familiar he was in the kitchen. "And do you really know how to brew good tea?"

"Not only can I brew good tea, but I know where the cakes and scones are!"

"Three days of confinement can work their own wonders," Genie said with a laugh.

"I wouldn't call it working wonders," Ezra said as he placed cups and plates on the table, along with a pitcher of milk, forks and spoons. He expertly warmed the teapot, added leaves, and when the water boiled, poured it into the pot. When everything was on the table he sat down across from Genie and was startled by the way she was looking at him. "What?" he exclaimed.

"This is a changed house since your arrival. If not working wonders—what? Miracles?"

He was shaking his head back and forth and looking frustrated. "Just observing, Genie, and helping when and where I could."

Genie nodded her acceptance of his words as she considered all the things he had done, had accomplished in Abby Read's house, in such a short time. She poured tea and cut cake, her thoughts a jumble though one took hold and stood out: Was it because he was a man and therefore able to get things done that a woman could not? She asked him and he considered before answering:

"You sent Eli to me, Genie, and you asked Maggie to help him adjust to a new . . . way to live. You got a horse cart, which is what put the idea into Abby's head, and it was Maggie who put into words that change—dangerous change—is coming to us. I merely assembled all those pieces into a whole."

"Merely." Genie gave him a hard look. "Donald is not merely a driver, is he?"

Ezra gave her a nod of acknowledgement and acceptance. "No. He is to provide protection to this house—"

"Why?" Genie demanded. "Why does this house need protecting? Who is safer than a wealthy white woman?"

"Because when Abby begins attending the women's anti-slavery meetings there probably will be people who will not be pleased. And when she and Donald are away from this house Maggie and Eli will be here alone." That reality hit Genie hard: not a wealthy white woman alone in a house but two Black people—one a woman, the other a runaway slave.

"I'm sorry, Ezra. I apologize—"

"No need for that, Genie, and no time, either." He paused, watching her, gauging her. "I want to share some ideas with you."

"Of course, Ezra, I'd like to hear them," she said, and meant it.

So he told her: Donald was a martial arts expert and in addition to speeding Ezra's own muscle recovery, he was to teach Eli to fight. Properly fight. And he and Genie would teach the boy how to use weapons. Donald also would help Ezra understand the threat to Arthur Cortlandt and his businesses and protect the man and his family. This shocked Genie.

"Cortlandt is in danger? Still?"

Ezra nodded and the frown on his face turned into a scowl. "The Cortlandt boy, when he recovered, told his father things he'd heard his captors discussing, things they could not and should not have known—" He stopped talking at the sound Genie made. "What is it?"

"William and I, and some of those we . . . work with . . . have been compromised. People knew things about us, too, things they should not have known, things that could have brought more harm to us—and to you, Ezra—not to mention to Mrs. Tubman."

He considered what she'd said: Someone with knowledge of Cortlandt's business dealings and family problems could not be the same person with knowledge of the operation of the Underground Railroad. Could it? "Do you know who betrayed you?"

116

Genie hesitated. Should she reveal what was only a suspicion, though one she believed William had confirmed? Certainly, she could trust this man—he'd more than proven that—but before she could respond he said the name: Job Mayes. Genie nodded. "He is the only new member of our group who had sufficient knowledge to damage us. How did you know?"

"All the stories I've heard of the man and his exploits—they all sounded too—"

"Unlikely?" Genie finished for him.

Ezra nodded. "For a Colored man to have done the things he's credited with, and done them to white people without retaliation? Yes, unlikely and, quite frankly, unbelievable." Ezra paused, then said, "Has he been confronted?"

"William said he'd been dealt with."

"Meaning?"

Genie shrugged. "I've no idea, Ezra, and I didn't ask. I already know more than I should."

"What would happen to someone who did what you think Mayes did?"

"As far as I'm aware we've never had a traitor among us, Ezra, so I don't know what would happen," Genie said. But she could well imagine. Their work was considered not just important but sacred among them. Slavery was an ever-present reality, and even living lives of relative freedom in Philadelphia did not diminish the ever-present fear that lived within every Black person. What would she do to Job Mayes if he appeared before her in that moment? She caressed the derringer that always was with her, always in a pocket, within reach. She would do to him what she'd been prepared to do to Montague Wright had she come face to face with him.

"Genie!" Ezra called her name loudly. He'd said something and she hadn't heard him.

"I'm sorry, Ezra. My mind was elsewhere."

"I asked if you are armed." She smiled and withdrew the derringer, and he recalled the night he met her: She had kept her hand in her pocket while they talked. Knowing her as he did now he had no doubt that she'd have shot him had she felt threatened. Her smile widened as she saw that he remembered. Then the smile faded and vanished when he said, "I think it would be advisable if you also had your revolver, especially when you are out alone."

"What do you know, Ezra? Why are you worried?"

Then he shared Donald's description of his train ride from Quebec to Detroit to Philadelphia—how the Blacks on board had been taunted and harassed and forced to move to the rear of the train once it crossed into the United States. Donald had pretended to be asleep so that he could listen without having to join in and therefore be forced to express an opinion. The topic was slavery. So heated did the conversation become that blows were exchanged more than once and the train conductor had to be summoned. Donald recalled a lengthy discussion about a court case that would decide whether Blacks could be citizens, but he said the men arguing about it didn't seem to understand the case and, he said, they certainly didn't understand the law. He said while it seemed that there was a general opposition to slavery itself, there also was a general belief that Blacks should not be citizens. He witnessed taunting and harassment of Blacks inside the Philadelphia train station, and he saw several Blacks flee when they were accused of being runaway slaves. One, an elderly man, was caught by two bounty hunters—that's what Donald called them—but several Blacks kicked and beat them until they released the old man and several other Blacks helped him hurry away. Chased by a group that Donald called mob-like, he blocked their path and then had to fight his own way out of the station, finding the weather both a curse and a blessing: The drifting snow meant that no one could chase him and he was able to jump onto a horse carriage. Unfortunately, it was going the wrong way though a fellow passenger convinced him otherwise.

"So, the danger is real," Genie said quietly.

"Yes, it is," Ezra replied in the same tone.

"How are we to protect ourselves, Ezra? Should I remain at

home? Should Eli and Maggie remain inside these walls? Should Abby, even though it is unlikely that anyone will attempt to sell her South?" she said bitterly.

"No, no, and no. You must all go about your daily business, just with much more caution. And Abby above all, for she can hear and learn what is being said and done out in the world, as can Donald and I—"

"And when we know what and where the danger lies, Maggie and Eli and I must rely on you and Abby and Donald to save us for the truth is, Ezra, that if I use one of my weapons to protect myself, I will hang." The combination of fear and bitterness that he heard in her voice so startled him that he could no longer sit across from her. He stood up and went to add wood to stove, which was necessary because it was getting cold in the kitchen. He added more hot water to the teapot and more cake to both their plates, all the while trying to think of something to say, something meaningful. He could not, and she saved him.

"You look to be healing well, Ezra."

"Thanks to Donald and the beastly weather, there wasn't much else to do, so he and Eli gave me their full attention. You should have been here two days ago when they decided to lift my arm!"

Genie winced. "I'm most relieved that I wasn't! That must have been excruciating."

"Only the first two or three times. Arthur's horse liniment could put doctors out of business," he said and described the process: Eli and Donald would lift his arm, he'd practically faint from the pain, they'd apply the liniment, Maggie would bring warm milk and brandy, and he'd sleep. "Now I can lift the arm myself, which means my next visit to Montague Wright will be the last time I will be required to see him."

"But I hoped you would be here when he comes to introduce his apprentice—"

Ezra shook his head. "Abby will not accept him. She has decided: No one who has harmed you is welcome in this house."

Genie was surprised—not by what Ezra said but by how the words made her feel. Someone was standing up for her, taking

119

her side, defending her! This was a new feeling, a different feeling, and she liked it, but since there was no appropriate response, she said, "And I have decided this: Eugene Oliver and his ... associates ... will be available to you whenever you need him."

Ezra smiled at her reference to herself as 'him,' and expressed his gratitude, for he knew that he and Donald would need the aid of Eugene and his assistants. "I wondered if Eli could—"

She swiftly halted his words, both with her raised hand and her own words: "Eli will not return to the streets. His place is here with Maggie, and with you." Genie had initially wondered whether it was wise to bring Eli in to care for Ezra, whether the boy would adapt and adjust after so many years of almost feral life on the streets. She knew that he would accept the job because she asked him to do it but she didn't know if he'd like it. What she also didn't know was that the street life terrified him. He was a farm boy. Yes, he was a slave and he hated that existence, but Philadelphia street life for an ignorant farm boy was a different kind of cruelty. "I hope that Maggie and I can teach him to read and write a bit, and with Donald's instructions—and yours—he can grow into a wise man."

"You're right, of course. I forget that he is but a boy—"

And at that moment they heard the joyful return of the boy and the others. Even Gerald produced an excited whinny as if he recognized home. Ezra rose to open the scullery door for Abby and Maggie, and Genie's heart rose when Abby cheered at the sight of the two coats hanging on the hooks there.

"I feared that you had gone!" she exclaimed as she rushed into the kitchen, arms wide open.

"And miss Ezra's tea making?" Genie laughed as she stepped into the embrace that was beginning to feel like home. Then she turned with a hug for Maggie. "You've taught him well. The tea making, that is, the cake, I'm sure, is yours alone!"

With a laugh Maggie insisted that if the snow had lasted another two or three days both Ezra and Eli would have learned to make cake as well as scones. Abby said watching that would be worth another few days of snow and Maggie said something in a language that none of them understood but which made them all laugh.

"What did you say?" Genie asked, still laughing.

Maggie was laughing, too, as she explained that it was something her husband said. "My Jack, his mama and papa were from the Homeland and still spoke their language. Jack remembers some few phrases, but he said he never knew what they meant."

"He should be home soon, shouldn't he?" Abby asked.

"He said by Christmas." Maggie's words were a prayer.

"Then not much longer," Abby said, adding her own prayer. She had met Jack Juniper many times over the years and knew how deeply he loved his wife and daughter, and they him. She did not understand fully why he chose a life at sea and the many months away from home it required though she suspected it was a matter of economics: A seafarer certainly would earn more than most ordinary men, Black or white.

"Perhaps now that we have a carriage," Maggie said, obviously attempting to contain and control her excitement, "we can fetch Elizabeth for the weekend."

"Yes!" Ezra exclaimed. "I'd love to see her again!"

"And I'd love to meet her," Genie said.

"You know who'll be enchanted by her?" Ezra asked.

"Eli!" Maggie and Abby said in unison, and they easily pictured the excitable boy playing big brother to the equally excitable little girl, and her being charmed by him.

"So many things will be possible with the carriage," Abby said. "Why didn't we think to do it before, Maggie?"

"Because we didn't have Genie and Eli and Ezra before," Maggie replied.

"Imagine Jack's surprise when you pick him up at the docks in the carriage!" Abby exclaimed, and Genie and Ezra watched the emotions and expressions roam across Maggie's face: surprise, shock, dismay, horror. Finally, she laughed and couldn't stop. She tried to speak but couldn't get the words out.

"He . . . he . . . he . . ."

Genie clapped her hard on the back while thinking that she very much wanted to meet Jack Juniper.

"Donald said that I'm now Gerald's friend since I fed him!" Eli exclaimed as he burst through the scullery door, a blast of very cold air following him. Then he saw Genie and his excitement tripled. "Miss Eugenie!" He hopped from foot to foot, still shy about touching her without a clear invitation. When she opened her arms he rushed into them, squeezing her breathless and freezing her at the same time.

"And did he give you the reins?" Ezra asked, and Eli beamed the answer. No, certainly this boy did not need to return to a life lived on the streets. "Where did you leave Donald?"

"He is at his home making hisself presentable to—" and here Eli stopped and struggled to recall exactly what Donald had said so that he could repeat it exactly, "—to some company," he said with a frown.

"To polite company?" Ezra finished for him, and Eli beamed even more brightly.

"Then perhaps you could go upstairs to your home and do the same thing," Maggie said with a gentle smile and a brief hug, and he loped off as she called out that he could then light all the fires and the lamps and make the house ready for the evening, as it was dark as well as cold. She followed his departing back with what could only be described as a motherly gaze. Then she looked at Genie. "He's a good boy."

"Yes, he is," Genie said, "and if Abby will grant you the time, perhaps you and I might teach him to read and write?"

"A splendid idea!" Abby agreed.

Maggie smiled. "He and Elizabeth can learn together."

"Miss Maggie and Miss Genie's school for girls and boys," Abby said.

"Wouldn't that be something!" Maggie said, gathering her coat, hat and scarf. To Ezra she said, "Donald is a wonder. Eli will learn as much from him and you as he will from Genie and me."

Ezra clutched at his chest with his good hand. "What a task you set for us, Mrs. Juniper!"

She dismissed him with a wide smile and a wave of her hand. "I'll go help young master prepare the house for the evening," she said, leaving them.

"And I'll prepare the kitchen for the evening meal," Abby said as she began clearing away the remnants of Genie and Ezra's tea. "And Maggie is right. Thank you both for what you've brought into this house. I hadn't realized how . . . empty . . . it was until you two filled it. I thought all I needed, other than Maggie, were gentlemen to occupy the rooms. Now, for the first time since my parents died, this huge house feels like a home." She looked all around. "I want all the lamps glowing and all the grates warm. I may even play the piano after dinner!"

"And I'll play—" Ezra began before he suddenly stopped himself, touching his wounded left shoulder with his right hand.

"What do you play, Ezra?" Abby asked.

"The violin—badly—but even playing badly requires two arms."

"When you are recovered, then," Abby said.

"May I help with dinner?" Genie asked.

"Yes, thank you, that would be lovely," Abby said.

"And perhaps I can talk about some things with you?" Ezra asked, and he began speaking. Since Genie had already had the discussion she remained silent while Abby alternated between listening and asking questions. She promised to learn, as soon as the next day, when she could attend an abolitionist meeting.

"My mother went with Florence Mallory down the street until Father no longer allowed it. Mother was so humiliated that she stopped speaking with Mrs. Mallory altogether. I'll go see her tomorrow. I'll ask Maggie to bake a cake for me to take." And she signaled Ezra to continue. She interrupted again to ask whether it really was necessary for Eli to learn to shoot and fight.

"Yes," Genie and Ezra answered as one voice, and Abby sighed deeply.

123

"He may be called upon to protect you and Maggie when both Donald and I are away," Ezra said calmly.

Abby frowned. "What did Maggie mean when she spoke of Eli learning from you and Donald? Have you already spoken to her of this?"

Genie was shaking her head. "I think she meant what Eli is learning from Donald about caring for horses and driving, and what he is learning from Ezra about—about what, Ezra?"

"Healing the body after an injury. About muscles and bones and about using laudanum, which is very dangerous if misused."

"Yes, I see," Abby said nodding her head. "The boy has learned a great deal in a very short time."

"And he's learned it well," Ezra said, "and faster than I've ever seen anyone learn. Now, if Arthur will teach him how to make that liniment, I'll retire from the private inquiry business and sell horse liniment for people!" He stood up. "Now *I* shall go and make myself presentable for polite company."

"Ezra," Abby said quietly, and he turned to look at her. "You are very concerned about violence being directed toward Black people, aren't you? And perhaps even about slavery being reintroduced into places where it has been banned? Places like here?"

"I think that I don't have enough information to give you a proper answer," Ezra said slowly. "However, until I do, I think that we must prepare ourselves for the worst," he said, and left them.

Then they were alone, Genie and Abby, a situation they both welcomed and feared. They did not know how to speak of the things they were thinking and feeling for and about each other. But this they both knew: Neither could bear the thought of harm coming to the other. "Will you teach me how to shoot, too?" Abby asked.

"Of course."

"Because I should know how, don't you think? After all, I may need to protect you one day."

"Then you absolutely should know how to shoot!" Genie said seriously.

"Will you stay here tonight? Or do you wish for Donald to take you home?"

"I would like to stay here. If you want me. And I will help you and Maggie with dinner."

"I want you to stay here as my guest. As my friend. With me. Not as a . . . an employee."

"Is that wise, Abby? Will Maggie be . . . concerned? And what about Eli?"

Abby smiled widely. "Maggie thinks you should live here, and Eli thinks you are an angel and can do no wrong."

"An angel!" Genie laughed. "And where will I sleep?"

Abby blushed a deep crimson. "With me," she said in a near whisper.

CHAPTER EIGHT

How long is all night? Not long enough . . . or too long? For Genie and Abby, it was both for a while. Now, as the cold dawn sought to penetrate the darkness, it was the latter. Genie opened her eyes to find the deep blue ones, inches from her own, gazing at her. Again. At least now she could see them. During the night she could only feel them. That's when the night had felt endless, when they lay close together, breathing deeply, not touching, not talking because they didn't have words for their feelings, yet not sleeping because—because they couldn't. Finally, Genie had thought of something to say.

"I haven't slept in a bed with anyone since I was a little girl and my little brothers and sisters and I all slept together."

"How old were you?" Abby asked.

Genie thought; it was so long ago and a memory so deeply buried. "I was perhaps seven or eight."

"And your brothers and sisters?"

"Younger than me," Genie said, regretting that she had spoken of it.

"I have never slept in a bed with anyone at all," Abby said, remembering what Maggie once told her: Jack said slaves did not speak of the past with each other, to say nothing of with strangers. Jack had revealed bits of his past only after several years of marriage, then only reluctantly. "I have no siblings so I can't imagine how sleeping with them would feel but I know that sleeping in the same bed with you is . . . something I want to do often."

"Yes," Genie said, and took Abby's hand and held it tightly. They awoke to the sound of wind rattling the windowpanes. It was now very cold in the room, the fire in the grate now little more than barely glowing embers. They wrapped their arms around each other, initially for warmth but ultimately for the deep, though so far unexplored, comfort it brought. "Where are they now?" Abby asked.

"Who?" a drowsy Genie asked.

"Your brothers and sisters." The pause was so long Abby thought she'd drifted off to sleep.

"I don't know," Genie finally replied. "They were sold off with my mother."

Abby cried out as if wounded. Then she began to weep. Genie held her even more tightly, grateful that someone could cry for her long-lost family because she no longer could. "Oh God Genie! How do you bear the pain?"

Again, Genie didn't reply for a long while and Abby waited, but it was she who finally dozed. Had she remained awake she would have known that Genie never replied because that was a question she could not answer. How did she bear the pain? She didn't; she buried it, so deep that it no longer could be touched. She barely remembered it and had never spoken of it. Why now, and why to this woman? Perhaps because she was able to shed the tears that Genie herself no longer could. And now those deep blue eyes were looking into her own dark brown ones.

"What do you see?" Genie asked.

"More than I ever believed possible," Abby replied, and before she could attempt to explain, Eli knocked on the door. Abby quickly pulled the covers up to conceal Genie and told him to come in.

"'Mornin' Miss Abby," he said. "Some kinda cold in here!" and he began heaping coals into the grate.

127

"More, Eli, please!"

"Yes'sum," he said and complied. "Be warm in here in a minute, Miss Abby."

She thanked him when he finished and said she'd see him downstairs. Then, when he'd closed the door, she uncovered Genie, who emerged like a beautiful brown spirit for an instant before pulling the covers over both of them where they remained for a few very pleasant moments before Abby broke the spell. "I must get up and go to work."

"I'll go with you. I can help. I know how to cook."

"Certainly not! You're not here to . . . to be a . . . cook!"

Genie jumped out of the big bed and ran across the room to stand beside the grate, thinking that Abby's bedroom was larger than her parlor, that Abby's suite of rooms—the bedroom, sitting room and dressing room—were larger than her entire house. "It will not offend me to help you, Abby," she said, moving a step closer to the heat as a gust of wind rattled the pane.

"Oh, I do so hope this wind doesn't mean more snow," Abby said, climbing out of bed and scurrying to the window. She parted the heavy draperies and peeked out. "No snow, thank goodness!" She crossed the room to stand beside Genie and put an arm around her. "I don't ever want to do anything to hurt you."

"And I don't expect that you ever will. Now let's get to work. How do I get to the back stairs?" And Abby told her. Much as she hated having Genie use the servants' stairs it would not do to have a Black woman, no matter that she wasn't a servant, be seen using the main staircase.

Breakfast was prepared and served in record time with the three of them working together—and they worked quite well together. Maggie and Genie were as comfortable with each other as if they'd been friends for years, and Maggie accepted Abby's friendship with Genie as if it were the most natural thing in the world. Donald ate in the kitchen with Genie, Maggie and Eli, while Abby ate in the dining room with Ezra and the other gentlemen guests after Maggie and Eli served them. It was generally accepted that Donald got the better deal. After breakfast, when they were all together again in the kitchen, they outlined their plans for the day, possible because there were now two modes of transportation: Eli would take Genie and Maggie to Genie's dress shop and Maggie shopping for food since Genie had said there were excellent places to purchase food and supplies nearby. Donald would drive the carriage and take Ezra to his office on Flegler Street and then to Dr. Wright.

Before they left, however, Abby had an errand for Eli and a request for Maggie: He was to deliver a message to Mrs. Florence Mallory six houses away where, if her expectations were met, she would have afternoon tea and cake that Maggie would bake. Lives were getting back to normal after the four-day halt caused by the blizzard and they were all thankful.

When the maid opened the door at Florence Mallory's home, Eli dipped his head in a gentle bow, extended the letter in his hand, and announced that he had a message for Mrs. Mallory from Miss Abigail Read and that he would like to wait for a reply.

Abby had told him that he might be invited in or not, and he was prepared to stand outside. However, the young maid asked him to step into the foyer and please wait. In a very few moments a harried woman came rushing toward him from the other side of the long hallway, brandishing Abby's letter. He knew that she was older than Abby and probably older than Maggie but having little experience with women, he could not guess her age. But he *could* tell that she was wealthy.

"Young man!" she exclaimed as she approached him. "You've come from Abigail!" It was not a question but he answered in the affirmative and waited for her to say more. "Is she well? Abigail. Is she well?"

Eli was confused. Of course, Miss Abigail was well. "Yes'um," he replied. "She very well."

The woman read Abby's note again, told Eli to wait a moment, then rushed back down the wide hallway that was so dark the gas sconces were glowing, even in the middle of the morning. He didn't ever light Miss Abigail's lamps until evening. He stood there studying the foyer, comparing it with Abby's: This one was larger and the staircase was on the opposite side, but they were otherwise very much alike. He pictured what he could not see: The kitchen, he knew, would be somewhere at the end of the long hallway; the dining room and parlor would be to one side, and the living room and library to the other. But there were more rooms on this floor than there were in Abby's house—

"Please give this to Abigail," the lady was saying, offering him an envelope with her extended arm as she hurried toward him.

"Yes'um," Eli said, accepting the envelope. He dipped his head again, deeper this time, and waited for the maid to open the door. He ran the six houses back home because he was anxious to finish his chores so that he could drive Miss Eugenie and Miss Maggie on their errands. He knew, without having to ask, that he could take carrots for the horse that Genie only ever called 'sweet girl horse.' Which was no proper name for a horse, Eli thought. The horse needed a name—like Gerald—except for a girl horse. He would give that some serious thought.

Adelaide was so happy to see Genie and Eli that she almost forgot that she was irritated with them for their protracted absence. Maggie's presence also helped—Adelaide couldn't express her anger in the presence of a stranger.

After hugging Adelaide, Eli rushed away to visit with William and Arthur and to regale them with stories of his recent exploits, and to tell Arthur how much Ezra had come to rely on the horse liniment. Genie, meanwhile, tried to tell Adelaide as little as possible about events in Abby's house, most especially about events to do with Montague Wright. Maggie did not interrupt or intrude and spoke only when spoken to. She was happy to answer Adelaide's questions and delighted to talk about Elizabeth and how excited she was at the prospect of her daughter coming home

130

for the weekend. "It was Genie and her horse cart who inspired Abby to get her carriage ready to roll again," Maggie enthused, "so it will be easier to pick her up."

"I heard about the horse Arthur got for her," Adelaide said, and laughed when Maggie told her the horse's name.

"If I had a horse I think I might name him after my pa, too," Adelaide said, "or maybe it should be a mule," and they all laughed at that. Then Adelaide apologized for asking but she wanted to know why Maggie's daughter lived apart from her, and Maggie told her how Ezra had rescued her from the clutches of slave catchers. Adelaide gazed in horror at Maggie. Of course, she had heard the story—how the same Ezra MacKaye whom Eli had believed was a slave catcher had rescued a little girl from slave catchers. Now the story had come full circle for Adelaide as she stood looking at that little girl's mother. She was speechless.

"Are you a native of Philadelphia?" Maggie asked Adelaide, as much to help her recover her breath as to learn something about free-born Blacks.

Adelaide understood the question. "I was born in Virginia but the man who owned the plantation where I lived with my parents freed us in his will when he died. His family tried to fight it but my father had a copy of the will. He loaded us into a mule wagon and we left in the middle of the night." She closed her eyes as she remembered.

"Were you frightened?" Maggie asked.

"I don't think so," Adelaide replied. "I don't remember fear— I was ten years old at the time and my brother was eight—and I don't think my father was frightened, but my mother was. She kept saying that it didn't matter what was written on a piece of paper, that white people would do with us what they wanted to do. But Papa said it would matter a lot up North what was written on the paper and he kept that mule moving. It felt like we were moving in circles because we were! There were lots of streams and creeks on that land and Papa knew where they were, even in the dark, and drove us through them, back and forth, to confuse the dogs."

131

Adelaide closed her eyes again and let the memories play behind her lids. "I don't remember how long it took us to get to Philadelphia. I do know that we spent some time in Washington, DC. There were a lot of free Blacks there, but Mama said there were more mosquitoes there than in Virginia and she didn't want to live on a swamp. So, we kept traveling. I do remember that it was cold when we crossed the river into Pennsylvania. Not as cold as what we just had but colder than anything we had known in Virginia."

Genie looked at her friend in wonder. "I always thought you were born free, Adelaide."

"I think I came to believe that myself, Genie. After so long a time, and especially after I married William—he is free-born, and I think I came to think of myself as like him." She gave a wry shake of her head. "I have never thought of myself as a slave."

"You're very fortunate," Genie said quietly, and no one spoke for several moments. Then Adelaide broke the quiet.

"I am, of course, very interested to know of your accent, Mrs. Juniper," she said to Maggie.

"Many are surprised to hear the voice of the colonizer come out of my Black face," Maggie replied—and then laughed, both at the absurdity of the truth of her statement as well as at Adelaide's expression.

Genie, thinking that Adelaide had most likely experienced enough truth for one day, interceded. "Maggie, would you like to take a look around the shop?"

"Yes!" Maggie exclaimed, and began an immediate exploration as Genie stepped close to Adelaide and, with a gentle hand on her arm, began to discuss the tasks confronting them. The donation pile was large and people were wanting, needing, and waiting for garments. Without accusation Adelaide made Genie's dereliction of her duties painfully obvious. Genie wished for the scolding she was due, but that was not Adelaide's way. Genie apologized for abandoning her duties. While the knowledge that she would not see Abby for several days pained her, she could not continue to ignore her responsibilities.

Maggie came toward them with several dresses. "May I purchase these?"

"Of course," Adelaide replied.

"And do you ever have items for girls and men?"

Genie gave her a smile that contained no mirth. "When I have attended properly to my duties we should have both."

"Do you not receive garments from your mistress?" Adelaide asked, and both Genie and Maggie winced.

"Abby is ten years younger than I and much less . . . robust," she said, patting her bosom and midriff. "Genie no doubt will benefit more from Abby's castoff wardrobe than I ever could."

Now Adelaide was confused. "Why would Genie—"

"And shoes," Maggie injected. "Do you ever have shoes?"

"Almost never," Genie quickly answered. "By the time people accept that a pair of shoes is beyond repair, the shoes are . . . well . . . beyond repair and good only for the rubbish heap."

"What size is your daughter?" Adelaide asked, and Maggie described Elizabeth with the expert detail of a loving mother while Genie explored the mound of donated goods, searching for dresses small enough to be cut down to fit a child.

"Do you like these?" she asked Maggie, extending three dresses.

"You can adjust these to fit Elizabeth?" Maggie asked with barely disguised disbelief.

"She could adjust them to fit your husband and he'd think they were men's clothes!" Adelaide exclaimed. "Genie Oliver is probably the best seamstress in all of Philadelphia."

Genie, uncomfortable with the attention, gave a modest chuckle and asked Maggie about her husband's size and suggested they explore the men's clothing. She was hoping to have a quiet conversation with her but Adelaide joined them. Genie said they should look for some things for Eli as well, and Adelaide mentioned how well he looked, that he seemed to have gained weight.

"I didn't think the boy would ever fill up!" said Maggie with wonder. "No matter how much he ate, he would still want more."

"How did you fill him?" Adelaide asked.

"Bowls and bowls of rice and gravy, potatoes and gravy, grits and gravy, and enough bread and butter for three people."

"That's what Genie used to feed him—bread and butter!" Adelaide offered. "Didn't you, Genie? You used to bake bread for those boys. You thought we didn't know but we did—"

Genie sighed. "Adelaide, please."

"I don't know why she wanted to keep it a secret," Adelaide said to Maggie as if Genie weren't standing beside them.

"I think to protect the boys," Maggie said.

"What do you mean?" Adelaide asked.

"I don't know the other boys though I've met them, I think?" She looked to Genie for confirmation. "But I have come to know Eli quite well and he works diligently. Did you know that he initially refused to accept payment from Abby and Ezra?"

Genie shook her head; she hadn't known that, though she did know Eli thought that living in a real house and having his own room was payment enough, and that caring for Ezra was a privilege. He did not expect to be paid.

"I think that Eli and those other boys did not want to be seen accepting charity from Genie—or from anyone," Maggie said.

Adelaide considered this. "Perhaps you're right," she said. Then the bell above the door tinkled, signaling the arrival of a customer and she hurried away.

"I should not have been away for so long," Genie said. "I should not have left her to manage on her own. It was selfish of me."

"Certainly she will forgive you," Maggie said kindly.

"Of course, she will," Genie said, "but she shouldn't need to and I'll have to make proper amends." Genie sighed. "Which means that I cannot return with you to Abby's. Eli will take you in my cart and I'll come when I can."

"Abby will be most disappointed but she will understand."

Genie studied her. "You are not . . . concerned—"

"About you and Abby? I am delighted!" Maggie said. "I have worried that she is too much alone, and I cannot be with her for much longer. But you must be careful, both of you! What you have between you, and what you do—"

"But we do nothing!" Genie exclaimed.

"Perhaps not now," Maggie said slowly and with great consideration.

"Maggie?" Genie prompted her. She needed to understand, and if Maggie knew—

But Maggie was shaking her head and holding her raised palms outward. "I don't know, Genie, really, I don't have answers. I know that there are women who . . . love each other. I've seen it but I don't know about it, I don't know what it's called or . . . anything. I just know that if you and Abby care for each other, that makes me happy. But it also makes me frightened. You really must take care."

Genie nodded. She had known that instinctively. "But it's not wrong, is it, Maggie? For us to care for each other?"

"Who do we ask, Genie? Is it wrong to hold slaves? Some say yes, others say no. Who do we believe? Or trust?"

Since there was no answer to that, Genie asked another question: "Does Abby know to be careful?"

The question startled Maggie, then she grew thoughtful. "I think perhaps I should remind her. She was strongly chastised for her decision to operate a rooming house though the loudest voices have since quieted. Abby may indeed think that she can continue to be bold and prevail, but this is not the same thing."

"Why isn't it?" Genie asked.

"Because it excludes men and men don't like being excluded." Maggie lowered her voice even more until she was whispering. She looked toward the front of the store. "And there are women who will always think that men should be included, always. Included and acknowledged and . . . obeyed."

Genie, too, looked toward Adelaide, her friend who had been kind to her, and generous, whose only fault was that perhaps she talked too much. "She is a good person."

Maggie nodded. "I can see that, Genie, but she will not understand and people usually don't like what they don't understand."

Genie nodded. Maggie was right. She lived her own life—and survived—by being careful. "Please remind Abby."

135

✳ ✳ ✳

Florence Mallory greeted Abby with great warmth and undisguised joy. "My dear Abigail! How wonderful it is to see you! And how beautiful you are! Your mother would be quite pleased." The maid took Abby's coat and the cake, and Abby followed her hostess down the hallway that was even more grand than she remembered, and into a sitting room fit for a palace.

"Was it always so beautiful and elegant here and I was too young to notice or appreciate it, Auntie Florence?" Abby said, then clapped her hands over her mouth, embarrassed. "I'm so sorry! I do apologize! I had no right to call you that—"

"You have every right, my dear, and I'm so very glad to hear you call me that. I've missed it."

Both women had been nervous about meeting again after so many years apart, but all reservations evaporated in those first few moments. "I'm so relieved that you agreed to see me," Abby said.

"Nothing could have prevented me from seeing you, Abby, though I must confess that I wonder why after so long a time."

At that moment the maid entered with tea and cake, giving Abby time to organize her thoughts. When she and Florence had refreshments, Abby inhaled and explained that recent interactions with Blacks, and learning of some mistreatment of them, made her wish that things were different. She recalled that her mother had attended abolitionist meetings and wished to do the same thing. "Are you still involved in that work, Auntie Florence?"

"Indeed, I am," Florence Mallory said without hesitation, "and it is more necessary now than ever before."

"Why?" a startled Abby asked. "I know about that awful fugitive slave law but are there other events that I should know of?"

Florence looked grave and a bit fearful. "There is a case being argued before the Supreme Court right now—the case of a man named Dred Scott—that will impact most if not all Colored people: your Maggie, her daughter, and the young man who brought your message this morning. Whether they and all like them will have the rights of citizens of this country is what will be decided."

136

And of course, Genie! That was all Abby could think: Genie would be affected, too! "And if the Court decides that they cannot have the rights of American citizens, then what?" Abby asked.

"Then they can never be more than slaves," Florence replied.

"Even if slavery is abolished?" Abby demanded. "If there is no more slavery, what, then, becomes of all these people?"

"Those are questions that will be asked at our next meeting," Florence replied.

"May I attend?" Abby asked.

"I will take you with me," Florence said.

Abby's excitement and gratitude were short-lived as she suddenly had the thought that perhaps she would not be welcomed at the meeting because of her mother's behavior: She had left the group without explanation or apology. "I can't imagine that everyone is as forgiving as you, Auntie Florence."

"You're not your mother, Abigail, and are not required to answer for her."

"Then there's the matter of my . . . occupation."

Florence sighed. "Yes, there is that." Then she brightened. "Several of us, however, admire you for refusing to accept a bad marriage just for the sake of being married. Too many of us know how badly that can end." And she laughed aloud at Abby's shocked expression. "Young people always think they're the first to have a radical thought."

"You knew, Auntie Florence?"

"Of course, dear, but since you didn't feel comfortable telling me, I didn't feel comfortable intruding."

"And we've both wasted so much valuable time, haven't we?" Abby said sadly. Then she asked what she'd always wanted to know: Did her mother really leave the group because of her father's insistence, or because she no longer believed in the cause?

"Your mother believed very strongly in the abolitionist movement, Abigail."

"And my father didn't?"

Florence shrugged. "Your father believed in making and

spending money. And that's not really a criticism, Abigail. Most men are similarly constructed, and having to pay for labor rather than getting it for free affects how much money businessmen earn. So, for many men, perhaps your father was one of them, morality was not the issue. Profit was."

"And Mother could not go against him."

"No. She could not. Not openly." Florence cut more cake. "Maggie is still a marvelous cook."

"And a marvelous friend," Abby said proudly.

"Is she still married to the sailor?"

"Yes, and she's been hopping from one foot to the other with excitement: She expects him home any day now. I'm almost as excited as she is."

"I often wondered whether your . . . friendship . . . was more . . . involved . . ."

"More in—" Abby was struck speechless.

"Don't look so scandalized, Dear. Many women prefer the companionship of other women to that of men." Abby could not speak. "That surprises you? Sickens you, perhaps?"

Slowly regaining her composure, Abby said that she certainly was not sickened. What surprised her, she admitted, was hearing of it spoken openly. Florence assured her that it was not spoken of openly but in the privacy of a lady's drawing room in a private conversation between ladies.

Did that mean she couldn't tell Maggie? And Genie? Needing to change the subject Abby asked Florence to tell her all about the abolitionist movement. "Pretend that I know absolutely nothing because I don't." And, with a fresh pot of tea delivered by the maid, Abby settled herself even more deeply and comfortably into the satin brocade armchair ready to take in all Florence would share. Then she suddenly sat up straight, horrified at her behavior. "Oh Auntie Florence," she exclaimed.

"Whatever is the matter, child!"

"Please forgive my awful manners but I haven't asked about your husband. I heard he died—"

Florence Mallory emitted such a loud peal of unladylike

laughter that the maid came running into the room, but Florence waved her away. When the poor woman saw that Florence was merely laughing hysterically and not *having* hysterics, she left. Florence wiped her eyes. "You don't remember his name, do you?" An embarrassed Abby admitted that she did not remember Mr. Mallory's first name, or even what he looked like.

"I don't, either," Florence said, and collapsed again into a fit of laughter. It was going to be a most interesting afternoon.

"Would you like to stay at my house with your family when Jack returns?" Genie asked Maggie, and the woman was so overcome with joy that she could not speak. They had heard Eli return and Genie knew there would be no further opportunity for a private conversation so she said what she'd been thinking. Maggie hadn't responded in words but Genie thought she correctly understood the emotion.

"Miss Eugenie! Miss Maggie! I got the cart! Y'all ready to go?" Eli came their way at a gallop, followed by Adelaide.

"You got some clothes!" he exclaimed, pointing to the bundle Maggie was hugging.

"For me, for Elizabeth, and for Jack," Maggie said, "though Genie will have to work her magic on some items."

"She got you something, too, Eli," Adelaide said, coming toward them. The looks she got from Genie and Maggie said more than their words ever could have. "I . . . I'm sorry, Eli, I think I spoiled Maggie's surprise for you."

"You don't have to buy for me, Miss Maggie—I got money! Miss Abby, she pays me, and Mr. Ezra, too." He stuffed his hands into his pockets to prove it and was momentarily confused. "But I give it to Arthur to keep for me," he said, brightening, "even though I know Miss Abby and Mr. Ezra will pay me real money and not like those other mens."

"What do you mean, Eli?" Genie had spoken almost sharply and Eli cringed a bit, relaxing when she reached out and put an arm around him, pulling him in close.

"Those places where I used to work, on the docks and in the city, what they paid me wasn't real money but I didn't know that until that first time Mr. Ezra paid me. Behind the church. You remember, Miss Eugenie?"

"Yes, I do, Eli. He gave you five dollars—"

"Naw, he didn't, Miss Eugenie. He give me those coins. Those other mens used to give me coins, too, but Arthur said they wasn't real like the ones Mr. Ezra give me."

Genie and Maggie looked at each other and knew they were having the same thought: reading, writing, and counting, and the sooner they began Eli's lessons the better. Genie took the clothes that Maggie wanted altered to her sewing table and gave the rest to Eli, asking him to put the bundle in the cart and drive it to her house. "Maggie and I will walk. I want to show her where I live." They donned their coats, hats and scarves and went to the front door where Adelaide was waiting for them.

"Will you be returning, Genie?"

"Yes, I will," Genie answered.

"Today?" a querulous Adelaide inquired.

"As soon as I have shown Maggie my house and how to get there." And they stepped out into a bustling Thatcher Lane where Genie exchanged greetings with practically everyone they passed. Maggie was mesmerized—and delighted! She knew, of course, that this part of town existed but she had never experienced it in this way: Walking with a resident. This was not Abby's world and since she went where Abby went, shopped where Abby shopped, walking about on Thatcher Lane was a new experience.

Maggie's eyes alternated between studying the stores and merchants and the people walking about. Of the latter it must be said that there was no hint of elegance or prosperity. These were working people, and the stores and shops catered to their needs—and their purses—Miss Adelaide's Dress Shop, too. Maggie suddenly stopped walking. Genie turned and gave her a puzzled look. "That's your store, isn't it? It bears Adelaide's name but it is yours." Genie didn't reply but her look remained steady. "How many people know the truth, Genie? Adelaide and her husband? And how many others?"

Genie resumed walking and turned into a narrow lane with small, neat houses on both sides, all with small, neat squares of dirt in the front—dirt that would be green grass in spring and summer.

She slowed her pace, and Maggie caught up with her as she stopped walking. Maggie heard her say, "One other," as she turned sideways into a space between two houses. Maggie could but follow. It was a very short journey. She stepped into the Back Street and into another world. It was darker, yes, but more than that, it was private. Only those who knew to look would know it was here. Of course this is where Genie Oliver would live!

"This is home," Genie said, stepping up onto a low porch that ran the length of the house. She lifted the handle and opened the door to an ordinary-looking but obviously well-built cottage. "Welcome," she said as Maggie stepped in.

"You may have made a mistake, Genie, for I may never leave."

Genie knew the feeling. She was very much looking forward to being here tonight—alone.

She heard Eli's arrival before she could say as much to Maggie, who clearly was reluctant to leave. Genie closed the door behind her and helped her into the cart. Then she said to Eli, "Please show Maggie how close this is to Elizabeth's school, to the docks, to Arthur and William, to good stores for food and supplies. No stopping and shopping—"

"Abby wants me to get some food and supplies, Genie. We need things for the house."

Genie sighed and looked up at the sky to determine the time. In winter, darkness came early, and a strong wind was beginning to blow. She did not want them out in the darkness. "Then please shop quickly, Maggie. And Eli, take the quickest and safest way back to Abby's. Be careful, Eli. Very careful. Do you understand?"

"Yes'm," he said gravely, and she saw that he did.

"Maggie, please tell Abby and Ezra that I shall return in three days' time if it is convenient to send Eli for me." Genie watched them until the cart turned toward the adjacent neighborhood and Elizabeth's school before she turned the opposite way and back to her shop and the mountain of work that awaited her, along with the mountain of questions that Adelaide would have, which Genie would answer as truthfully as possible.

Abby walked home from Florence Mallory's slowly, hoping the combination of the cold wind and her wet feet would help order her thoughts. Florence had wanted to send Abby home in her dry, warm carriage, but Abby refused. It was such a short walk and the fresh air would do her good. Besides, there was no danger to confront, walking on her own street. But nothing good was coming of her obstinance. She was ruining a pair of good shoes and the hem of a good dress and her thoughts were a messy jumble. She must get them ordered before attempting to speak with Ezra to tell him how correct he was to be concerned.

Florence had made it very clear: While the work of the abolitionists was more necessary than ever, success, at least in the near term, was less likely than ever. How would she ever say these things to Genie and Maggie and Eli? She could not! She would not! She was so glad they were not at home when she arrived that she didn't wonder why they weren't.

She lit the wall sconces and lamps on the sideboard in the dining room and the stove and lamps in the kitchen. Then she hurried up to her suite, taking the back stairs because they were closer. She noticed for the first time the absence of wall sconces. If there should be light anywhere it should be in the passages where the servants lived and worked, the people who must be up before dawn to make the house livable for everyone else. She was weeping by the time she reached her suite of rooms, having lit all the wall sconces and table lamps along the way, as well as those in her suite. Though she was chilled to the bone she did not light the fire in the grate; there was no need since she was going back downstairs after she changed her clothes. She'd had her fill of tea and cake but she wanted to be in the kitchen, surrounded by the memories of the talking and laughter of the people she cared most about.

The hall clock struck the hour, and she felt a tiny fear crawl through her as she envisioned Maggie, Genie and Eli in the horse cart, the illusion of their safety able to be shattered at any moment for no reason.

Then she heard them. She rushed to the scullery door and flung it open in time to see Eli help Maggie down. But Genie! Where was Genie? Eli was leading the horse and wagon into the carriage house and Maggie was coming toward her.

"She had to remain at her shop and work, Abby. I'll tell you everything while we prepare supper."

Abby didn't even try to hide her disappointment. "I have things to tell you as well."

"So your visit with Mrs. Mallory was pleasant?"

"More than pleasant, Maggie. She harbored no ill will—"

Eli burst through the scullery door, his arms full, a strong, cold wind blowing at his back. "You can't have stabled the horse so quickly, Eli," Maggie exclaimed.

"No, ma'am, Miss Maggie. I just wanted to bring all these things in first—"

"And maybe get a carrot?"

Trying without much success to stifle a grin, the boy deposited his armload on the table, rushed into the scullery and grabbed a carrot from the vegetable bin, and hurried back outside. Abby began to sort through the paper bags. "My goodness, Maggie, you could not have purchased so much with the money I gave you!"

"I did, and I have change left over! We should have been shopping there all along."

"Two bags of flour, two bags of sugar, coffee and tea—and vegetables—"

"And three chickens and a joint!" Maggie exclaimed. "And the butcher will have a turkey for us for Christmas!"

143

"Do you think Genie will come for Christmas dinner?"

Maggie laughed and hugged her friend. "If you invite her, most certainly. And Abby, she'd be here now—she wanted to be here—but her absence left all the work on Adelaide," and Maggie went on to explain how Genie apparently was a seamstress of more than ordinary skill and how she actually owned the shop that bore Adelaide's name. "I asked her directly, and she didn't deny it, but she was very guilty and apologetic for leaving Adelaide to cope on her own for so long."

"She seems to have an enormous capacity for caring for other people," Abby said. "Perhaps that was the reason for the guilt."

Maggie acknowledged the possibility but she didn't believe that to be the reason for Genie's guilt. Whatever the situation, though, it was Genie's story to tell, and if she wanted them to know the details of her life she'd tell them. It was wrong of Maggie to speculate. But that Genie owned her house was indisputable. Maggie described the house and the neighborhood and its proximity to the dress shop. "And she said that we can stay there, Abby—Jack, Elizabeth and me—which means that she'll have to stay here with you. If she's invited, that is."

Abby was so excited she could barely talk. She told Maggie about her visit with Florence Mallory in fits and starts, hopping from one subject to the next like an excited child. *Just like Elizabeth does*, Maggie mused. Abby chose not to tell Maggie what Florence said about the case being argued before the Supreme Court; that's a conversation she would have with Ezra.

She laughed throughout the telling of how and why Florence claimed not to remember her dead husband's name: "He was foolish enough to fall in love with an Irish house maid who was foolish enough to believe that he would leave me and his society life and marry her! Of course, he had neglected to tell her that the house and the money were mine, which infuriated her." Abby imitated Florence's haughty, aristocratic tone as she repeated the story, practically choking with laughter. "Did I mention that the girl was nineteen? They were cozy and comfortable in a cottage on the Irish coast when she got the news that she'd not be moving into the mansion and riding in the carriage. So while he slept she took every cent he had, along with his watch, rings and cufflinks, Phi Beta Kappa key, his overcoat and his shoes!" Abby said, adding more details of the story.

Maggie was appalled. "How did he get home?"

"He didn't, not for weeks, and Florence didn't know where he was because he told her he was going to visit his sister in Scotland. She said that initially she was worried. Then she was frightened, then hysterical, and finally angry. She said she told herself that if he wasn't dead she'd never speak to him again."

Maggie tried to understand that. Certainly, she could understand the emotions. She experienced them all when Jack was at sea and she didn't know—couldn't know—for months whether he was well and safe. But to never speak to him again if he were alive? The only reason that Jack would not communicate with her would be that he could not. "Suppose he couldn't communicate?"

"As it happens, he could not. He'd gotten pneumonia from wandering around the Irish coast barefoot and without a coat. It's very damp in that part of the world—"

"How did she learn all of this if she wasn't talking—or listening— to her husband?" Maggie asked.

"From his sister," Abby answered. "She's married to a lord or something in Scotland, and he harassed the police until someone noticed someone selling items they shouldn't have had access to: the watch, ring, cufflinks, overcoat and shoes of a wealthy American, which got the attention of authorities. It wasn't long until a very ill stranger was found in a farmhouse on the Irish coast. By the time his family transported him to Scotland he was extremely ill. He managed to tell his sister what happened to him, and the police arrested the disappointed maid and several of her relatives. It was too late, though, to make a difference to Florence Mallory's husband, who died in Scotland."

"But why does she claim not to remember his name?" a confused Maggie asked. She found no humor in the situation.

"Ah!" Abby exclaimed. "You don't believe that she doesn't remember his name?"

"I certainly do not!" Maggie said. "She might wish that she could forget it, but I assure you that she remembers everything about the man, even the smallest detail."

"But why, given how he hurt and humiliated her?"

"That's why," Maggie said sadly, "and it's why she laughs when she speaks of it: to keep from weeping."

Abby considered Maggie's words and concluded that she most likely was correct. She'd been so happy to be in Auntie Florence's company and so grateful to be welcomed by her that it was easy to accept her words as truth. Yes, her husband's death meant that she didn't have to figure out how to forgive his transgression, but it didn't erase the pain of his betrayal. "You're right, of course," she said to Maggie. "I suppose not having a husband means that I wouldn't understand—"

Maggie shook her head and gently touched her shoulder. "If I betrayed you so horribly it would hurt just as much."

"But you would never!" a horrified Abby exclaimed.

"And your trust is why my betrayal would be so devastating."

They both turned, startled at the sound of the scullery door opening, and surprised when Ezra entered the kitchen. They hadn't heard the carriage arrive. "Good afternoon, Ezra," Maggie managed.

He looked at them, worry creasing his forehead. "What has happened? You both look . . . stricken."

"I'm learning things from Maggie that I should already know," Abby said. "Did you have a productive day?"

"A most enjoyable day," he replied, noticing with satisfaction that they both reacted to his description of his day. "Which is why I've come in the back door—so that I could tell you imme-diately." He looked all around, sniffing the air, for Abby and Maggie had been working toward dinner preparations while they talked. "But all I've done is make myself hungry. May I eat now?"

"Only if you like raw chicken," Maggie replied. "Would you accept tea and cake?"

"We have cake?" an excited Abby exclaimed.

"Of course," Maggie said equably. "Did you think I'd make just the one?"

Ezra made the tea while Abby cut the cake. Maggie finished braising the chicken, covered the pot, and joined them at the table. Ezra accepted compliments on his tea-making ability and Maggie on her cake, and they enjoyed their repast in companionable silence for several moments until Ezra broke it.

"I'll accept that I cannot eat raw chicken if you'll kindly tell me what it will be when it's cooked."

"You're every bit as annoying as Eli," Maggie said, feigning exasperation. "Chicken fricassee."

"Do you think Mr. Juniper would mind if you took a second husband?" Ezra asked meekly, causing Maggie to roar with laughter, surprising Abby, who said she'd never heard Maggie laugh like that.

"That's because I've never before heard such foolishness! You're *worse* than Eli!"

Ezra smiled contentedly and began to tell them of that part of his day they were most interested in: his visit to Montague Wright. "He was, to use his words, surprised and amazed that I was so well healed, given the care that was available to me. I told him that I would not have had better care in a hospital and he bristled at that, as I knew he would. Then I told him that all his patients should be so fortunate as to have Mrs. Juniper and Eli care for them, which rendered him speechless. Which was my intention."

"I'm sure you appreciated even a brief respite from the sound of his voice," Abby said bitterly. She'd never erase from her mind or her memory of Genie's reaction to hearing the man's awful voice.

"But it's when I gave him your letter that his longest silence reigned. He must have read it through four times, and each time he opened his mouth to speak but no words came. Finally, he managed to say that he didn't understand and he gave me the letter to read, as if I could explain what he didn't understand."

Ezra, who was clearly enjoying himself, described how he took

147

the letter and read it through, as if he didn't already know its contents. Then, with a puzzled look, he returned the letter and said *he* didn't understand what it was that the good doctor didn't understand.

"Does she mean that she won't accept my apprentice or she won't accept his slave?" the man had whined.

Abby was on her feet. "He said *slave?* He actually said that word?"

"He did," Ezra replied. "Then he seemed to realize what he'd said and he began to sputter. I left him then."

"He wanted to bring a slave into this house," Maggie said, and got up to go attend to her chicken fricassee, the dish that would net her a second husband if her first one approved. The thought allowed her to push the ugliness from her mind and give in to a smile. Then she thought only of Jack and the fact that he'd be home any day now and that the three of them—she and Elizabeth and Jack—would live like a family in Genie's beautiful little house. And Genie! How glad Maggie was that she hadn't heard Ezra's words—that the man with knowledge of Genie's own slave past wanted to bring a slave into this house. She hoped Abby wouldn't tell her. She'd make certain that Abby didn't tell her. She didn't need to know.

Eli came in then, with hurried and harried greetings as he unwound his scarf and removed his hat. He headed for the stairs at a trot, informing Abby that he'd have the lamps and fires lit and the house bright and warm as quickly as possible. The adults watched him go with the same thought: that they were watching a boy become a man. In the short time that he'd been in Abby's house he had become taller, straighter, more confident. He also had become a member of the household, as had Genie. Oh, how they missed her!

And Genie missed them. Her work with Adelaide had gone swiftly and smoothly. They'd gotten a lot done and, for a change, they'd had more paying customers than not. Genie had promised alterations for three women and she'd stay late to complete them. For the first time she didn't want to rush home to be alone.

Working would occupy her mind so she wouldn't think so much about Abby and Maggie and Eli and Ezra and being with them. Adelaide told her half a dozen times how much she liked Maggie, and each time she'd marveled at the fact of friendship with Abby. That she lived in the woman's mansion as her friend, not as her servant. "I didn't believe Colored could be friends with them. Do you think you'll be friends with her too, Genie? Is that why Maggie said the woman would give you her old dresses?"

Genie did not want to discuss Abby with Adelaide but ignoring or deflecting her questions would only make her more curious. "I think we already are friends. And Maggie's comment about the dresses is due to the fact that Abby and I are the same age and size. And Ezra MacKaye is my friend, too, and I think if you ask William and Arthur, you'll find that they think he's worthy."

"I think you're right about that," Adelaide said thoughtfully, and they worked in companionable silence until Adelaide said she thought they should stop for the day. But Genie told Adelaide to go, that she would finish the alterations she'd promised. "Shall I bring you some dinner, then?" Adelaide asked.

"That is most considerate and generous, Adelaide, but I have food here that I can eat. Please give William my best regards." She locked the front door after Adelaide left and turned out the lanterns. She worked at her big sewing machine in the back room near the wood stove, which she stoked. She had noticed how strong the wind had become when she opened the door for Adelaide. She would not stay here too late, she promised herself, though she knew she had lost track of time when she heard a firm knock at the back door. The ever-present derringer was in her pocket but, as Ezra had suggested, she now also kept the revolver close and that was what she held when she went through the storage room to the back door.

"Yes?" she said in a lowered, almost guttural voice.

"It's Arthur, Miss Eugenie," she heard, and she hurriedly unlocked and opened the door.

"Are you all right, Arthur? William? The boys?" In truth his unexpected arrival frightened her.

"I didn't mean to scare you, Miss Eugenie. I'm sorry," he said, following her in to stand beside the stove.

"Have you eaten, Arthur? I've got bread and cheese and some ham. And tea, if you like."

"Yes, ma'am, thank you. I appreciate it," he said, and took a seat at the rough table she and Adelaide used for meals.

Genie fixed two plates and quickly made tea as the water already was hot. She joined Arthur at the table and began to eat as she waited for him to talk. "Oh! I forgot, there is milk but it's on the window sill and I'm sure it's frozen—"

"Don't need it, thank you," he said, and he was ready to talk. "It's about your friend, Miss Maggie. Eli said her man works on one of them across-the-ocean sailing ships, is that right?"

"Yes, it is. In fact, he's due in any day now . . ." The look on his face froze her words. "Arthur? What is it?"

Then he told her that he'd heard a ship from England that was blown off course by the bad weather had decided to dock further south—either in Baltimore if possible, or it would go on down to Charleston if necessary. "The Colored men who work on the boat—I guess they're sailors? They most naturally didn't want to get off a boat in Baltimore or Charleston so they jumped ship."

Oh Maggie! Genie's heart was in her throat for her friend. "How do you know this, Arthur?"

"A man I know works in the telegraph office and he said they been clickin' and clackin' back and forth all day about it. Where did the boat come from, the one Miss Maggie's man works on?"

"Liverpool, England."

Arthur nodded. "That's the one. Got a lot of passengers, too, who're gonna have to figure out how to get to Philadelphia. Won't be too hard from Baltimore, but Charleston?" He paused. "Where's that?"

"South Carolina," Genie said.

"Oh, dear God in heaven! Ain't no Colored man in his right mind gonna get off a boat in South Carolina! He'd be a slave in chains before the cargo was off the boat."

"How do we find out, Arthur? I can say nothing to Maggie until I know something for certain. And she's so excited about having her daughter this weekend." She stood up. "I must complete this work tonight so that I can go to the docks tomorrow."

"You can't go down to them docks, Miss Eugenie! That place ain't safe for big men with pistols!" Arthur spoke forcefully. It was an order, not a request.

Genie withdrew the pistol from her pocket. "I have a pistol, and thanks to you I know how to use it."

"One of them well-fed wharf rats could take that from you before you could fire it. You cannot go down there!" There was no deference in his voice but there was a hint of fear. Arthur had issued an order that was also a plea. "It would be better—and safer—if Mr. MacKaye went. A white man can learn things from other white men that we can't."

He was right and Genie knew it. "But he'll have to go tomorrow, Arthur. If I write to him tonight will you make certain he gets it?"

"I'll take it to him myself, Miss Eugenie," Arthur said, heading for the back door.

"Thank you for letting me know, Arthur. As helpless as I feel, I'd rather know than not know."

"I'm real sorry, Miss Eugenie. But we'll find out where that boat is. And them men, too."

Genie heard the neighing horse outside the following morning, and she opened the door to find Arthur on horseback, a light dusting of snow covering him. She gave him the letter she'd written to Ezra, thanked him, urged him to be careful, closed the door, and walked briskly to work. She expected that the turn in the weather would mean a heavy volume of business and she was correct: She and Adelaide were occupied from the moment they unlocked the door until well past time for the midday meal. Genie was glad because it meant there had been no time for thinking and wondering and worrying.

The people that she was thinking, wondering and worrying about had those same thoughts on their minds, but the weather was the cause. Not wanting to be snowed in again, Cornelius Eubanks, who had announced at dinner that he'd be leaving because his job had transferred him, announced at breakfast that he'd leave immediately to visit his family for Christmas before assuming his new posting. And Henry Carson said that he, too, would leave that day for warmer weather to the south, while Josiah Jones was going further north, to New England, where he would remain with his newly widowed sister who now was alone—all decisions which made Abby and Maggie relieved and happy.

They wouldn't have to look after boarders for a while and therefore could enjoy each other for the Christmas holiday. Neither of them considered Ezra a boarder or a guest and while they didn't know if he planned to be away for the holiday, they would be pleased if he remained. At least Abby and Eli would. Maggie would be at Genie's with Elizabeth and Jack, and Genie would be here with Abby, Ezra, Eli and Donald.

Breakfast was ending when Eli ran to answer a knock at the scullery door to find a snow-covered Arthur, who thrust an envelope at him with whispered instructions to give it to Mr. MacKaye, "quick-like. I'll be in the stable."

Eli hurried back to the dining room with the letter and leaned in to whisper to Ezra, who had recognized the writing. He stood quickly, excused himself, and was on his way to his suite while reading the letter. He turned and headed quickly back to the kitchen where he grabbed Donald, who'd been enjoying breakfast with Maggie and Eli, and the two of them hurried out in the thickening snow to where Arthur waited in the stable. Ezra read Genie's letter to Donald then asked Arthur to tell all that he knew. "We'll dress for the docks and take Genie's cart," Ezra said.

"I'll get it ready and y'all can follow me," Arthur said.

They dressed in record time. Ezra stopped in the kitchen to apologize for rushing away. "I don't know what time I'll return so you need not worry about a meal for Donald and me," he said. Then he looked at Maggie. "I don't know how bad the weather will get so perhaps you'd like for me to pick up Elizabeth and bring her here?"

Maggie hugged him tightly and whispered that she'd saved some chicken fricassee for him, and he left, determined to find out where Jack Juniper was.

CHAPTER NINE

Every piece of information that Ezra and Donald could gather suggested that Jack Juniper and two other men had escaped the packet ship *Rosemary* in the ship's dinghy at least a week ago, in the middle of a storm with fifteen- to twenty-foot seas and devil winds. The general consensus was that they could not have survived. But Donald had heard enough speculation to the contrary to give him and Ezra hope.

Donald had made a nuisance of himself in and around the shipping office, posing as the brother of a passenger on the *Rosemary* unwilling to accept the fact that the ship had docked in a place called Charleston, South Carolina—a place he'd never heard of—and that his sister was obligated to get herself to Philadelphia however she could. It was when he was prowling the docks and boat slips, asking how he could bring someone to Philadelphia from Charleston, that he heard men talking about how good a sailor Jack Juniper was and that if anyone could bring the dinghy to shore, it would be him.

The question was, where would or could he come ashore in a dinghy? Where would the storm have blown the small boat? Ezra and Donald both had taken ocean voyages from their native Scotland to America, but neither man was well versed in the ways of the sea. Since Donald by now was well-known as the brother of a passenger blown off course, it was left to Ezra to find out where the dinghy might have washed ashore. He had made some decent contacts while looking for Edward Cortlandt. He hoped he'd be remembered. He also hoped he had sufficient funds to properly show his appreciation. Seamen and dockworkers didn't do favors.

"Maggie gave us too much money," Adelaide said as Genie completed the alterations to the dresses Maggie had selected for Elizabeth. Maggie's own dresses were ready and Genie was about to begin on the items for Jack, tasks she didn't expect to take very long as she was only opening and then tightening seams in three pairs of trousers, and shortening the sleeves in three shirts. She wanted to have everything ready by the end of the day because she was hopeful that Ezra and Donald would find Jack.

"I'm sure she'll visit us again and we can have her choose something to make up the difference," Genie said, then added, "or more likely, knowing Maggie, she'll have us apply her surplus to someone in the opposite circumstance."

"You really think a lot of her, don't you?" Adelaide asked.

"Yes, I do," Genie answered as she folded and packed Maggie's purchases, which she would take to her own house so they would be there for the Juniper family when they arrived. And as if she could read Genie's thoughts, Adelaide said what she had been thinking but had not expressed: "But do you know her well enough to leave her in your home?"

"I know her well enough that I don't wish that she and her family should have to live in a rooming house."

"But you don't know her husband at all—"

"Enough, Adelaide, please. I've extended the offer and it has been accepted. There is nothing further to discuss."

"And a very kind and generous offer it is," Adelaide said, "and I admire you for it."

Genie had stopped listening to Adelaide and was thinking of Maggie and Abby, Ezra and Donald, feeling helpless because she was doing nothing to help find Jack. Of course, she knew there was nothing she could do but that didn't stop her from wishing there was. The bell over the front door jingled. That and the sound of Adelaide's voice returned her to reality.

They were busy for the next couple of hours during which the weather put on a varied display: It snowed heavily and the wind howled for a brief but furious fifteen minutes. Then the snow stopped and the sun shone so brightly it could have been a spring day. Except for the temperature: It was frigid. But it was still and quiet, which everybody preferred to heavy, blowing snow and the threat of a paralyzing blizzard. Then, after an hour or so of clear, sunny calm, the sky darkened and a light snow began falling. It was a slow fall of tiny flakes that would take hours to accumulate but accumulate it would, if it lasted long enough. Such snow, however, carried no threat and no one was worried.

No one but Ezra and Donald, who learned where Jack and his mates might have made landfall—if they had survived. There were coves all along the rocky shoreline where the land eventually led to farms and homesteads that were only reached by roads and lanes that were not in Philadelphia City proper. Instead, they were out in the countryside, an area totally unfamiliar to Ezra and Donald and which most likely would be rendered impassable by a heavy snowfall. Then there was the fact that there were but a few hours of daylight left.

"We don't know if that's where Jack Juniper is, or even if he survived," Ezra said to William and Arthur. They hadn't known where else to turn for help, and they'd believed—correctly—that if anyone could or would help it would be these two men.

"I know where you mean," William said thoughtfully, "and those farmers along there are Amish and Quakers. If Jack and the other men washed up on their land, they'd be taken care of."

"Might we go looking?" Donald asked.

Arthur nodded. "But not today. Those roads out there is not a place you want to be lost, especially at night."

"If they're out there and one of those farmers found them, they're safe," William said. "We can set out at first light tomorrow."

"But if it snows all night—" Ezra began.

"We'll take the horses," Arthur said.

"And if someone is hurt and needs a cart, we'll come back for him," William said. Then he took a close look at Ezra. "And you look to be in need of a meal and a bed."

Ezra had to admit to being in a great deal of pain after the day's exertion. What he wouldn't give for one of Eli's horse liniment massages! "We'll spend the night at one of the places on the dock."

"You'll sleep here in the stable where you'll be dry and warm, and that'll be after a meal at Joe Joseph's place. And don't argue, Ezra," William said. "This is a most wonderful thing you and Donald are doing for Maggie Juniper."

"The way that she and Eli cared for me—I'd sail to South Carolina for Jack Juniper if I had to!"

Donald added, "She feeds me at her table like she's known me all my life."

"I promised Maggie I'd take Elizabeth to her," Ezra said. "I have Genie's cart—"

"Eugenia can take her," William said in his quiet way that brooked no argument. "That way she'll have her cart with her."

"Is it safe for her and the girl alone?" Ezra asked.

William nodded. "If they go now. You go get Elizabeth and I'll fetch Eugenia."

The joy that erupted when the snow-covered Genie and Elizabeth entered the kitchen could have been surpassed only if Jack Juniper had been with them. The absence of any guests to feed meant that Abby had joined Maggie and Eli at the kitchen table for a meal of sweet potatoes, greens and fresh baked bread with butter and jam—only Eli among them eating the latter.

Hugs and kisses and Elizabeth hopping from one foot to the other, interspersed with shouts and cheers of joy, lasted for a while. Maggie held her daughter so tightly that the girl yelped as all the air was squeezed out of her. Eli and Maggie gave their seats at the table to Genie and Elizabeth. While Maggie prepared plates for the newcomers, Eli went out to stable the horse and cart. Elizabeth chattered the entire time—about school and what she was learning there, about school friends and teachers, and at length about Ezra MacKaye. Genie, who initially had attempted to converse with the girl during the snowy ride, gave up and resigned herself to listening, as Abby was doing now. Genie cleared the dishes from the table while Abby served tea and cake, and Elizabeth chattered. Finally, Maggie put a stop to it, either because she realized that Genie and Abby were feeling overwhelmed or she herself was.

"Enough talking, Elizabeth."

"But Mama—"

"No buts, Elizabeth. Finish your food so we can get you ready for bed."

"No, not bed! Not yet, Mama!"

"Yes, bed, Elizabeth, and we can go now if you don't wish to finish eating."

Elizabeth hurriedly began to eat. She spread jam on her bread as Eli had, but without the butter. She drank her tea without sugar but lots of milk. She seemed finally to have calmed her excitement and, in doing so, seemed to become a bit drowsy, as if agreeing that going to bed was a good idea.

Then Eli returned, recharging the energy in the room, and it was well over an hour before calm returned. A whispered conversation between Genie and Eli resulted in two decisions: He would spend the night in the carriage house, and Genie and her revolver would sleep on the sofa in the parlor. Eli filled and lit the grates in Maggie's and Abby's suites and the one in the parlor before he exited the scullery door to cross the yard to the carriage house. He carried a lantern so that Genie could watch his progress, and she didn't lock the scullery door until she saw the carriage house illuminated. Genie then checked to be certain that all of the outside doors and windows were shuttered and locked. Abby had brought blankets and linens to the parlor and was waiting for her there.

'I'm so glad you're here."

"As am I," Genie said, taking her hand.

"I need to ask you this but I won't be upset if you can't answer: Where are Ezra and Donald?"

Genie hesitated only long enough to ensure that Maggie was safely upstairs before answering. She told Abby everything she had discussed with Ezra, Donald, William and Arthur—and Abby's fear matched her own: Maggie!

"And if they have no success with the farmers along the coast roads, then what?"

"Ezra said he'll go to Charleston if necessary, and if the worst has happened, he'll buy Jack back."

"Then we must hope and pray that Jack and his mates survived in their dinghy," Abby said resignedly.

"Of course, we must," Genie agreed.

"Though I can't imagine how," Abby said, fear in her voice. "I still recall the Atlantic crossing with my parents when we left England. We encountered a storm and the wind and waves tossed the ship about as if it were a child's toy—and it was a huge oceangoing vessel! My mother was sick for weeks afterward and I wasn't much better—and we were on land in Philadelphia!"

"You must remember that Jack is a seafarer with many years of experience."

"Yes. Yes, I must keep that in mind," Abby said.

"They will send word tomorrow as soon as they know something whether good or bad," Genie said. "So, let us imagine giving Maggie good news and imagine her happiness."

"At least she has Elizabeth to keep her occupied."

"And a good job she does!" Genie exclaimed, and they both enjoyed a light, though brief, moment.

"Will you be all right down here?"

"I'll be quite all right."

"I so quickly came to feel safe with Ezra down here and Donald in the carriage house. I don't miss the other men—the boarders—but I do miss Ezra and Donald. I won't sleep with you down here alone."

159

"I'll likely not sleep much, either, and I'm quite accustomed to being alone." Genie walked with Abby to the stairs. "Take the lamp. The upstairs hallway is in darkness."

"Thank you for being here, Genie."

"There's no place I'd rather be," Genie said, stepping into the circle of Abby's arms. "I'll watch until you're upstairs." And she did until the darkness absorbed the flicker of the lamp. She then lay on the sofa, wrapped in the linens and blankets. Her final thoughts before drifting into a restless sleep were how pained she would feel if Ezra and Donald needed to travel south to locate Jack and she could not be there to help—because under no circumstance would she voluntarily travel south.

The other side of that painful thought was that such a journey would be a fool's errand because if Jack and his mates remained on a ship that docked in a southern port, they already would be slaves by the time Ezra and Donald arrived and nothing they said or did could or would change that. *Please let them be on some farmer's land here in Pennsylvania* was her last conscious thought before sleep.

And those were the first thoughts of William and Arthur as they left the city of Philadelphia in the snowy dawn for the farmland that followed the banks of the Schuylkill River. Unlike the white men, they didn't need to try to imagine the fate of the Black seamen if they landed in Charleston. They knew exactly what would befall them. Arthur led the way on horseback. Ezra rode beside him and William and Donald followed in a horse-drawn cart large enough to transport three men if that proved necessary. As grateful as William and Arthur were for the effort to locate Jack Juniper and return him to his wife, and as amazed as they were that white men would put forth such effort to benefit a Colored family, they would not, for any reason, go south. Though they had known him but a short time they had come to like and trust Donald Bruce. If he was inclined to believe those who said that Jack Juniper had the skill to steer a dinghy to shore in a storm, then they were inclined to accept Donald's belief as good enough reason for this morning's search.

Overnight snow had been light and sporadic so roads, streets and lanes in the city were passable. Such was not the case in the countryside where the rutted lanes were filled with snow, making it impossible to do more than inch forward cautiously. Since no one had traveled the road before them there were no tracks or trails to follow. Ezra rode to the front door of each house they passed and made inquiries. Only once was he gone long enough to raise hope among his companions, hope that quickly became excitement as they saw the farmer of the house hurriedly pull on boots, coat and hat and climb up behind Ezra.

"This is Amos Yoder," Ezra called out when he and his passenger were close enough for conversation. "He is accompanying us because the farmer who rescued Jack doesn't speak English."

It took a moment for the words to resonate, and when they did, there was a great cheer and William, who was closest to Donald, hugged him and thanked him. "Where is he? We may be able to get the man home in time for dinner with his wife!"

"You passed the house—you can't see it from the road. You must turn around," Amos Yoder said, which was not a problem for those on horseback. Turning the cart around was a different story. Arthur climbed down and immediately stumbled and fell to his knees. Yoder saw Arthur's damaged leg and quickly slid down from his place behind Ezra. "Allow me to help, please," he said to Arthur.

"I can manage," Arthur growled.

"Please, sir, allow me to assist you. This road is—"

Before Amos could complete his sentence, Arthur went all the way down. William, Ezra and Donald were on the ground with him in a matter of seconds. No one spoke and no one touched Arthur—they knew of the man's pride—but they stood around him in a semi-circle, ready to offer assistance if he needed it. Muttering unintelligible curses, he pulled himself to his knees using the cart wheels for leverage. Then he looked beyond his circle of friends to Amos Yoder. "You're right about this road, sir, whatever it is you were about to say. I'd appreciate your help turning this cart around."

Yoder knew his rutted road well. He advised the men to walk their horses, then he backed the cart into a path the visitors had not known was there and led the horse forward, a task that proved much easier when Yoder offered the carrot that Arthur gave him. "The horse belongs to a woman who thinks feeding it is a good idea."

"It is a good idea," Amos Yoder said, stroking the appreciative horse between her ears.

They were wet and freezing when they turned into another path they'd not have known existed without Yoder's help and guidance. Their unusual procession had almost reached the front door of a farmhouse that was set well back from the road when the front door opened and a very tall, very thin, very old, heavily bearded man stepped out. Amos greeted him in a foreign language and the man replied in the same language. Yoder introduced him as Elmer Briskey, and he looked even older than he had appeared at a distance though there seemed nothing infirm about him. Amos and Elmer talked for a long while. Occasionally they both would look at Ezra and Amos would say something to him. Ezra would reply, and Amos would then interpret for Elmer.

After a while Elmer looked at the people in his yard, raised his right hand as if taking an oath, and beckoned them forward and everyone followed him around the house to the barn. En route, Ezra quickly shared what he had learned: Three days ago, Elmer Briskey had found two men and a capsized boat washed up on the shoreline behind his house. The two men were barely conscious. He had them brought to his barn. He was about to drag the dinghy into the yard when beneath it he discovered the body of a man. That had been two days ago. Yesterday a second man had died without regaining consciousness. Both of the dead men were in the dinghy covered with snow. The third man, who Amos believed was Jack Juniper, was alive but barely.

"Why does Amos believe he's Jack Juniper?" William asked.

"Because the only word he has uttered is *Maggie*."

"That's good enough for me," Arthur said. "Let's get him an' take him home."

162

"He's not a man you'd want to take home to his wife," Ezra said, repeating what Elmer said: The sea and the rocks had beat the man badly. And though they hadn't known Jack when he was healthy, not one of them wanted to take this man to Maggie Juniper. Not in his current condition.

"First he's got to wake up, then we got to clean him up and fix him up," Arthur said.

"We'll get him home, and if he's still alive we'll wash and shave him and cut his hair so that he looks like a man instead of a beast. Then we'll get Maggie and let her fix him," William said. "She'd want to be the one to get him back to health." And since he was the only one of them who had a wife, they deferred to him.

They put Jack on the cart and wrapped him in the blankets and rugs they'd brought. William sat in the cart with Jack's head in his lap to protect him from the worst the country roads had to offer as Arthur started slowly forward. Ezra was still talking with Amos and Elmer and trying to offer them money, which they were refusing. Ezra continued to talk, and, by all appearances, to beg and plead, until Amos and Elmer reluctantly accepted money from him. Then old man Briskey gave Ezra a parcel and the three men shook hands. Ezra made his way as quickly as possible to his horse and to William's, which was now tethered to his. It didn't take long for him to catch up to and overtake the cart, and he led them back to Philadelphia. Just as day had been breaking when they left that morning, it was fading when they returned. They were tired, cold and hungry but they could not see to their own needs until they took care of Jack Juniper.

It took them an hour to get Jack clean and to rid him of several weeks' worth of head and facial hair. Adelaide brought beef broth and hot milk with honey and brandy. "What a handsome man!" she exclaimed.

"You should have seen him an hour ago," William muttered.

Jack swallowed most of the broth and opened his eyes but without recognition. He slept again, then took the remainder of the broth. He opened his eyes again and tried to focus them and make some sense of what he was looking at, but the effort was too great. By the time he was halfway through the hot milk and brandy he was sleeping deeply, the way Ezra had slept after his injury.

"He'll be all right," Arthur said, and opened a bottle of horse liniment. And the following morning he was all right enough to ask who they were. When he understood they were Maggie's friends, tears filled his eyes.

"Please," he whispered.

"We'll go get her now."

"Elizabeth?" Jack whispered.

"They're both at Abby's," Ezra said, and Jack smiled and fell into a deep sleep. When they were convinced that he was just sleeping and not dying, Ezra bought dinner for everyone at Joe Joseph's restaurant where the waiter greeted them warmly before demanding to know where Miss Eugenie was.

Reverend Richard Allen had never seen any of them without Genie being present and it wasn't a circumstance that he wished to become familiar with. Both Ezra and William tried to reassure him that Genie would have been with them if she hadn't been busy but he wasn't to be mollified. "I want her to see what a good job I'm doing! She got me this job and I want her to know that Mr. Joseph, he says I'm doing good and I want her to see!"

"We will tell her because we can see what a good job you're doing," Adelaide said.

"And when she's not working, she'll come see for herself," Ezra said, thinking he was helping.

"She ain't working at that dress store this time of night, 'specially with Miss Adelaide here," he said darkly.

"Miss Eugenie does all kinda work, boy, you know that, don't you?" Arthur growled, giving Reverend Richard a hard look, and he took the meaning. He knew very well that Genie did more than sew.

"Yessir, I know," he said quickly. "Y'all enjoy your dinner."

And they did enjoy dinner, and breakfast, too, the following morning—all except William and Adelaide who ate at home.

Then, rested and fed and assured that Jack Juniper was alive if not yet well, Ezra and Donald went to get Maggie.

"You will be quiet Elizabeth Juniper, or you will go to your room!" Maggie's frustration with her daughter's unbridled exuberance finally spilled over, startling Abby who had entered the kitchen at just that moment. She had been in the front of the house supervising the thorough cleaning in preparation for Christmas—as well as keeping the hired cleaners well away from the kitchen where four Blacks were studying.

Genie, Maggie, Elizabeth and Eli were seated at the kitchen table for Eli's lesson and they were using Elizabeth's alphabet book. She had agreed to help—was, in fact, excited at the prospect of helping this boy she had come to think of as a big brother—but she could not restrain her inclination to show off. She knew more than her big brother! Whenever Genie or Maggie queried Eli, before he could answer Elizabeth would proudly recite the correct response in defiance of all attempts to convince her that not only was she not helping but she was making it more difficult for Eli to learn. She had not understood why a boy older than she was could not already read and write the alphabet and Genie and Maggie had explained that he'd had to go to work, not to school, a fact she had seemed to both understand and accept. The challenge was allowing him to learn at his own pace.

"I'm sorry, Mama. I'm sorry, Auntie Genie."

"It is Eli to whom you should apologize," Maggie snapped, "for it is his lesson you're ruining."

Elizabeth hung her head. "I'm sorry, Eli. I won't—" The neighing of a horse interrupted her words and the two children leapt to their feet as one and were out the scullery door in an instant. Ezra and Donald had returned! Genie and Abby shared a look that mixed hope and fear, which Maggie didn't see as she was collecting the paper and pencils and clearing the table.

Ezra entered then, smiling, and Genie and Abby gave an excited whoop, startling and confusing Maggie, who was even more startled when Ezra came to stand before her. "Jack is at Genie's waiting for you," he said.

It took a moment for Maggie to understand but when she did tears sprung to her eyes. "But how?"

"Donald and I went to get him," Ezra replied blandly. Too blandly apparently, for Maggie now was on alert.

"From where, Ezra? And why didn't he just send for me when he returned like always?"

And so Ezra had to explain, as cautiously and gently as possible, but Maggie's tears flowed and her chest heaved, though she stifled the sobs that threatened to break free at any moment. When Ezra began to explain the ship's detour to the ports of Baltimore or Charleston, Maggie's knees buckled. Abby and Genie caught and held her until she regained her balance. She kept trying to catch her breath so could she speak. It proved difficult but she managed a few words between sobs. "He couldn't go back to Maryland. He's a runaway from there. He'd rather die than go back there!" Genie and Abby continued to support her on either side but did not speak or attempt to halt her tears. Eventually Genie brought a cloth to wipe her face, and she finally controlled her breathing and managed words: "First you saved my daughter and now you've saved my husband. I will never be able to thank you, Ezra, and I will forever be in your debt."

Ezra smiled as he took her hands. "After meeting the man, I can understand why you laughed at the thought of me as a husband, but I'd be grateful if you'd agree to make me chicken fricassee on occasion—"

Maggie hugged him then, laughing through her tears. "Please take me to my husband, you silly man!"

While Maggie ran upstairs to pack bags for herself and Elizabeth, Ezra quickly told them what he could and promised complete details later. "We'll take the carriage and Eli if that's all right?" Ezra asked, and Abby immediately agreed as Maggie bustled back in and they all helped her take her things to the carriage. When Maggie explained where they were going, Elizabeth alternated between excitement and trepidation. How badly was Papa injured and would he be all right? Maggie told her to get into the carriage and be quiet while she turned her attention to Abby.

"I'm sorry to leave so suddenly and without proper preparations—"

"Please don't apologize, Maggie—it isn't necessary. We will be fine. See to Jack and if he's well, perhaps the three of you will come for Christmas dinner?"

"Oh, I won't be away for so long!" an appalled Maggie exclaimed. "Besides, I must cook Christmas dinner. Or at least assist. And don't forget that the butcher is saving a prime turkey for us!"

"I won't let her forget," Genie said, "now go!"

Maggie's tears started again as she embraced Genie. "And I can't thank you enough. We've never had a place to be a family."

"Now you do," Genie said. "Please make it your home."

"You three will return for supper?" Abby asked Ezra.

"Can you make chicken fricassee?"

Abby laughed and Genie, with a shrug, allowed that perhaps she could—but not tonight. "But I will bake bread and make a cake." And with that a happy Ezra climbed into the carriage with Maggie and Elizabeth and pulled the curtains while Donald and Eli sat up top like the professional drivers they were, taking their passengers safely to their destination. Back inside Genie and Abby sat at the table, quiet for a few moments, too emotional to speak. Then Abby got up to brew a pot of tea.

"I keep trying not to allow myself to think what Jack must have been going through, fighting that rough sea in that small boat."

"I keep trying not to allow myself to imagine being returned to Maryland. I'd also choose the sea and I hate water." Genie had spoken quietly but Abby flinched as if she'd screamed at the top of her lungs.

"Genie . . . ?"

"I am a runaway slave from Maryland. That is how I know Montague Wright. His sister was my owner and she is more evil than he. He is merely vain and stupid, though apparently, he is a good physician. She is good only at creating misery for others."

Something deep within Abby fractured, shattered, broke. "Genie." She whispered the word as a prayer.

167

* * *

"I don't want her in my house!" Matilda Wright Will shrieked. "I hate niggers, Montague, you know that!"

"Yes, I do know that," her brother said, "but I also know that you have no interest in caring for your child—"

"Don't call her mine. She belongs to Gilbert. He's the one who wanted a child, not me."

"But it is you who had her, Sister."

"Don't remind me of that horrible experience, or of the even more horrible experience that led to her existence."

Montague Wright gave his sister a pitying look. She was miserable but that wasn't his fault and there was absolutely nothing he could do about it. Their father had married her to Gilbert Will who was old, ugly, and richer than anyone in the county. For her part, Matilda, at twenty-four, no longer was young, and while she never had been pretty, she was the richest girl in the county—only because there were no women of marriageable age in the Will family. The marriage of the Will and Wright fortunes made Matilda a very wealthy woman. Montague had chosen medicine over plantation management, which destined him to a life of genteel poverty. It was only due to his sister's generosity that he was able to enjoy external manifestations of wealth: expensive clothes, jewelry, artifacts, and travel to exciting—and expensive—locations, a gift that Matilda now refused him because she no longer was allowed to accompany him. "I'm giving you a girl to care for the child, Matilda, and unless you'd prefer to do the job, the girl's mother to nurse the child."

A horrified Matilda screeched and clasped her bosom. "Most assuredly not."

"The girl is about ten years old and she'll move into the nursery immediately—"

"I told you, Montague, that I don't want some filthy nigger upstairs near me!"

"They cook your food, Matilda, and wash your clothes and clean your house—"

"And they do it all downstairs where I can't see them, not up here where I can. And they're stupid."

Montague sighed. "Then hire the tutor for your child now and have her teach the slave to read and write and speak properly. That way the slave can help the tutor teach the child. And I'll see to it that she bathes daily."

Matilda sighed her acceptance. "What is her name?"

"What is whose name?"

"The filthy nigger, Montague! Who have we been discussing?"

"You know that I don't name them, Matilda. I have no need to since I don't talk to them unless absolutely necessary."

"The tutor will have to call her something, as will the child."

"Then you may feel free to name her, Matilda. You choose a name."

"I will when I've seen her," Matilda said, and made it clear that wouldn't be until after Montague had hired the tutor, not an easy task since they lived outside Baltimore in what he called the country. Words like plantation and farmland, to Montague, meant country. There were cities—Baltimore and Philadelphia and New York and certainly London and Paris. Everything outside those cities was the country, and lettered tutors were loathe to take jobs in places lacking cultural enticements. Unless they were old and penniless and without family. Rebecca Tillson was her name and she had more education than anyone Montague had ever met. She also was weary of cities and welcomed the calm and quiet of the country. She was initially confused to learn that the pupil was an infant. When Montague explained what his sister wanted from the tutor, Miss Tillson initially was resistant. Then she met Matilda and learned that part of her job was to take the infant downstairs to the wet nurse several times a day so that Matilda wouldn't have to see "her Black ugly face," and that tutoring the ten-year old girl was so Matilda wouldn't have to "put up with her Black, ugly, ignorant self," and the old tutor's resistance faded. She was no abolitionist, but she did not understand such virulent hatred of people who had no ability to harm. Besides, she knew quite well that Blacks were as intelligent as anyone else if they were properly taught. She made up her mind that the girl Matilda called

Clara "*because she looks like that black, ugly mule out in the yard named Clara,*" would be the most accomplished student of her long and varied teaching life. And she was. The slave girl loved learning as much as Rebecca herself did, and she learned faster and more proficiently than any previous student.

Gilbert Will named his daughter Victoria after the queen because he admired all things British, and because his wife said she didn't care what he named the girl. She was not as good a student as Clara, nor was she as interested in learning, but she had her father's temperament rather than her mother's, so she was not unpleasant to be around. More importantly, she didn't interfere with Rebecca's teaching and Clara's learning. Because Matilda insisted that her daughter—whose name she could never remember—had only the most fashionable wardrobe, she had Gilbert hire the best seamstress he could find. He found Beate, a German from Philadelphia. She spoke minimal English and no one in the house spoke German—except Rebecca, who agreed to teach the seamstress English if the seamstress would teach Clara to sew. In a very short time the girl named after a mule became as adept as her teacher, making all of little Victoria's garments and most of Matilda's while Rebecca and Beate kept each other company, speaking in German so no one knew what they said to each other.

"You cannot leave me, Monty. You simply cannot. I won't hear of it!" A furious Matilda was weeping and throwing things.

"I will visit as often as possible, Tilda, but there's a practice in Philadelphia that I can assume. It is a marvelous opportunity. It is in a well-to-do area and it comes with a prosperous patient list. The doctor's house, too, is available—"

"But what am I to do here alone?"

"You have friends, Tilda—"

"I have no friends here! Take me with you to Philadelphia! Please, Monty, take me with you!"

"You have a husband and a child, Tilda. You can't just leave them."

"I can and I will," she insisted. But Montague knew that if she did *that Gilbert Will would cut her off financially. She would be destitute and totally reliant on him for her upkeep, and that he could not have.*

"Let me think about it," he said, giving her hope while he packed his belongings and moved to Philadelphia, funded by a generous contribution from his brother-in-law who was glad to see the back of a man he considered a braying fool.

Matilda refused to leave her rooms for weeks after she learned that her brother was gone without a word of good-bye. She refused to eat or dress or bathe, behavior which distressed no one, especially her maids who disliked being referred to as ugly, ignorant Irish slags. And certainly no one missed her brother. More disruption and distress were caused by the joint resignations of Rebecca Tillson and Beate whose last name no one knew because no one could pronounce it. Both were well liked by the household staff, Black and white, and they would be missed. Before she left Rebecca whispered these words to Clara: "If you ever get away from here go to Philadelphia. Many of your people are free there, and educated, and some are wealthy. Get away from here if you can." It was months before Matilda knew they were gone, and she didn't care because she didn't remember who they were.

"How can you possibly love me after that?" asked Abby.

"I can because you are not that. You can't even understand that."

"No. I can't. I can, however, be your avenging angel. I can . . . I can . . ."

Genie took Abby's hands and looked into eyes too kind to be able to conjure an appropriate vengeance. "Don't bring that upon yourself. Besides, that would put her out of her misery and I wouldn't want that. She is a miserable woman, and her misery is of her own making though she is too evil to see it. I wouldn't want you to release her from that," Genie said with a gentle smile that belied the harshness of her words.

"I wish she could see you and see that despite her best efforts you emerged a strong and beautiful woman who has given her life to helping others. Would that knowledge add to her misery?"

Genie laughed and hugged Abby. "More than you can know." Then she sobered, released Abby, and set about making the cake and bread she had promised Ezra. "Despite what she always said, it still amazes me that I was so well educated and that I learned such an important skill. She had to know those two things would improve my life."

"And despite all the evil you know to live within her you still search for the good."

"I don't believe there's any good within her to find," Genie said. "But there is a reason . . ."

"You have thought a great deal about this. What, then, have you concluded?" When Genie didn't respond immediately, Abby pressed. "Genie? You have reached a conclusion, haven't you?"

Genie nodded. "She believed that I'd always be a slave and that having knowledge and skills that I could not use would make me as miserable as she. That's what I concluded, but with a huge caveat: She'd have to know how much I learned, and I don't think she ever did because I never was real to her."

"What a truly awful woman," Abby said, more to herself than to Genie, as she began to cut onions, carrots and potatoes that she would add to chunks of meat for the stew that she knew was a favorite when the weather was frigid. A hearty stew, which managed to fill even Eli when served with loaves of bread and cakes of butter.

"This soup is really good," Eli proclaimed as he finished his second helping. Abby remembered that Maggie advised serving Eli plenty of rice and bread, and she had served his stew atop the rice, generous portions of both. The grown men had watched the boy eat in amazement, no doubt having forgotten that they, too, once possessed stomachs that were bottomless pits.

"Thank you, Eli, I'm glad you enjoyed it," Abby said.

"I'm glad Miss Maggie told you I like rice," he said.

"So am I," Abby said, and the boy smiled along with the adults, though not understanding why they were so amused. The rice apparently had done its work because Eli could eat only one piece of cake with his glass of milk.

"How is Jack?" Genie asked.

"All the better for seeing his Maggie," Donald responded, "though I'm not certain he'll survive his daughter. She is a most agile and enthusiastic child."

"Enthusiastic I understand," Abby said. "But agile?"

"He was standing on the porch when we arrived," Ezra explained. "She saw him and was out of the carriage and running for him before Maggie could stop her. She flung herself at him, and to his credit he caught her. But it cost him dearly. Donald saw that he was about to collapse, and he ran and caught him just in time."

"Maggie must have been—I don't know what!" Genie exclaimed.

"It was only her joy at seeing Jack that saved that little girl from a certain thrashing," Donald opined.

"But how is Jack?" Genie asked again. "Does he appear to be recovering?" She knew that her own fear of the sea was coloring her reaction but she could not help herself: She had to know if he would survive.

"He is remarkably well, and he is anxious to meet you," Ezra answered. "Yes, he is still very weak, and Arthur thinks he may have a few broken bones—"

"A few!" Abby exclaimed.

"Arthur is watching him closely and reporting to William regularly. There is a Colored doctor ready to attend to him if that becomes necessary," Ezra said. He explained that Jack's injuries were a result of being tossed against waves and rocks. He said Jack had managed to cling to the dinghy for a while, but in the end he had to try to swim to shore. Arthur said Jack's back and chest were badly battered and bruised, and now that Maggie was there she would tightly wrap him the way Dr. Wright had wrapped Ezra. "She can give him a few drops of laudanum and the milk with brandy and honey for a couple of days."

"But what about the broken bones?" Abby asked.

Ezra said the only one Arthur was really worried about was a leg bone. "If it's more than just badly bruised, William will have the doctor come to set it."

Genie and Abby sat quietly, allowing what they'd learned about Jack Juniper's condition to ease their worry for Maggie. They must have visibly relaxed because the two men and the boy at the table also relaxed. Ezra told them Maggie promised to come tomorrow or the following day because she could not ignore her duties any longer. Abby, knowing there was no point complaining to Ezra about Maggie's stubbornness, said nothing. Genie wondered whether Maggie and Jack had found everything they needed and if they were comfortable. Ezra and Donald had not been inside so they couldn't say. Ordering Elizabeth to remain on the porch, Maggie had taken Jack inside and put him to bed. She had returned with a bundle she said was for Genie.

"Oh! I forgot!" Eli exclaimed with a sheepish look. "Miss Maggie said to put it in her suite 'cause you and her was in each other's homes." Then he frowned. "Did I do right?"

"Yes, you did," Abby and Genie said in unison.

Looking relieved, Eli stood. "Then I'll go make the grates in the suites ready for the night."

"You can sleep in my sitting room, Eli, so prepare the grate in there," Ezra said. Even though Eli really preferred to sleep in his own room the absence of any kind of heat source on the servants' quarters floor made sleeping up there very uncomfortable.

"I'll keep him with me if you don't mind," Donald said, "so we can have a lesson before he starts his work for the day."

"I didn't know you were instructing him as well, Donald," Abby exclaimed.

"Not that kind of instruction, dear," Genie said, stifling a giggle that was bubbling up.

Confused, Abby was about to ask what other kind of instruction was there when she remembered. "Oh! You're teaching him to fight," she said dryly. "How—"

"Necessary, Abby," Ezra said gently. "You did agree."

"Yes. I did. I just hope you'll be careful, Donald, and remember that he's just a boy."

"I'm almost a man!" the boy insisted, puffing out his bony chest.

174

"Donald certainly is a gentle man," Abby said when he and Eli left, "but a paternal one?"

Ezra grinned. "More like big brotherly. Donnie is the eldest of nine and he helped raise them. He also misses them."

Abby looked relieved. "Then he knows to treat Eli like the boy he still is and not the man he thinks he is."

But the man-boy still had much to learn about fighting, as the left side of his face proved the following morning. Abby was with Genie in Maggie's suite, which faced the back garden. Genie awoke to unusual noises outside. She got up to look, and though it was a dark, snowy dawn, she could see Eli in the garden bending down, seeming to search for something in the snow banks. Shivering violently in the frosty air, she pulled on her heavy robe.

"What is it?" A sleepy Abby asked.

"Eli is out in the garden looking for something. And it's snowing." She hurried out of the room and turned the wrong way, almost getting lost in the vast, dark hallways; she had failed to bring a lamp. She met Abby as she retraced her steps—Abby who carried a lamp—and pretended not to hear the comment about her sad sense of direction. The downstairs was frigid because Eli had not yet lit the fires. Now they both were worried—and one look at him as he entered the scullery door said they were correct to be.

"What on earth happened to you?" Genie reached out to touch his closed-shut left eye and swollen left cheek, but he flinched and backed away. He had rocks in one hand and packed snow in the other and was alternately placing them on his damaged face.

"Mr. Donald told me to keep cold things on my face. These rocks is real cold," he said, letting Genie touch the frozen stones.

"Did he also tell you to duck?" Gene asked, and was pleased to see the boy's wide smile.

"That's not funny!" Abby scolded them, but she was relieved to see that Eli was well enough to laugh at himself, and to busy himself with his morning chores. The house soon would be

175

brightly lit and warm. She went into the scullery to look out at the snow. It had not been snowing for very long and it was not, at least for the moment, a heavy fall.

"I must hurry and dress. I must go to work today—"

"But what if it snows heavily and you can't get back? This is your home now, you know." And she could see that Genie had forgotten that the Juniper family now lived in her house.

"I will keep watch on the weather, and if it begins to look bad I'll leave work and come home." She hugged Abby and ran for the stairs. She asked Eli to ready her cart and horse when he'd finished his inside tasks, and she was dressed and ready to leave in short order. Abby insisted that she have tea and bread and butter before leaving, which gave Eli and Donald time to ready the cart. She told Donald that she hoped Eli's face meant that he was an apt pupil and Donald scowled.

"He's not nearly mean enough! He won't hit me back when I hurt him!"

That worried Genie—but just a bit and just for a moment. "Tell him to imagine that you are attacking me or Maggie or Abby or Ezra and that we are being harmed. That might spark anger in him."

Donald nodded and smiled widely. "An excellent idea, Miss Eugenia," he said, before suddenly sobering. "But I fear the lad might kill me in a scenario like that."

Genie feared that he was right but did not say so. Instead she wished him a pleasant day and accepted his hand up to the seat of her cart. He urged her to take extra care due to the weather, and she told him she'd return quickly if the weather worsened. He looked relieved and she didn't understand why until he said Ezra would be pleased to know that. She wrapped herself from head to toe as Donald opened the carriage house doors, and she drove out with a feeling of warmth and gratitude that she had so many people in her life who cared for her welfare and for whom she cared. That feeling was reinforced when she drove up to the stable door in the alleyway shared by the ironworker and the blacksmith Arthur and William, both of whom ran out to greet her, both wanting to talk to her as they had much to tell. But duty first.

"I must go to Adelaide. Perhaps we can eat together later? I'll buy food from Joseph's for us if one of you will fetch it."

Adelaide, too, was very pleased to see Genie. She wrapped her in a warm embrace. "I was afraid the weather would keep you away," she said.

"If it worsens I will leave for home," Genie said, "but until then I will be here. And William and Arthur will join us for lunch so that will help us speed the morning's work along."

Adelaide looked stricken. "You call that place home now, Genie?"

"Yes, Adelaide, I do, and I will, as long as the Juniper family calls where they now live their home."

"I still can't believe you just turned your home over to strangers!"

"Not strangers, Adelaide, people in need. Like Carrie Tillman took me into her home within an hour of meeting me, and where I lived for three years. It is from Carrie Tillman that I learned kindness."

Genie's words shocked and wounded Adelaide. Genie had intended to give her friend something to think about, but she had not intended to hurt her. In hindsight she should have known better, for Carrie Tillman was Adelaide's now-deceased mother-in-law. Her first impulse was to try to make amends, but she decided against that. Best to leave well enough alone.

"What must we do first, Adelaide? Alterations that customers already have paid for?" Genie knew that Adelaide still felt wounded, but if that was what it took to elicit politeness from her then Genie would suffer the other woman's stiff silences for the next several hours. They would last no longer. Fortunately, one of Adelaide's best qualities was that she did not hold grudges.

"I put them on your sewing machine," a hurt-sounding Adelaide said.

"Then I'll get to work," Genie said.

"I thought Maggie would have come to say hello."

"I'm sure she will when her husband no longer is at death's door."

That remark had the desired effect, allowing them both to work in silence throughout the morning. The time sped by so quickly that the knock on the back door startled them both. Genie rose to open it, and her stomach growled at the sight of William and Arthur with bags of food. "Who's minding the shop?" she asked.

"Reverend Richard Allen, and he knows to come for one of us if necessary," William said before going to look for his wife.

Genie prepared the table in the back room as she and Arthur chatted about Jack Juniper and his gradual but certain recovery. He proudly accepted the compliment that his horse liniment, which Maggie applied regularly, was a major factor. They were laughing heartily, imagining Ezra telling Montague Wright that horse liniment was responsible for what the doctor called his 'remarkable recovery' when William and Adelaide came in and they sat to eat. The good food and good company made it difficult for all of them to return to work but return they must. The bell over the front door announced a customer whom Adelaide went to greet while Genie and Arthur cleaned up and William whispered that he had a job for Eugene Oliver.

"Do you remember the slave family being held by Dr. Wright?"

"Of course I do!" Genie exclaimed.

"We have a place for them to live and there's work for the women. Arthur and I may hire the man, depending on the kind of man he is, now that Reverend Richard is almost full-time with Joseph."

"Genie!" Adelaide was calling so William and Arthur quickly left and Genie hurried to the front of the shop where she was kept busy for the next few hours, but she also kept watch on the weather. The snow was intermittent and not heavy, but the ground was gradually being covered. Genie decided to leave.

"I'm going now, Adelaide, and I'll return tomorrow, weather permitting."

"Will you go to visit Maggie?"

"Perhaps," Genie replied. She opened the front door. "Why don't you lock the door behind me and prepare to leave as well?"

Adelaide nodded and wished Genie a pleasant evening. Genie stepped out into the lightly falling show, wishing that William would share more with Adelaide so she'd stop seeking information from Genie. Perhaps she'd make that suggestion to him . . .

"I'm glad you're here," William said when she entered the blacksmith shop. The forge was calm and quiet, and William led her toward the back where her cart was ready. How did they know she was coming? He told her that Peter Blanding's back room was empty because Arthur's nephews had moved out so the newly freed slave family could live there. He told her that Blanding had married the former Mrs. Carpenter and the couple wanted household help—a maid and a cook. "If the snow gets deep enough, you and Reverend Richard will go free those slaves." And he explained the plan. It was a good one. However, Genie had to ask: "How likely is it that I could come face to face with Wright?" That was Genie's primary—in truth, her only—concern.

"Not at all. We don't go forward if he is at home. The logistics will be finalized tonight, and we go in the next couple of days."

Genie nodded agreement and took her leave. She did want to visit quickly with Maggie before going toward home, and happy as she was to have the Junipers in her former home, she felt a pang of loss as she knocked on the door.

"Oh Genie!" Maggie exclaimed when she opened the door. She pulled Genie inside and embraced her tightly and at length. "It feels an age since I've seen you and it's been less than two days!"

"You are very much missed as well, especially by Eli."

"Auntie Genie! Auntie Genie! Papa look—it's Auntie Genie! Come see!"

"I don't know what I'm going to do with her," Maggie whispered. "She seems incapable of being calm. Or quiet."

"Miss Oliver," Genie heard in a deep voice from the bedroom

179

door as Jack Juniper emerged. He was a big man and indeed a very handsome one—Adelaide was right about that, and she'd seen him at his worst. He walked very slowly toward her.

"Mr. Juniper. I'm so sorry to have disturbed your rest, but I am most pleased to meet you."

He extended both his hands to her, and it was clear that the effort cost him as he winced in pain. Arthur had indeed wrapped his ribs very tightly. "I am so grateful to you for so much. To you and Mr. William and Mr. Arthur and the two other gentlemen whom I hope to meet again soon. Now that I am more alive than dead, I am able to properly thank them."

"We were all very pleased to be able to do something to help Maggie."

"That you could care so much for my family—" He was overcome with emotion.

"Your family has become like my own, and I hope that I may include you in that feeling."

"I will be injured if you do not!"

Genie squeezed his hands then took her leave. Maggie tried to say that she would return to Abby's in a day or two but it was clear that Jack was in no condition to be left alone. "Yes, we miss you, but we can manage. We feed Eli rice and bread at every meal, and I've promised to attempt chicken fricassee for Ezra. I just hope the bleedin' Scotsman won't want to marry me!"

Maggie, stifling the kind of laugh that surely would incite her husband's curiosity, pushed Genie outside and followed her. She let herself laugh then and said again how much she missed the residents of the Abby Read household, including "the bleedin' Scotsman." Then she grew quite serious, which concerned Genie, until she learned the reason for it.

"I sent some of your things with Eli—"

"Yes! You did and I forgot to thank you—"

"Then you didn't find it . . . rude?"

Now Genie was puzzled. "Rude, Maggie?"

"What I thought to be your most personal and most special belongings—I removed them from your home, Genie! It felt like

I was taking over your home, moving you out of your own home!" Maggie was upsetting herself, and she was shivering. The shawl she had thrown around her shoulders was no real protection against the frigid air.

"You were wise enough to recognize and gather the things I care most about, Maggie, and kind enough to send them to me in my new home. I never thought ill of you."

Maggie gave her a speculative look. "You think of Abby's as home now?"

An exasperated Genie told Maggie she sounded like Adelaide. Maggie grasped the meaning immediately. "She thinks that not only have you abandoned your home but maybe you left your people behind as well."

"Home for me, Maggie, is where I can live without fear, surrounded by people who care for me. I was happy that I could give that to you and your family. Now I must go." The snow had abated but Genie still wrapped herself tightly and warmly anyway and drove away with a wave. Maggie remained on the porch waving back at her. The tears in her eyes froze there.

Dinner was ready when Genie arrived home but they were waiting for her. Donald and Eli rushed outside to take the cart into the stable, unhitch the horse and brush and feed her, and to clean and dry the cart, then rushed back inside as if they feared all the food would be eaten in their absence. Genie told them of meeting Jack Juniper and told Ezra and Donald of his expression of gratitude to them. She described his movement and his appearance and assured them that he seemed out of danger and well on the road to recovery. No, she told them, Elizabeth still had not calmed down and probably would not for a while. Eli wanted to know when she would return so his lessons could resume, and Abby told him that she and Genie would resume his instruction the following day. They both studiously ignored his all but swollen-shut left eye, and Genie realized that she'd forgotten to tell Maggie about it. Abby was scheduled to attend a meeting with Florence Mallory the next day, and Ezra had a meeting with the Cortlandts at their home: He had questions for young Arthur and he knew the boy wouldn't answer truthfully, if at all, unless his parents were present, especially his mother. Donald had been to the telegraph office at the docks to learn of the weather report and the news was not good: Another blizzard was headed their way. Not good news for any but the slave family—Robert, Josephine and Mary—in Dr. Montague Wright's house, Genie thought.

Ezra surprised them by volunteering to help clean up the kitchen while Eli tended to the grates and lamps. His motivation soon was apparent when he asked if Genie would join him in his sitting room for a few moments when the fire was lit.

"Of course," she replied matter-of-factly. Abby's heart sank. He had something for her to do, some work that would endanger her, and if he asked for her help she would willingly give it.

"I need your thoughts," Ezra said when they were seated before the fire in his sitting room. The wind rattled the window-panes, a sure sign that the bad weather was approaching. He told her that Donald had overheard snatches of conversations when he was prowling the docks searching for information about Jack Juniper, conversations that Ezra now believed were about the aborted attempt to take control of Arthur Cortlandt's railroad. "Young Cortlandt repeated bits of conversation that he recalled from his captivity when he was too drunk or drugged to think properly and which made no sense at the time."

"But now you think differently," Genie said.

Ezra nodded. "Based on what Donald overheard, it is likely that servants in someone's employ supplied the information about the location of that train car, where to move it, and why it was parked where it was."

"The servents who knew that Cortlandt owned the train and that . . . someone . . . was expected to take refuge there," Genie said.

"More than one someone," Ezra emphasized.

"But both working where they could overhear information—"

"And both giving that overheard information to the same person," Ezra concluded.

"I can find out who Job Mayes was working for but how do we find the other two people involved?" Genie asked.

"That's where the Cordlandts come in. If young Edward can remember exactly what he heard, his father likely can figure out who had such knowledge."

"And his mother," Genie said slowly but wisely, "can learn who the servants are in that house."

"Information for which the Cortlandts will pay handsomely," Ezra said, "since the betrayals almost cost him his railroad and her the son she worships."

They were quiet and reflective for a moment. Genie then told him of the rescue of the slaves from Montague Wright's home, which probably would occur tomorrow or the next day, depending on the weather. "That means that I most probably will not be able to return here tomorrow night," she said.

"Then I will make certain that Donnie or I will be here."

Genie stood to leave. "What kind of fighter will Eli make?"

"Donnie says a very good one—if he has a proper target for his anger."

"But first he must have two good eyes to find the proper target," Genie said dryly as she left, though she heard Ezra's chuckle before the door closed completely. Abby was waiting for her in the kitchen, a pot of tea brewing and cake slices on a plate.

"Eli and Donald took their cake with them," Abby said.

"What did you say to Donald about Eli's eye?"

Abby looked put upon. "What makes you think I'd say anything?"

"The fact that you think young Eli is more noble than the Prince of Wales is what."

Abby sniffed. "It's not sporting for a grown man to pummel a boy."

"Did you happen to notice that Donald didn't have full and proper use of his left arm this evening?" Genie asked.

Abby, pouring tea, halted with the pot midair. "I did notice that he seemed a bit stiff." A smile lit her face as she continued with the tea, and Genie began to feel sorry for Donald.

"Am I correct in thinking it's possible that Mrs. Cortlandt would know if one of her equally wealthy friends was having difficulty with a servant?" Genie asked Abby.

Abby nodded slowly. "If the two women are good friends. A troublesome servant can wreak havoc on an entire household and a woman naturally would consult her friends for a solution."

"What about the men—" Genie started to ask, but a most unladylike snort by Abby stopped the question.

"Men think servants, like wives, somehow appear via divine intervention to make their lives easier."

"So a man wouldn't hire a servant?"

"Not unless he's a single man, and then his mother or sister or aunt would send servants from their households."

"Thank you," Genie said. "That's useful information. Will you tell it to Ezra in the morning?"

"Why can't you tell it to Ezra in the morning?"

"Because I must leave at first light," Genie answered, and explained why.

"But you're not . . . you can't . . . you won't confront Montague Wright!"

"Oh no!" Genie exclaimed. "He'll never see me and I'll not see him." And she explained how the rescue would work. "I'll be hidden in a carriage within sight of Wright's home. Several minutes after his carriage leaves and he's well away I'll run to the scullery door and tell Josephine and Mary this is their chance for freedom. They either will leave immediately with me or we will leave them, their chance at freedom likely gone forever. At the same time that I run for the scullery door, Reverend Richard runs into the stable to await Robert's return where the same scenario will play out: He'll be told that his wife and daughter already are gone and it's his turn. This all is possible, by the way, because of the falling, blowing and drifting snow and because all we Black people will be wrapped in white sheets. Robert, Josephine and Mary will be hidden in a nearby house until it is safe to take them to their new home, and Richard and I will be taken back to William and Arthur."

Abby was silent for a long moment. "That is a very good plan. In whose home will Robert, Josephine and Mary be sheltered? And in whose carriage will you and Reverend Richard be hiding while waiting for Montague Wright to leave?"

Genie shrugged. "I don't know," she said, and stopped Abby's question before she could ask it. "If they were not trustworthy, they would not be a part of the plan. And each of us knows only what we need to know to execute our part. I need only to get Mary and Josephine to the carriage that will take them to safety, and then to get myself to the carriage or cart that will do the same for me."

"And what about Richard?"

"Richard is responsible for himself," Genie said.

"And when will you return here?"

"As soon as the weather permits, and I hope and pray that I won't have to sleep in William's barn for four days!"

Genie had to pound on the scullery door before it cracked open a sliver. "I've come to take you and Mary to freedom, Josephine, and a friend is waiting in the barn to take Robert when he returns!" Genie was shouting to be heard over the howling wind and through the tiny space in the door, which eased open a bit more. The face that peered at her was both terrified and hopeful. "You and Mary quickly grab a few belongings and let's go. *Now.*"

"We don't have no belongings," Josephine said.

"Then let's go," Genie said. "Where's Mary?"

Another terrified face emerged from behind Josephine and peered at Genie. "Is you really come to get us?"

"Yes! Let's go! Here—wrap yourselves in these sheets, head to toe, so you're white like the snow—" She looked down at twenty bare brown toes. "Where are your shoes?"

"We ain't got no shoes," Josephine said. "Dr. Wright said we don't need none."

"You can't go out there barefoot!" Genie exclaimed as an unaccustomed curse rose in her throat.

185

Josephine, wrapped head to bare toes in the sheet, pushed her aside. "I don't need no shoes to run to freedom! My feets got wings! Come on, Mary, let's go 'way from here!" And they were away, leaving the scullery door standing wide open now, and Genie delighted at the thought of Montague Wright returning to an ice-cold house.

Genie led the way. Mary held the back of Genie's sheet and Josephine held the back of Mary's. Every few steps Genie shouted at them to confirm that they were still there. "We still here!" she heard yelled back, but weaker each time. Up ahead she saw what she hoped was their waiting carriage but covered as it was in snow it was hard to tell. Then the door opened and she saw William's face.

"We're here," Genie said. "Come on and get in the carriage."

The two women hesitated briefly. They'd never ridden inside a carriage, but frozen feet, wings notwithstanding, and imminent freedom propelled them. As soon as they were in, the door closed and the carriage moved quickly away. Genie looked in the opposite direction, into the blowing snow, for the carriage that was to transport her, but seeing nothing, she began to walk. Because her head was down, she did not immediately see the carriage until it was upon her. She gratefully opened the door and climbed in. A pile of rugs and blankets on the seat meant that she could remove the now frozen sheets and soaked clothes and shoes beneath, but she knew it would be hours before she was warm again. Then she had an awful thought: She didn't know where this driver was ordered to take her and she was practically naked. Not only that but she didn't know where she was, not being familiar with Montague Wright's neighborhood. But she soon got her bearings, and it became clear that she was destined for Arthur and the stable and she let herself relax. She awoke when the carriage pulled into the stable. She climbed down, careful to hold the blankets and rugs close, and Arthur retrieved the wet clothes and sheets. Then Adelaide appeared with clothes for her, and Arthur told the driver to wait just a moment for the blankets and rugs and have a cup of hot mead while he waited.

Adelaide led her inside to a stool beside the stove and somehow managed to dress her even though she shivered uncontrollably. She folded the rugs and blankets and gave them to Arthur and then returned to give Genie a cup of hot mead. She sipped until her insides began to warm up and she stopped shaking. Adelaide's face then relaxed though she still looked worried.

"Thank you, Adelaide. I was never in danger, just cold."

"In danger of freezing to death," Adelaide snapped.

"Not if everyone did their jobs, and everyone did," Genie said. And because she thought Adelaide deserved to know what they were doing since she was expected to help, she told her.

"Slaves! In the middle of Philadelphia?" She was stunned. "I had no idea."

"Nor had I," Genie said, and then told Adelaide about Wright's apprentice who wanted to rent a room in Abby's house and bring his slave with him.

Adelaide grew very quiet. All the anger and worry left her and she just looked sad. "Will it ever be different for us?"

Genie shook her head impatiently. She had stopped having that thought years ago. It did no good to wonder if or when things ever would be different for people born with dark skin. She could fight only one battle at a time. Today that battle was against a known enemy and she had won. She would learn later whether Richard had won his battle. Now she wanted only to eat and sleep, and Arthur and Adelaide made those things possible. She awoke to Adelaide shaking her.

"Ezra is here for you, Genie. He wants to take you . . . back to Abby's."

Genie stood up quickly and was about to ask where Ezra was when she heard his voice. She ran out to the forge to see Arthur, Ezra, Donald and Reverend Richard Allen. "Ezra?"

He walked over to her and explained that Donald had again checked the weather forecast, and the calm they now were experiencing literally was the calm before the storm. Unaware that the blizzard she'd traveled through earlier had abated, she went to the door and looked out on a calm, clear late afternoon. "But some time tonight a second storm is coming and bringing half a foot of snow, high wind and low temperatures, so if you want to be home for Christmas you should come with us now."

Christmas was tomorrow! Ignoring Adelaide's accusatory look, she turned to Richard. "Did you get Robert out?"

Richard gave a whoop. "What a sight that was! That doctor made him wear a top hat and tails to drive the carriage and first thing Robert does is throw that hat on the ground and stomp it flat! Then he does the same with the coat. I tried to tell him that coat could help keep him warm but he didn't care and he wanted to leave the shoes but I wouldn't let him. I wrapped him in the sheets, and we had opened the barn door when we heard the doctor screaming for Josephine! Then Mary! It sounded like he just stood in one place and screamed. Then he started screaming for Robert and we ran. He wanted to leave the barn door open but I closed it. Better to let the man think, at least for a few more minutes, that Robert was still there." Richard shook his head. "That man's voice . . . I never heard nothin' like it . . . and them poor people had to listen to it all the time."

"Not any more they don't," Genie said, trying to expunge its sound from her memory. "Good work, Richard."

"You too, Miss Eugenie," he said, and gave her a shy hug.

"Has anyone seen Maggie today?"

"I was over there a little while ago, after the snow stopped," Arthur said. "Mr. Jack was up helpin' Maggie and the child bring wood in. Couldn't hardly stand up to say nothin' of haulin' firewood, but there he was! I made 'em all sit down, and I stacked enough wood to last a week." He looked at Genie. "He's a lot stronger. Miss Maggie feeds him good and rubs the liniment in the worst places." Then he looked at Ezra. "You got any laudanum left?"

Ezra nodded. "I wish I'd thought to bring it. I will when the next storm lets us."

Arthur nodded. "The first few days he slept 'cause he was almost dead. Now that he's better he don't sleep much, but he needs to sleep. Miss Maggie, she knows how to give just the right amount."

"I'll make sure she gets it," Ezra said. "Now we should go before it gets dark. Merry Christmas everybody!"

There were hugs and handshakes all around and then Genie and Ezra climbed into the carriage, and with Donald in the driver's seat they left the warmth of the barn. The snow might have stopped but it was cold, and the ride was slow so it was dark when they got home. Abby and Eli were watching and waiting for them. Eli rushed out to help Donald, and Genie and Ezra hurried inside to get warm, and inside was where they remained for the next three days. Most of them anyway, for Eli and Donald romped and played in the snow like puppies under the pretense of snow removal and fight training. The first two days, however, they all enjoyed each other and ate as much food as Genie and Abby could prepare, accompanied by Abby on the piano, Ezra on the violin, and Donald's very fine tenor.

"How beautifully you sing!" Genie exclaimed on Christmas morning when he finished a verse of "Silent Night"—in German!

Donald took a modest bow, wet his throat with some mulled cider, and performed several more carols, this time joined by Abby's lilting soprano. Genie and Eli did not know any of the Christmas hymns but they were a most appreciative audience. In the middle of "God Rest Ye Merry Gentlemen," Abby suddenly stood, opened the piano bench, and withdrew a hymn book. She paged through it until she reached the Christmas hymns and gave the book to Genie. "Now you can sing with us."

"But I can't sing!" Genie exclaimed.

"You probably sound better than Ezra," Abby said. "Good thing he plays the violin so well."

Christmas and the following day were spent eating, singing, and, for the men, sleeping in front of the fire that burned constantly to protect against the wind and snow that battered the windows and doors as if seeking entry. On the third day Donald and Eli set out to clear the snow from doors, windows and walkways, though it sounded as if they played as much as they worked. He reported what they already suspected: Job Mayes and an unknown man in the temporary employ of one of Cortlandt's

189

rival bankers were responsible for providing the information about Cortlandt's railroad to his son's kidnappers, as well as the information about the expected arrival of Mrs. Tubman.

"Both Mayes and the other man have gone missing, so we may never know who else they told," Ezra said.

"But Cortlandt now knows enough to protect his investment," Abby said, indicating a knowledge of business workings.

Ezra nodded, impressed. "He also knows that having an alcoholic, spendthrift son roaming freely around town is a danger he cannot afford, so they're sending him to England to live with poor relations."

"How is Mrs. Cortlandt taking that?" Genie asked.

"Surprisingly well since any threat to her husband's fortune is a threat to her way of life," Ezra reported with a small smirk, not having forgotten the beating he'd taken because of the younger Cortlandt.

"He won't fare well there," Abby said almost sadly, not having forgotten how her family had to flee England because of her father's spendthrift ways. At least Papa wasn't an alcoholic, she thought, surprised that her memory of him no longer was clear.

"Speaking of faring well," Ezra said to Genie, "I hope as much for your freed family."

"As do I," Genie said. "I hope to learn something tomorrow, weather permitting, if you and Donald will drive me to William's? I left my cart there."

"Of course," Ezra said.

"And after I see to the family—whose name I don't know—and to the Juniper family, I will go to the market, Abby. Perhaps our turkey is still there and we can have it to ring in the New Year since we didn't have it for Christmas."

"I do truly miss Maggie!" Abby said.

"And she misses you and she misses being here, though she seemed well. Of course, she's obviously exhausted, caring for Jack and keeping up with Elizabeth. Or trying to keep up with Elizabeth."

"And based on what Arthur said, Jack Juniper isn't exactly a model patient," Ezra said.

"Look who's talking!" Genie and Abby said in unison and watched Ezra raise and lower his left arm and shoulder without pain as proof that he had healed.

Jack was with William and Arthur when Genie arrived the next morning, intent on proving that he was healing, too. He greeted Genie with a tight embrace and Ezra and Donald with strong handclasps. "I am most pleased to see all of you," he said, sounding more robust and looking well fed, though he was still weak. They could tell by the way he stood beside a tool cabinet for support.

"You're looking much better, Jack," Genie said in a show of support.

"Did you bring that laudanum?" Arthur growled.

"I don't need laudanum!" Jack snapped before Ezra could reply.

"We'll see what Miss Maggie has to say about that," Arthur replied darkly, knowing exactly where the balance of power rested in the Juniper family.

Jack ignored the comment about his wife and looked from face to face. "I owe you good people my life, and while you will have my gratitude as long as I draw breath, it is money that men—and women—need and I have money to pay—"

"We don't want your money, Mr. Juniper," William said.

"Well, you're getting it!" Jack snapped. "And if you don't need or want it, give it away, but I'm giving it to you, and I have it to give because I took it from the ship's captain. I stole it," he said, and took a deep breath. "And I stole it because we learned that he could have docked here in Philadelphia. He could have ridden out the storm, but he went south just to sell us. The three Colored crewmen. We would have brought him a fine payday, money he would have kept in his own pockets, along with our nine weeks of pay he owed us." Jack took another deep breath. "We couldn't go back south, none of us, so we jumped him in his cabin just before daybreak, emptied the safe, bound and gagged him, climbed into the dinghy and released it into the sea. We almost perished then, for while the ship could have ridden out the storm, that little dinghy . . ." He closed his eyes against the memory.

"Drink this." Arthur gave him a cup.

"Is that your damn laudanum?"

"No, it is not! It is a bit of whiskey," Arthur growled at him.

"Oh. Well, then," Jack said, swallowing it in a single gulp. "Now I want to tell you why I did what I did, and I speak only for myself since the other two can no longer speak for themselves." He took a breath though not so deep a one. His tightly wrapped rib cage prevented that. "I am a runaway slave from Maryland's Eastern shore where I became a waterman at eleven years of age. My name then was Jacob Sweetwater."

"That boy of yours is a tadpole, MaryMae," one of the other laundresses said to Jacob's mother as they watched the boy jump in and out of the water from their vantage point in the wash house.

"I don't know where he gets it. I hate the water and his papa hates it worse than me. He still have night sweats about comin' cross the big water chained hand and foot in the bottom of that boat. He rather burn up in the fields and chop t'bacco than walk over here by the water where it be cool."

"The Master don' mind the boy playin' in the water all the time?" another woman asked.

"He seem not to care and I don' want him thinkin' on it 'cause Jacob bring food from the water for us to eat. Better than to eat animal guts all the time."

"That much is true. Still . . ."

"Still what?" MaryMae asked.

"The boy look to be enjoyin' hisself and us enjoyin' ourselfs is not a thing the Master likes to see."

MaryMae nodded. She knew this to be true. She would keep the boy closer to her or send him to work with his father. But they both spoiled him because he was the only one they had left. The others had been sold off.

Jacob brought home crabs and shrimps that evening, enough to share with their near neighbors. Pots of rice and beans and pans of fried cornmeal cakes along with the boiled seafood made for a fine dinner. MaryMae told him that night not to spend so much time in the water because the Master didn't like it.

"He likes to watch me dive deep and swim way far out."

MaryMae felt a chill breeze in the hot, still night. "Who?"

"The Master."

MaryMae and her husband shared a look of fear and dread.

"When he told you that?"

"That time when the fishing boats came back in. You 'member when I brought all them bluefish home?"

She remembered. So the Master had been watching her boy all that time. Why?

She found out in less than two weeks' time. She kept Jacob away from the water and the Master came to learn why.

"Where 'bouts is that fish of yours, MaryMae?" He stood outside the wash house and called in to her. The other women froze.

"He's workin' with his papa," MaryMae answered.

"Well, I don't want him workin' with his papa, I want him workin' on one of my boats. The boy is a natural on the water."

MaryMae did not reply. She didn't know what to say so she remained silent. "I'm gon' send him out on the next boat," the Master said, "and we'll see how he does."

"Yessir," MaryMae whispered.

Jacob sailed on the Master's fishing boats for the next three years. The sun bronzed his skin, and the work built his muscles, and the seafood diet made him tall and strong. "Just like the juniper trees in my homeland," his papa said, and Jacob liked hearing that. He liked hearing anything his papa said about his life before the awful ride on that awful ship.

"I can't believe that a boy of mine is workin' on a boat on the water. But if you find a way to take me back home, let me know, I'll go," Jacob's papa always told him. "Find a way to take me back home."

But Jacob didn't know where his papa's home was and he didn't know where the Master's fishing boats went. He was not permitted to sail them, only to put out the nets or the traps and bring them in when they were full. Jacob enjoyed the work, he liked being on the water, and he liked learning the names of the creatures of the sea—those who lived in it and those who flew above it and dove down for their food. Jacob even liked storms, liked watching them form, liked watching them come dancing across the water sending the message that men and their boats should leave if they wanted to live. And Jacob didn't think it was wise to disobey the storm.

The boat's hold was full and dark, and dancing cloud formations were sending messages at the end of what had been a good trip for Jacob . . . good because for the first time the captain had let him take the wheel. He had been watching the sky for years and he knew how to read the clouds. He also had closely watched the different captains steer the fishing boats over the years and he'd always thought that, if given the chance, he could manage a boat. Even in a storm. And he proved it this day, impressing the captain and the others who were watching. He couldn't wait to tell his parents!

Off-loading the catch was Jacob's least favorite part of the job, especially in a storm, but the fish couldn't be left to rot. When they finished, he was too tired to run home. He walked slowly and let the rain bathe him so his mother wouldn't complain that he stank. She couldn't say that she knew he was coming because she could smell him. He smiled and walked a bit faster. He became aware that he was being watched, that his neighbors had stopped whatever they were doing to watch him walk home. He waved and most returned the greeting though some did not, which he thought was strange. The women in the wash house did not call out to him and when he looked closely, he realized that he did not recognize them. That, too, was strange. Then there were the people on the front porch of his house that he didn't know and who, judging from their expressions, didn't know him, either. He heard his name. A woman who worked in the wash house with his mother—he called her Aunt Avie—was running across a field toward him, calling his name and waving her arms. He stopped walking and waited for her, no longer aware of the rain beating down on him.

"They gone!" she screamed at him, trying to be heard over the howling wind. "They ain't in there!" he heard as she got closer. "Your ma and pa. They gone." She was breathless as she spoke the words, standing close to him now, rain pounding her. Then she was weeping. *"They ain't in that house, Jacob. They gone 'cause he sold 'em. Master done sold your mama and papa."* She gripped his arm and wept, howling with the wind.

Jacob didn't say or do anything for a very long time. He just stood on the road looking at the small house he had raced a storm to get back to. His parents had been sold by the man he was catching fish for. *"Will you do something for me, Aunt Avie?"*

"Yes, baby, anything you need."

"Shave my head? Mama always cut my hair down to the scalp when I came home 'cause she said I stank like fish."

She nodded. *"I remember and yes, I'll cut off all your hair."*

"And she made me soak my hands and feet in lye soap 'cause she said they stank, too."

"I remember," Aunt Avie said again, *"and I got some lye soap, and I got some clean clothes for you to put on, too."*

Before dawn the next morning, when Jacob no longer stank of fish and when he had eaten and slept, he quietly stole away from Aunt Avie's tiny shack and went down to the dock where all the fishing boats were tied up, riding out the storm. He carried a huge, heavy hammer and he let its weight carry him quickly down until he was beneath the boats. Then he swam from one to the other beating holes into the hulls until they all were destroyed. He surfaced twice to breathe before going under again until the job was done. Then he went to the area where the nets and traps were stored, and he beat the traps to pieces with the hammer, which he then dropped into the water. He took his fish knife from his belt and sliced all the nets to shreds, then threw it into the water where it sank like the hammer. Then he swam to the secluded cove where the Master kept his racing sloops, beautiful boats that Jacob had helped build. He untied them and watched two of them drift away to be battered by the storm. The third sloop, the best and fastest one, he guided safely out of the cove and into open water before boarding it. He took the tiller and, keeping the shore in sight, he headed north, looking for a cove to sail into and hide until the storm passed. The following day he sailed up to Delaware where he sold the sloop and caught a ride from the docks on the back of a cart to a road where he could get another ride north with a farmer. He got rides on the backs of carts all the way to Philadelphia.

"I was fifteen years old when I got here. I changed my name to Jack Juniper and I didn't have any trouble getting work on boats and ships of all kinds," Jack said to his listening audience. "But I have sailed my last voyage. I don't know what I will do. I have no other skills but seafaring, but I do know that I will never again leave my family and I will never again work for a boat captain."

"I hope that evil bastard never caught another fish," Arthur said.

Jack stood up and swayed, and three pairs of strong arms steadied him. He nodded his thanks, suddenly looking exhausted, but untied a leather bag from his waist.

"I will take no money from you, Jack Juniper. I have done nothing to earn it," Genie said.

"I live in your house, woman!" Jack thundered. "That is not nothing! That is something! A lot of something!"

Before Genie could respond Peter Blanding entered through the back door, raising worry in Arthur and William, but it was Genie he wanted. "I heard you were here, Eugenia. I need your help, please. The family you rescued—they will not speak or open the door or come out. I don't know if they're all right because they won't answer when I call out." Peter was frantic.

William grabbed his coat but Genie waved him off. "I'll go, William. Ezra, will you and Donald be here for a while?"

"We will take Jack home and visit a while with Maggie and Elizabeth, then we will return here."

"Good," Genie said, and left with Peter, knowing that her friends would fail in their attempts to refuse Jack Juniper's money.

Most of the walks fronting the stores on the main street were cleared of snow so Genie and Peter walked quickly to his clock and watch repair shop. Genie went around to the back, to the entrance of the apartment there and knocked on the door.

"Robert. Josephine. Mary. I'm Eugenia Oliver. I'm the person who brought you away from Montague Wright's house. Please open the door." She had spoken softly, her mouth against the door, so as not to frighten them. She knocked again and waited. Finally, she heard the latch released and the door opened a crack.

"Hello, Robert," she said. "May I come in?"

He didn't respond but neither did he close the door, so Genie pushed it slowly open. The three of them were huddled together in the middle of the floor, terrified. They wore different clothes from the last time she'd seen them, and they had shoes. She knew they had arrived the previous night, but the beds had not been slept in nor had breakfast been cooked, although the stove had been fed because it was warm. It took a moment but she finally understood that these people did not know how to be free. All of the runaways she knew, herself included, had survived in spite of the fact that there had been no assistance. It was survive or perish. She closed her eyes. Was it a mistake to free them?

"Mistress?" Josephine whispered, her voice shaking.

"My name is Genie and I want to help you, to answer your questions, to make sure you understand that this is your home. This is where you live now. The food here is yours. The clothes in the drawers are yours. You can open the door and go outside whenever you like. Do you understand?"

They looked at her wide-eyed, processing her words, looking for truth in them. "We ain't slaves?" Mary said. "We really ain't slaves no more?"

"You are free people. You will never see Montague Wright again. He does not know where you are or how to find you." She went to the door and opened it. "Come with me and I'll show you where you live." She walked out, leaving the door open, and took several steps away from the building. They followed timidly, ready to turn and flee if necessary. "Close the door, Robert, so you're not heating up the outside." She walked around the building to the main street, then to the front door of the watch repair shop and opened it. She beckoned to the three frightened people and they slowly approached. "This is the front of where you live. The man who owns this shop, Peter Blanding, has given you the place where you live."

Peter saw them and hurried from behind the counter. "Good morning, friends," he said, extending his hand, and one by one his new friends shyly shook it. "Do you like your apartment?"

"Yessir," they said in unison.

"We're going to walk a little, Peter, then I'll take them home so they might eat breakfast and sleep."

"Thank you, Genie," Peter said. "Robert, Josephine, Mary—if you need anything, just ask."

"Yessir," they said again, and followed Genie out into the street. They walked in silence, looking and watching.

"Probably half the Black people you see around you once were slaves—you have no way to know which ones because they don't act like slaves! But they all will know you for slaves if you continue this behavior."

She knew that her words were harsh. She also knew as well as anyone how difficult it was to abandon the slave mentality.

And the behavior that came with it. Carrie Tillman had taught her that truth. Looking back Genie could see that it was a difficult task, but Carrie never gave up. *I'm not telling you to forget you were a slave, Eugenia. You couldn't if you wanted to. What I'm telling you is to forget acting like one.* At the time Genie didn't know what that meant. She knew now. And she knew it was necessary to teach these slaves how to act free. Fortunately, there were people to help, including Jack Juniper. He was the only one of them who had the time to spend with Josephine, Mary and Robert. He could make them understand this simple truth in these complex times: If one behaved like a slave, one would be recognized as a slave.

Robert wanted to speak, began to speak, but the words wouldn't come. Josephine looked ready to faint from fear. Finally, Mary spoke. "You, too, Mistress? Was you a slave?"

"My name is Genie," Genie snapped, "and yes, I was."

"Mistress Genie, can we go back now?" Robert asked timidly.

"Back to Montague Wright?" Genie asked.

The three newly freed slaves shrank into themselves. "N-n-no, ma'am, back to where we just come from," Robert managed.

"And where was that?" Genie asked.

"That new place," Mary said. "Home. The place you said was our home."

"Robert. Josephine. Do you want that place to be your home?" They nodded.

"Robert and Josephine, yes or no: Do you want that place to be your home?"

"Yes," Robert said.

"Yes," Josephine whispered.

"Then go home," Genie said, and turned away from them and walked in the opposite direction, hating herself in that moment for her cruelty but knowing that it was necessary, and also hoping that freeing them had not been a mistake. Mrs. Tubman had discovered that slave behavior was so deeply ingrained in some runaways that the reality of freedom was less desirable than the horror of slavery. But Josephine had sounded so certain! Her feet, she said, would have wings because she was running to freedom! And now that she was free she was petrified. Genie turned to look for Robert and his family. They were gone. To their new home she hoped. She would leave it to William to explain the concept of being paid for their work. And to Jack Juniper to explain how to be free.

CHAPTER TEN

"How delightful to have you welcome the New Year with us, Abigail," Dorrie Woodhull enthused. "I do hope that your presence is a harbinger of what is to be."

"Indeed, Abigail! We have missed you."

"And you are as beautiful as ever. Your mother would be so proud," someone said.

"She may be even more beautiful than her mother, and her mother was a real beauty," said another.

Abby stole a glance at Auntie Florence who correctly read the message and interjected. "Ladies please! If you continue to overwhelm Abby, she may absent herself again and never return! Now in all fairness, let us not forget the reason for Abby's absence."

There was a stunned, confused silence, which Abby broke.

"May we put the past behind us and begin 1857 on a positive note? I will always miss my mother and I will never be as beautiful as she was, but I share her belief in and commitment to abolishing the horrible, disgraceful practice of slavery in this country."

Shouts of *hear, hear!* rang out among the dozen or so assembled women of the Philadelphia Women's Abolitionist Society. Not all were as wealthy as Dorrie Woodhull or Florence Mallory or Abigail herself, but none had been required to take in boarders, and Abby's decision to do just that had been a gross violation of propriety. She honestly did regret having offended them, but she knew she'd do it again to avoid having to marry a man she didn't want or need. Or love.

"How do you take your tea, Abigail? As your mother did, I'll wager."

Abby smiled, nodded, accepted a cup of tea, sipped, then said, "May I share with you some things I've recently learned?" And she told them most of what Genie, Ezra and Donald had told her about freeing Robert, Josephine and Mary. The room went airless. Then a woman Abby didn't know exclaimed, "I don't believe it! I know Montague Wright and I don't believe it! Whoever told you this . . . this . . . tale . . . is lying. Montague is an excellent doctor!"

"But that's not the issue, is it?" Florence asked. "The issue is his holding slaves—"

"That is a lie!" Sheilagh Callahan practically shouted.

Abby controlled her temper and gave the woman what she hoped was a pitying smile. "I was speaking with Montague Wright myself when he asked if his apprentice and his slave could live in my house."

"Why should we believe anything you say? You don't have the most sterling reputation."

"That will be quite enough, Sheilagh," Auntie Florence hissed. "You may not remain in this group if—"

"I don't want to remain if this is the kind of thing you do," Sheilagh said.

"What on earth do you mean, the kind of thing we do? We are an abolitionist group! What did you think we did?" an astounded Dorrie asked.

"That a doctor, right here in the middle of Philadelphia, would hold slaves—" someone said.

"I didn't think you engaged in character assassination!"

"As you just did?" Auntie Florence was scathing. "I think it would be best if you left."

"Now Florence—" Dorrie began.

"Or Abigail and I will leave."

"No." Dorrie stood, holding herself as upright as if she wore a crown. "Mrs. Callahan apparently will not be comfortable with what we do and we'll not temper our discussion for her comfort. It would be best if you left," she said.

"You should have seen the look on her face!" Abby was telling Genie and Maggie that evening as they prepared dinner. "She most certainly had never been asked to leave a gathering before—"

"Especially one where defense of a fallen woman over the reputation of an honorable man was the cause," Genie said bitterly.

They worked in silence for a while until Maggie said, "I am glad they took your side over hers, fallen woman that you are."

"Perhaps I'm not the only fallen woman," Abby said with a raised eyebrow, "and they were merely looking after their own interests rather than mine?"

"Now there's a thought worth considering," Genie said. "Who else do you imagine sleeps in the same bed with her Black escaped slave house maid?"

Maggie gave a whoop, covered her face with her apron, and ran into the scullery for vegetables.

After dinner, when Eli was driving Maggie home, Ezra provided a very different thought for consideration, one which left them no room for laughter. "I think Sheilagh Callahan was a spy," he said, "who allowed her true feelings to sabotage her mission."

"Sabotage her mission!" Abby was aghast. "What mission? Surely, Ezra, you can't be serious!"

"Indeed, I am serious, Abigail," a very grave Ezra replied. "There exist spies in most, if not all, anti-slavery organizations. Job Mayes almost got me and the Cortlandt boy killed and Mrs. Tubman caught and hanged. And if Sheilagh Callahan were not a novice she would have feigned both horror and interest long enough to learn whether you knew who stole Montague Wright's slaves from under his nose."

Genie was first to recognize and accept Ezra's suspicion as truth for she, too, had been betrayed by Job Mayes. It was their good fortune that Abby had not revealed all she knew about the disappearance of Wright's slaves, but before they could feel relieved Donald articulated the real danger. "That Wright, he's not the kind to leave well enough alone. He'll be looking for vengeance."

"You're right about that, Donnie. He'll want someone to pay," Ezra said, adding, "He already harbors resentment for Abby for rejecting his apprentice. Her having knowledge of his escaped slaves will be too much for him to bear. Genie, you must not remain here," he said gravely. "Leave tomorrow."

"But . . . but . . . ." Abby sputtered, "where will she go? She's given up her home!"

"I can stay at the dress shop for several days at least," Genie said. Ezra was right, and she knew it. "How long do you think, Ezra?"

"I think Dr. Wright will make his presence known sooner rather than later. He's not a . . . contemplative man." Anyone who had spent more than five minutes with the man knew that. Whatever came to his mind came out of his mouth, no matter whether right or wrong or true. He talked to hear himself talk and he listened to no one. Yes, Ezra was correct: Abigail Read was the only person Wright could connect to his slaves and, bully that he was, he would confront her.

Three days later, shortly after breakfast, a furious and blustery Montague Wright pushed Eli aside and strode into the front hall. "Where is she?" he brayed distinctively. "I demand to speak with her!"

"Is Miss Abigail expecting you, sir?" Eli asked politely.

"You damned impudent Black bastard, you get out of my way!" Wright thundered and brushed past Eli.

"If you'll wait here in the foyer, sir—"

"Get out of my way!" he screamed at Eli and raised a hand to hit him. Eli quickly grabbed the arm as Donald had taught him and just as quickly twisted it behind the angry man's back with such force he screamed in pain and fell to his knees.

Abby came running down the stairs, hair flying behind her, and Ezra came running from the opposite side of the foyer, from his suite, pulling on his jacket. "What on earth is happening here? What are you doing here, Dr. Wright?"

"Tell this Black bastard to release me immediately!" He meant for his words to be a thundered roar, but they were a whimpered plea—or prayer—for the pain to cease.

"I'll not have that kind of language in my home, nor will I have it directed at someone in my employ." Abby emphasized the word *employ* and noted its effect on the good doctor, who was still in Eli's grip and still on his knees.

"I will not be treated in this manner," he brayed.

"Then you should have waited in the foyer as requested," Ezra said, buttoning his waistcoat as he approached.

"I don't take orders from niggers," Wright said in his best snarly voice.

Ezra nodded at Eli who released Wright and stepped back toward Abby. "Then get up off your knees and walk your arse back to the front door or I'll throw you back there."

"I'm surprised you didn't come down from the boudoir behind Mistress Read," Wright said in his now recovered, braying voice.

Ezra slapped him with his open hand across the face, hard, and Wright stumbled backward into the wall, knocking over a table and a vase of flowers. "Get up," Ezra ordered, "and get out, and don't ever come here again or I'll beat you like you beat slaves."

"Who took them?" Wright whined. "Who took my Robert and Josephine and Mary? Where are they? They're mine and I want them back!" He had struggled to his feet and was backing toward the front door. "You had no right!" He was whining piteously.

"You had no right to think you could own human beings," Abby said.

"They're not human beings! They're niggers!"

Ezra slapped him again, opened the front door, pushed him out, and slammed the door. Then he stood and watched through the glass to make sure Wright left, pleased to notice that he was in a hired carriage.

"What an odious man!" Abby exclaimed. "I'd never have believed I'd hear myself say such words but I am so glad you struck him, Ezra. I understand now why you wanted Eli to open the door when Wright came instead of Maggie."

Donald and Maggie came silently into the hallway, Donald grinning, Maggie weeping. Abby rushed to embrace Maggie and to assure her that all was well.

"And Master Eli handled himself quite well, did he not?" a beaming Donald asked.

"That he did," Ezra said with a pat on Eli's back that made the boy beam proudly.

"Would he really have struck Maggie?" Abby asked, and both Donald and Ezra nodded assent.

"That's who he is: a coward and a bully," Donald said with disgust. "You said as much, Ezra, and while I believed you, I also hoped you'd be wrong, so he'd put up more of a fight. Then I could have been of some assistance."

"I don't know what I'd have done if he had hit you, Maggie!" Abby was now weeping, too.

"I'd have kilt him," Eli said quietly, sounding very much like Ezra.

"As well you should have done," Donald said, drawing the boy in close to him. "It's what a man should do to the bastard who hurts his mam."

"Or burn his boats," Ezra muttered, earning him a speculative glance from Maggie and a puzzled one from Abby.

"What if he returns, Ezra?" a worried Maggie asked.

"He won't," Ezra said. "The coward in him won't allow him to have to defend himself physically again."

"Perhaps I should take fighting lessons," Abby mused.

"You are safe as long I am here," Eli announced, and stretched into his constantly increasing height and breadth, making himself as tall as Donald if not yet as broad.

"I think you should visit Mrs. Mallory today, Abby, and tell her what happened. She should know that Sheilagh Callahan is a spy, and she and her friends should look carefully at any other new members."

"Why don't I ever think of these things on my own!" Abby berated herself.

"Because you're not accustomed to there being treachery around every corner," Maggie said.

"What's treachery?" Eli asked.

"It's when someone you trust betrays you," Donald said, then asked, "you know betrays?"

Eli nodded. "Turns on you, cuts you in the back." And all the adults nodded at him. "Somebody betrayed me once. He was my friend. I thought he was until he betrayed me." Eli sounded as sad as if the betrayal had occurred yesterday.

"What did you do?" Donald asked.

"I pushed him in the river," Eli answered. "He couldn't swim." They watched him retrieve the memory he had long ago put into a hole dug deep.

"You tole Boss Johnny I goes to stay with my ma at night. Why?"

"Why you such a baby you got to sleep wit your ma?"

"You just mad 'cause your ma ain't here no more, but that ain't no reason to hurt mine!"

"Don't nobody need a ma! You just a stupid baby."

"Everybody need their ma and you the cause my ma gon' get whipped, 'Zekiel. You 'spozed to be my friend."

"My onliest friend is a extra piece of fatback at suppertime. Anyway, we's niggers and niggers don't have friends."

"What kinda talk is that?"

"It's what Boss Johnny say. I tole him you was my friend and he say niggers cain't have friends 'cause we ain't people."

"Well you for sho' ain't my friend no more."

"Put me down, Eli! This bridge rail ain't that strong and you know I cain't swim! Put me down, Eli! Please!"

Eli watched as his former friend coughed and gagged on the dirty river water as the strong current carried him along. It wouldn't be long before people saw him. Perhaps he would be saved but Eli doubted it because only other slaves would see him and niggers didn't swim. Everybody knew that. Which was why Eli could swim: His ma always told him to be able to do one thing that white people didn't know you could do. Eli's ma could read—not a lot, just some few words—but she would never let Boss know that. She also could understand some of the African words spoken by the cross-the-water people and even they didn't know that about her.

"Niggers is scared of water," Boss Johnny tole the other Bosses. "So that's how you keep 'em in line: Say you gon' throw 'em in the river and they'll do whatever you tell 'em to do. They scared of the water! Don't know why but it's so."

Eli was, too, but if one of the Bosses ever threw him in the river he would just keep on swimming to freedom. So, he learned how to swim by secretly watching the Bosses, how they either pinched their noses closed or took in a deep breath before jumping in the water. Then the ones who had taken in the deep breaths moved their arms back and forth and kicked their legs up and down. So, at night, Eli practiced, frightened of the water snakes but determined to learn to swim. Once he understood that the held breath kept the water out of his lungs— kept him from drowning—that's what he practiced, for longer and longer periods of time until he could hold his breath for many minutes. Moving the arms and legs was not easy but he learned it, practicing until he could swim.

'Zekiel had stopped screaming and fighting the water and was bobbing along on top, taken by the current. What would happen when he was discovered? They will look for me, Eli thought, especially Boss Johnny, and the Boss would want to know how 'Zekiel got in the water he was so afraid of. Eli took the deepest breath he'd ever taken and jumped off the bridge from which he'd thrown his friend. He went under and stayed there, letting the current carry him along. But his pants and shirt were ballooning around him and slowing and

pulling him to the surface! He undid them and swam away from them. Soon enough he heard people screaming and shouting and calling for help—Colored people—but not one of them entered the water to save 'Zekiel who probably was past saving at this point, or to investigate the floating clothes. No one knew that Eli was bobbing along naked beneath the surface. Just as he believed his lungs were about to explode, the motion of the water changed; it slowed and smoothed. Eli surfaced to find himself at a gentle bend in the river. He swam quickly to shore and climbed out. He no longer could see the plantation he belonged to and no one from there could see him.

He heard a whine and a rustle of the underbrush, and a floppy-eared hound emerged and approached slowly. "Hey, dawg." The dog's tail swished and she crawled on her belly to Eli. He scratched the top of her head and rubbed her back, glad that he had no real scent; the water had cleansed him. Eli liked dogs and they liked him, but the perverse Boss Johnny wouldn't let him work in the kennels with the hunting hounds. Believing that Eli feared horses; he was sent to the stables. Eli neither disliked nor feared horses, he just didn't know them. However, he was happy to let Boss Johnny think that stable work was punishment.

"Where you live, dawg? Can I steal me some clothes and some food and a hoss?" The dog gave him a short bark and disappeared into the brush the way she'd appeared. Eli followed. He gave no further thought to 'Zekiel or Boss Johnny but he never stopped thinking about his mother. Not yet anyway.

"Where were you, Eli?"

"How did you get to Philadelphia?"

"How long did it take you to get here?"

Eli didn't know how long it had taken or how he had managed. "I knew to go north and I knew not to get caught."

"But where were you, Eli?" Maggie asked. "Where was the river?"

"Virginny somewhere," Eli said, and wondered why they all looked at him wide-eyed. The boy—still a child—had made his

208

way to Philadelphia and freedom alone, all the way from Virginia. Maggie held him tightly, hoping and praying that it felt comforting, as if it were his mother's embrace. The others marveled at him, knowing that they never could really understand how a slave could and would risk everything for freedom, could and would even kill to attain that freedom, but knowing that they would do all in their power to end slavery, to make freedom possible, even to kill in the pursuit of that goal.

"I'll change and go to Florence," Abby said.

"I'll clean the kitchen," Maggie said, "and make a cake for later."

"Eli and I will clean the stable and feed the animals," Donald said.

"I need to visit my bookkeeper," Ezra said, "and I'll walk. I need to breathe some fresh air into my lungs and get rid of all traces of Montague Wright."

Much later that evening Donald drove Maggie home and brought Genie back. As had become their habit the Black women lay down on the bench for the journey—this for the same reason that Eli did not transport them at night: For their safety. Genie quickly learned that she had missed important events, none more so than Eli's account of his run to freedom. She also regretted missing the sight of Montague Wright being brought low. A man who took pleasure in humiliating others being humiliated. She told them about Robert, Josephine and Mary and how she wondered whether freedom was the correct path for them.

"But you can't think slavery is better!" Abby said, horrified.

"Slavery, no. But I'm not sure they can live on their own. I hope I'm wrong."

"But why couldn't they?" Ezra asked. "If they're free?"

"Slavery destroys . . . personhood. It destroys the self. It destroys the ability to decide to do or be. The entire self is enslaved, not just the body—the mind, the spirit, the will . . ." They could never understand. They wanted to, she knew they did, but even if she could find the words to explain what slavery did to a person, how could she make them feel what it was like?

"How long have you been free, Miss Genie?" Donald asked.

"Eight years," Genie said. "I was sixteen when I . . . escaped."

"You were little more than a child!" Abby exclaimed.

"I was older than Eli and Reverend Richard and Absalom," Genie said, "and I could read and write, which saved me."

"You can't sell her, she's mine! My brother gave her to me!" Matilda did not look at her husband when she spoke to him.

"You don't even know her name!" Gilbert snarled. "You don't even know what she looks like."

"She's Black and ugly, like all of them," Matilda said.

"I've already sold her, Matilda, and gotten a good price—"

"You can't sell her, I told you! She's not yours to sell!"

"She lives in my house, and she's mine to do with as I choose. So are you, for that matter, but I couldn't sell you because you are worthless. You have no skills or abilities."

"And I suppose she does? What skills does she have?"

Gilbert laughed at his wife. She really was quite ridiculous, even more so than her ridiculous brother. "She's a very fine seamstress, Matilda, worth her weight in gold in places like Charleston and New Orleans, or Philadelphia or New York, where women look and behave beautifully."

"If anyone is going to Philadelphia it will be me," Matilda said.

"You're not going anywhere, but Clara is going to Washington, DC. I'm taking her there myself. We leave tomorrow."

Now she looked at him, her eyes wide. "That Black nigger is going to Washington while I languish here in this . . . this backcountry no man's land? That is most unacceptable, Gilbert."

He didn't bother to respond. He went in search of her maids, indentured Irish servants, both of whom would earn their freedom soon! He found them folding sheets in the linen closet and told them what he needed: "Get Clara ready to travel tomorrow morning, early. Carriage to Baltimore then train to Washington."

They stared at him as if he spoke a foreign language. Finally the older one said, "How, sir? Does she have a travel bag, travel clothes? How many days will she be away? And is Mrs. Will going as well?"

"Mrs. Will is not going and Clara will not be returning. As to what she has, probably nothing of her own so you'll have to use something of Mrs. Will's, something she no longer uses."

They left at dawn the next morning, Clara and Gilbert Will, Clara seated on the bench beside the driver, Gilbert inside the carriage. Clara and the driver did not know each other so there was little conversation aside from his answering her question about knowing the way to the Baltimore train station—he'd driven the Master there many times. No, he did not know where Washington was. Why was she going there? After she told him why there was no further conversation between them.

The train station frightened Clara—more people and carriages than she had ever seen in one place and more Colored people than she had ever seen. But if the station frightened her the trains were terrifying: huge and black and smoky and noisy. Then she had a thought that stopped her: Did the Mistress hate trains? They were black though not ugly, Clara thought. Master followed a Colored man in a suit to the front of the train while another led Clara to the rear. She was shaking now, and crying.

"Is you ever rode a train?" The man leaned down and whispered to her.

"No sir," she said, shaking harder.

He grabbed her shoulder and squeezed. "You gon' be awright, girl, but you got to take hold. You cain't let people see your fear. You unnerstan' me?"

Clara shook her head. She did not understand anything and she certainly could not control the fear that was making her want to vomit everything she'd ever eaten. "I'm going to be sold," she managed to say.

"Then you CAIN'T show no fear, girl! Somethin' about fear makes people want to hurt you. Try to look mean. You know how mean niggers look? Try to look like that." And he lifted her up into the train car because there were no steps at the rear of the train for Colored people. No seats, either—just hard wooden benches. The train whistle blew and smoke billowed, and Clara tried to call up the image of the only mean Colored person she'd ever seen, a man who tended the cows

211

and hogs. Her granny said he was "mean as a whip snake. He done worked up under white mens so long he come to act like 'em. Mean as a snake that man is." Clara called up his face, sweat running down like water, a scowl permanently etched into his visage. Clara tightened her face into a scowl as the train lurched forward and willed herself to keep it there. She would not show fear. She would not let anyone hurt her.

When the train stopped everyone got off, so Clara did, too. There was no one to help her so she threw her bag down and jumped, landing so hard she didn't have to work to bring the scowl to her face. She swung around when she heard her name called.

"Come on, girl! Hurry!" Master Gilbert was waving her forward. She picked up her bag and ran toward him, then followed him past so many huge, black trains that she lost count, and into a station that made her stop and catch her breath. So many people, many more than in Baltimore! And so many Colored people! "Come on!" Master grabbed her arm and pulled her along behind him.

One of the Colored men in the suits was following, pushing Master's things in a wagon. Master was walking very fast to a long line of carriages in front of the station. He raised his arm and the driver of one of the carriages jumped down from his seat and opened the carriage door. Master climbed in and the driver closed the door. Then the driver and the Colored man got Master's things from the wagon and strapped them to the back of the carriage. Master threw some coins out of the carriage window at the Colored man and his wagon as the carriage driver climbed up to his seat. "Where to, sir?" he called out.

"Hotel Washington," Master replied. Then he seemed to remember Clara. "Get up there with the driver," he ordered.

Clara clambered up, the driver offering no assistance, and they drove away. Clara's eyes couldn't keep up with all there was to see. Everything was larger and grander and different from anything she'd ever seen—except in books belonging to Rebecca Tillson and Beate. How she wished they were there to explain what she was witnessing! And what would she do in a hotel?

"The porter will take her to the servants' quarters in the basement," she heard the desk clerk say to the Master.

"She'll stay in my suite," the Master said. "She can sleep on the floor in the sitting room. She'll belong to another tomorrow."

The hotel was huge and grand, the people inside it grand and glittering, the suite larger than the ones in their home. What would the Mistress think of this?! Clara thought. The Master ordered a large meal, eating most of it quickly, telling Clara she could eat what was left. Then he went into the bedroom and closed the door. Not knowing what else to do, Clara picked up the newspapers that were on a table and sat on the floor near the fireplace and read until her eyes burned and watered: It had grown dark and the fire had burned out. She returned the newspapers to the table just as the Master entered the sitting room, dressed to go out.

"Do you know what poker is, girl?"

"No sir."

"It is what some call a game of chance but I call it a game of skill, and I am very skilled at it. With the money that I will win tonight, and the money I will be paid for you, I will be able to purchase all the remaining land in the county. I will own the largest plantation in Maryland. Then I will send my ridiculous wife to live with her ridiculous brother."

He opened the door to a knock, and servants came to light the lamps and candles and to lay fires in the grates. He waited until they finished then asked Clara if she knew the duties of a lady's maid. She shook her head. "No sir."

"Your mistress never taught you how to ready her boudoir for sleep?"

"No sir."

"What did she discuss with you?"

"Nothing sir."

"She talked to you, didn't she? What did she say to you, girl?"

"She said to get my Black, ugly, ignorant self out of her sight, that she didn't want to look at me."

"Her brother spoke to you. What did he say?"

"He told me not to ever look directly at him, not to speak unless spoken to, never to make noise in his presence—"

"Stop! Enough! They're worse than I thought." He turned back to the bedroom. "Come with me, girl. Look there—I want the bed turned

down, I want my night clothes on the bed and my slippers beside the bed, I want a glass of water on the table there and the bottle of laudanum beside the glass—" He stopped speaking and looked closely at her. "Did you understand what I said?"

"Yessir."

"Good, because though the hotel would send someone to do these things, I do not want strangers handling my belongings."

"Yessir."

"I hope to return by midnight," he said, and left the suite.

Clara had followed him from the bedroom into the sitting room, and watched him leave without a backward glance. She stood frozen for a moment, not knowing what to do. Then she understood that she should do what she was told so she returned to the bedroom and turned down the cover and the sheets. She lifted the suitcase onto the chair and opened it. He had said nothing about the suits and shirts. She opened a closet and saw hangers so she put the suits and shirts on them. Then she saw the night clothes which she put on the bed and the slippers, which she put beside the bed. There were several leather cases inside the suitcase. She opened one. Money. A lot of money. She closed it and opened another in which there was a razor, brush and soap. She placed the case on the stand with the wash basin. She had just opened the third case when the door opened and the Master rushed into the room. He stopped and stared at what he saw and Clara began to shake with fear.

"Calm yourself, Girl, you've done exactly as I asked. Even more: You've hung the suits and shirts. If I didn't need the money you'll bring I'd keep you myself and rid myself of a useless wife. But seamstresses are more valuable than maids." Then he grabbed the case with all the money and hurried to the door. He stopped suddenly. "I'll have some food sent up to you. When you hear a knock on the door ask who it is. If the man says it is room service you may open the door. If it is anyone else, do not open the door. Understand?"

"Yessir. Thank you, sir."

But he was gone before she finished thanking him. She closed the door and returned to the bedroom to complete her tasks. She opened the last case, smaller than the others. In it were two bottles of pills and *the laudanum, which she recognized because Rebecca used it every night—a miracle drug, she called it. "One or two drops soothe the pain in my joints and allow me to sleep. A drop more makes me sleep too long and everyone is awake before me and I am the lazy one! A drop more than that and—one never wakes."*

Clara put the laudanum beside the glass on the table and was about to close the suitcase when she noticed a packet of papers in the back pocket. She lifted it and saw the only thing that interested her: A map. She hurried into the sitting room with it. Rebecca and Beate had shown her maps and how to read them: North, South, East and West. She opened the map and quickly found Baltimore. She knew that Washington, DC, was north of her, and she quickly found it. How close they were, which was why the train ride was so short. Then her eyes, acting on their own, saw PHILADELPHIA. So close to Washington. As close as Baltimore. "Get to Philadelphia," Rebecca had told her. She looked at the other papers and found the name of the hotel, found the name of the train station.

She returned the map and papers to the suitcase as she found them and closed the case and put it on the floor. She hurried to ask who was at the door when she heard the knock and opened it when the man said "room service." He was a tall Colored man in a white jacket and black pants and he said good evening to her. She replied in kind and asked him to please put the tray on the table next to the sofa when he asked where she wanted it. She thanked him and followed him to the door. Just before he opened it she took a deep breath and asked him if the train station was too far to walk to.

He looked at her closely. "Not for a strong young girl. Walk downstairs to the servants' quarters in the basement. Go down the hallway and out the door and turn right and keep walking. You will hear the trains."

"Thank you, sir."

"It is good that you won't let yourself get sold."

She was astonished. "How did you know that?"

"Your Master told the desk clerk, and he told everyone else."

Clara closed the door. She had not decided until the man spoke the words that she would not allow herself to be sold. That she would go to Philadelphia. She ate the bread and cheese that the Master had ordered and lay down on the sofa. She did not know what time it was or how long she had until midnight. She did not expect to sleep because of all the thoughts in her head, but she jerked awake at the sound of the door opening and the Master stumbling in. He groaned as if in pain as he threw off his jacket.

"Put two drops of laudanum in that glass of water, girl. Do it quickly!"

"Yessir!" she said as she hurried into the bedroom where she quickly put three large drops of laudanum in the glass and swirled it around as she'd seen Rebecca do, "because it is most bitter." She was swirling it when the Master stumbled into the room and snatched it from her. He gulped it down and fell onto the bed, groaning. She waited for him to say something, but he did not, and within what seemed a matter of seconds he was snoring. She backed out of the room and closed the door.

The Master's shoes and jacket were in the sitting room. So was the leather case that had held the money. She tiptoed to the door but she need not have bothered—she could hear the loud snores before she got there. She turned back to the leather case and opened it and her eyes grew wide: There was even more money than before. Much, much more. Bills and coins and, folded inside a heavy, white linen napkin, two diamond rings and a gold watch on a heavy gold chain. She pulled her battered travel bag from beneath the sofa and from within it claimed an even more battered and soiled reticule bag. She didn't know if the servant girl who had packed it was being kind or insulting but since Clara had never had occasion to need a reticule she hadn't given the matter much thought. Now she wished she had a handkerchief or a comb but all she had to put in it was money. She chose three bills and half a dozen coins. She did not know their value and she had no idea what the money could or would buy but she would learn.

Before she zipped the money case closed she removed the watch from its chain and dropped it into the reticule. She had once known how to tell time—Rebecca and Beate had taught her—but there was no opportunity or need to practice since they left. Now, however, she thought it would be wise to know the time of day. She looked at the watch. Sometime before one o'clock in the morning. Then she had a thought that propelled her to her feet: Master had said that the man who now owned her was coming at nine o'clock to get her. She zipped the case and put it into her travel bag. Then she pulled the strings of the reticule, closing it tightly, and put it into her bag, closing it tightly as well. Now to make a plan that would get her to freedom without getting her caught or killed. The first part was easy: all the way downstairs to the servants' quarters and out the door to the right. Then walk to the train station.

Nobody stopped her. Nobody even seemed to notice her as she made her way through the hotel's servants' quarters to the back door. The same was true all the way to the train station where she expected to face her first real challenge: Which train was going to Philadelphia? However as soon as she entered the cavernous station signs pointed to all the trains and their destinations. She had only to follow directions, and once she found the correct train she followed a group of white people accompanied by several Colored people and, as Clara and her Master had done the day before, the two groups separated at the train and Clara followed her people and climbed into the servants' car at the rear of the train. The ride was longer this time, but Clara was filled with anticipation and something entirely new: the thought, the realization, the knowledge that she was free! She no longer was a slave or a servant. If she got off the train in Philadelphia she would be a free woman of Color!

The Philadelphia train station felt different from the Washington, DC, station both inside and outside, but Clara could not spend time wondering and thinking. One thing that was the same was the line of carriages waiting for passengers. And here was a new thought: Now that she was in Philadelphia where would she go? She knew not to attempt to hire one of the shiny black carriages, especially one with a white driver. Then, off to the side, she spied a single, beat-up and battered mule cart with a Colored driver. She hurried over to it and the driver smiled and tipped his hat.

"Morning, miss. Where 'bouts you goin'?"

Clara smiled and returned the greeting and asked to be taken to dine. "Some place with very good food," she said.

"I know just the place," the driver said as he reached for her bag. But she gave him her hand instead, and he pulled her and the bag up to the seat beside him. Clara held her bag in her lap and tried not to call attention to herself by memorizing her surroundings. Thankfully the mule's slow progression made noticing landmarks easy. The driver's constant chatter also helped, especially when he announced that they were entering South Philadelphia, the part of the city where many Colored people lived. "And a gentleman by the name of Joseph got a small eating place but the food is real good," the driver said, and it wasn't long before he slowed the mule to a stop, allowing Clara to jump to the ground.

"How much do I owe you sir?" she asked, pulling her reticule from the travel bag.

"Your ride is free if you'll buy me a meal, miss," the driver said.

Clara looked askance at the little shack behind them, then the wind shifted and she got a whiff of cooking food and it smelled wonderful. Clara nodded and followed the driver to the door of the shack, which he held open for her. Half a dozen people were seated on benches at two long tables, and a huge cookstove was visible at the back of the room. A bearded man came toward them.

"How're you, Mr. Joseph?" the cart driver said jovially. "This young lady is gon' buy me a meal 'cause I just drove her here from the train station. Ain't that right, miss?"

"Yes it is," Clara said to Mr. Joseph. "And he says this is the best food in Philadelphia."

Joseph gave her a searching look. "I'm sorry to ask but can I see your money, miss?"

Clara opened her reticule and when Joseph saw the bills and coins he begged her pardon and pointed to a place on the bench at the front table. Then he led the cart driver to a seat at the back of the place. Then he returned to Clara and asked what she wanted to eat as he told her what was available. "Fried chicken, rice and gravy, beans and greens. And sir? I'm very hungry."

Joseph nodded and walked away and Clara examined her surroundings, noticing a pile of newspapers on the floor near the front door. Nobody was paying attention to her so she went to the pile of *papers and took a handful and brought them to her table. She couldn't believe what she was seeing and reading, page after page of words that she knew but forming concepts that were completely beyond her comprehension. "You never seen a Colored newspaper before?" Joseph was standing at the table with her food, but even as hungry as she was her attention was captured by the newspapers.*

"No sir," she said. "I never have."

"Well, you eat first and you can take some of them to read when you go." He walked away and Clara faced food that engaged all her senses at once. She had never eaten food like this before. She'd never even seen food like this!

Joseph said eat, and Clara did eat, more and better than she ever had, hoping that the food would strengthen her mind and spirit as well as her body so she could think where and how she would live in this city. She initially ate rapidly, as if the man, Joseph, would come and take the food away before she could finish. But the food began to do its work. Her insides began to calm and quieten. She now ate slowly and savored the food. Could she eat food like this, in a place like this, all the time? Perhaps if she had a place to live—money! She had money! Was it enough to buy a place to live?

Joseph returned with a woman before Clara's thoughts about money were in order. She watched their approach with something resembling fear though she realized that she hadn't been afraid since leaving Baltimore.

"This is my wife," Joseph said, "and she knows a lady who will rent you a room."

"It's a clean, safe, quiet house and Mrs. Tillman is a good, God-fearing woman," Mrs. Joseph said.

"And it's not far so you can take your meals here," Joseph said with an appreciative glance at her empty plate.

"That's very good news and I thank you both," Clara said.

"What is your name, child?" Mrs. Joseph asked.

With only the slightest hesitation the reply came, "Eugenia Oliver."

* * *

"And that's where and how Genie Oliver came to be," Genie said.

"How did you decide Eugenia Oliver was your name?" Abby asked. "Had you already chosen it?"

"I liked the name Eugenia," Genie said slowly, remembering. "I first heard it from Rebecca and Beate during one of their many arguments about whether or not saints were real." Genie laughed at the looks on the faces around her and explained that Beate, a Catholic, often referenced saints, especially female ones, as sources of strength and courage. St. Eugenia, who, in the third century, disguised herself as a man to escape persecution, was one of Beate's favorites.

"Why was she persecuted?" Eli asked. "And when was the third century?"

"Well we live in the nineteenth century," Donald said, "so the third century—"

"Was a way long time ago," Eli said, "but what did she do to get persecuted?"

"Let that be a story for another day, please Eli," Genie said.

He was disappointed but he nodded. "When did you stop being scared, Miss Eugenie?" he asked instead.

"I thought all the fear had left me, Eli, until that morning I heard Montague Wright's voice in the kitchen, just as I thought all vestiges of slavery had left me. But perhaps it never does."

"I didn't stop bein' scared 'till I come to live here," Eli said, "and I ain't been scared since."

"Haven't," Genie, Abby and Ezra said in unison, and they all laughed.

"What about the Oliver part?" Eli asked.

"Another saint—" Genie began but Donald began to sputter.

"Not that bleedin' Irishman!" he exclaimed.

Ezra quickly changed the subject. "The Mrs. Tillman you rented a room from—"

"William's mother," Genie said, "and I didn't rent it. She gave me a place to stay the day I met her. She refused to accept any money. She told me I was safe. Constantly, over and over, she told me I was safe, told me not to be afraid, until I finally believed her."

"How long before you believed her?" Eli asked.

"It took years."

"What made you believe her?"

"When she told me the Master was dead," Genie said.

Carrie Tillman was a tall-ish woman, and very thin. She was not young, but Eugenia could not assign an age to her. She stood straight as a fence post and looked as strong. White hair, gentle, dark brown eyes, and a soft, low voice. She led Eugenia into the parlor and invited her to sit down. Genie had never sat in a parlor. She felt the fear begin in her stomach. She felt it grow. She put on her mean face, which startled Carrie Tillman. Until she laughed.

"Little girl! Why you make yourself so ugly like that?"

"I'm scared, miss."

Carrie was taken aback. "You fear me, little girl?"

Genie looked closely at Carrie. Then she looked all around. The parlor was very pretty. Genie was still standing in the middle of the room. She dropped down into a side chair because her knees buckled. "I fear everything and everybody."

Carrie knelt down beside the chair and wrapped her long, strong arms around Genie. Genie went rigid. Carrie tightened her grip. Genie stopped breathing. If she'd ever been held she didn't remember it. Carrie held on. For a long time. Finally, Genie inhaled deeply, and when she exhaled, the fear bubble burst. She leaned sideways, putting all her weight on Carrie's shoulders. Carrie held her there as if she were a young child. Again, for a long time they remained like that until Carrie's knees could take no more.

"Are you tired, little girl? Would you like to sleep?"

Genie sighed. "Yes, ma'am. I would."

"Then stand up, little girl, and help me stand up, and I'll take you to your room."

Genie's room—Clara's room—in the Will manse had been a space

221

beneath the back staircase. She could neither stand nor lie straight. Her room in Carrie's house was a room with furniture, windows and a door. Genie looked at the bed and almost fell asleep right then. "This is . . . a very beautiful room, Mrs. Tillman."

Carrie smiled at her. "Would you like to wash—can you keep awake that long?"

"Oh yes, ma'am, I want to wash! Please can I wash?" Of all the slave things Genie hated, never being clean was at the top of the list. She would stay awake for another day if it meant she could wash herself clean. With hot water! When finally she was ready to sleep, she asked Carrie what time she should rise. "I have a timepiece and I can read it."

"You're not here to work, little girl. You rise when your body says you have slept enough."

Fifteen hours later Genie rose. For several frightening seconds she did not know where she was. Then she remembered. On the chair beside the bed were a dress, shoes, and a piece of paper. A note from Carrie. I know you can read, it said. Put on these clothes and come to the kitchen. C. Tillman. Genie did and found Carrie seated at the table, two books and several newspapers in front of her. Carrie smiled at her—something she did often and which Genie would have to get used to. Beate and Rebecca were kind to her but they did not smile at her. "Would you like tea or coffee?" Carrie asked.

"I never had coffee."

"Then you shall have it. Would you like cream and sugar?"

"I never had cream and sugar."

Carrie fixed the coffee and gave it to Genie. She took a big gulp just as Carrie warned her that it was hot. It burned her throat but it was so good that she took another big gulp. Then she laughed. And Carrie seemed to know exactly why Genie was laughing because she laughed, too. Then she fed Genie ham and biscuits with red-eye gravy and more coffee. Then it was time to talk.

"Tell me about yourself, Eugenia Oliver, and how you came to be in Philadelphia." And Genie told her. Everything, every detail that she remembered of her life on the Will plantation in Maryland, up to and including the train journey with Master Will to DC to be sold. She told how she drugged him, and took his money. And how she fled *to the depot, and became a stowaway on a train bound for Philadelphia. Carrie listened to every word, never interrupting and never commenting. Ten days later, when Genie was altering some dresses for Carrie, the older woman bustled into the room more animated and excited than Genie had seen her. She extended a newspaper and pointed to a story.*

"Is this a Colored newspaper?" Genie asked.

Carrie shook her head impatiently. "It is the Washington Star. Read this," and she pointed. Genie read. Then she read it again. Then she looked up at Carrie. She knew what she had read but she didn't know what it meant.

"Gerald Will, the man who was your master, is dead from a laudanum overdose following a night of poker and drinking. The men he played cards with say he cheated. The police said he was robbed: There was no money in his room, or the watch, rings, and other jewelry his poker-playing friends lost to him. But more importantly, Genie, there is no mention made of you. Which means no one is looking for you. Clara does not exist, and Eugenia Oliver is a free woman."

"I lived with Carrie Tillman for three years," Genie said into the stunned silence. "She taught me how to cook and how to take care of a house. And when the time was right, she introduced me to the man who built my own house." Genie was still and quiet but they saw that she had more to say. "She also taught me how not to be afraid all the time. She taught me that fear was a tool to be used to save and protect myself and others if necessary." She paused again, seeing and hearing Carrie: *Use the fear, Eugenia, but never show it.*

"How did she find out?" Abby asked. "What happened to Gerald Will, and that you truly were free?"

"She sent William to Washington. The air was abuzz with the story of the wealthy Maryland plantation owner who was found dead in his hotel room of a laudanum overdose. How he might have been a card cheat as well, who was robbed of his winnings. It was a fantastic story that lent itself to all manner of gossip. But he was puzzled that no one mentioned a Colored slave girl who was traveling with him." Genie paused, thinking and remembering. "Few people wanted to discuss a man who'd come to Washington, DC, to sell a slave girl. It was whispered about but not discussed in polite company or published in the newspaper." However, the Colored hotel staff in the basement knew about the slave girl who was brought to town to be sold, but that was not information they shared with white people, so no one was looking for her. Genie did not tell them that it was she who had robbed Gerald Will. Carrie and Abby knew but no one else needed to.

"That's why you always help us boys, Miss Eugenie? 'Cause Miss Carrie helped you?" How wise Eli was becoming.

"Yes, Eli. That's why."

"I wish the world would repay kindness with kindness!" Donald exclaimed. "A better world it would be. Though I still wish you hadn't named yourself after that Irishman! Surely Scotland has men worthy of—"

"We have many worthy men, Donnie. What we don't have is the Catholic church. Now Abigail: How did Florence respond to your information?" Ezra asked, removing the focus from Irish saints.

"Her face blushed so purple I thought she'd explode!" Abby answered truthfully because Florence *had* practically ignited when she learned that Sheilagh Callahan apparently was a spy in their abolitionist group. "And she said since they don't know if other new members also are traitors—her word—she will recommend that they disband the group."

"Oh that would be a shame!" Ezra said.

"Perhaps not," Genie said sadly, explaining that even before Abby told Florence of Sheilagh's treachery they had talked of how things were changing for the worse, how hope, even among the most committed anti-slavery stalwarts, was dimming. "She said there once was a really strong belief that slavery in the entire country could be ended but that many no longer believed it likely."

CHAPTER ELEVEN

"St. Eugenia, wake up. Eli is beginning his rounds and Maggie will be here soon."

"Shouldn't saints be permitted to sleep later than mere mortals?"

"Saints *are* mere mortals until they are put to death, dear."

Genie groaned and opened her eyes to the sight that brought her such great joy: Dark blue eyes, just inches away, staring back at her, filled with love and amusement. "I don't wish to be put to death but I also don't want to get up."

"Well you could always explain to Eli how Eugenia came to be a saint and that way perhaps he'd understand finding us in the same bed."

"Have I told you how very annoying you can be, Abigail Read?" Genie huffed and threw back the covers as she jumped from the bed and scurried across the room, nightshirt flapping in the breeze, and ran from Abby's suite across the hall to her own, entering her room and running to the bedroom and managing to jump into bed and beneath the covers, just seconds before Eli's knock at the door.

"Good morning, Miss Eugenie," Eli called out as he entered her suite.

"Good morning, Eli. How cold is it this morning?"

"Very cold, Miss Eugenie. Ice sticks hanging from the north side of the house."

"But no snow?"

"No ma'am, no snow."

"Well that's something," Genie said as Eli shoveled coals into the bedroom grate, lit it, and took his leave. She waited a few minutes until warmth could be expected before getting out of bed and going to break the layer of ice on the wash water. She would need to be dressed when Maggie arrived so that she could leave with Jack and go to her own place of work. Business was good and she and Adelaide were kept busy.

Ezra and Donald, too, were busy, and had been able to hire Absalom to help with several assignments. Abby, still saddened and upset by the dissolution of the abolitionist group, kept herself occupied with attending social and cultural activities and events that provided some opportunity to learn what was happening in the political circles of the wealthy, and it was from one such event that she rushed home on the evening of March 6, hoping that the denizens of her residence would be present. They were, though Maggie and Jack were leaving, Jack having recently returned Genie home.

"Don't leave yet, please," she called out as she hurried down the front hallway. Maggie and Genie were rushing to her.

"Is something wrong, Abby?" Genie asked, and the answer was on Abby's face: Something definitely was wrong, and whatever it was troubled Ezra as well. He and Donald had run in the scullery door as if chased by the devil.

"Genie!" he called out. "Maggie! Jack! Where are you?" And they all ran back to the kitchen.

"You heard, too," Abby said to them, her voice heavy with unshed tears.

Genie grabbed her hand and looked steadily at Ezra. "What on earth is the matter?"

"That damnable Supreme Court decided the Dred Scott case today," Abby said, and Eli drew in breath at the sound of the profanity for which she did not apologize.

"What did they do?" Jack asked, and Ezra explained it while the four people in the kitchen affected by the Court's ruling froze in place, barely breathing as they struggled to understand how their lives were about to be affected. The highest court in the land had decided that Blacks were not, could not, and never would be full citizens of the United States of America. Furthermore, the Court said that the Constitution never intended they should be.

No one spoke for long minutes. They stood and looked at each other. Then Jack Juniper took his wife's hand.

"Come, Margaret," he said softly, and Maggie Juniper, with tears in her eyes, looked at each of the people that she loved so dearly, and followed her husband out into the night.

"Will we have to live scared again, Miss Eugenie?" Eli asked.

"I don't know, Eli," Genie said quietly. "I honestly don't know, but we will do whatever we must do together."

"And we will be there with you and for you," Abby said, speaking for herself and Ezra and Donald.

Ezra said good night and walked slowly to his suite. Donald put his arm around Eli's shoulders and they left, locking the scullery door behind them, something they'd never done before.

Genie and Abby stood looking at each other, hands tightly clasped. "I don't know what to feel, Abby. I don't feel fear, not the kind I felt as a slave, though I suppose that technically I still am a slave." She shook her head hard, as if to shake the thought out of her mind. "What I feel is . . . broken. Like a bird with a broken wing being pursued by a cat or some other predator. The poor bird cannot ever get to safety because it cannot fly with one wing, so its fate is sealed. It will be destroyed."

"I will be your other wing, my dear," Abby said, "and together we can and will fly to safety if that becomes necessary."

"Do you think it will become necessary?" Genie asked.

"I think we must prepare for that eventuality," Abby said.

"And you will fly with me?"

"Two wings are necessary to fly, and I am your other wing, my dear Genie."

Genie's heart soared, as if already winged. "As grateful as I am that you feel so much for me, Abby, you cannot leave your home." She waved both her arms around to encompass all aspects of the elegant mansion that was Abigail Read's home. "You cannot simply walk away from all this. I will not, I cannot—"

Abby smiled at her, tears glittering like stars in her eyes. She touched a finger to Genie's lips to halt the words. "I'd be flying, not walking, my dear. And until recently it was a rooming house, not a home. It now is a home because of the people who live in it with me, and three of you cannot live in peace and freedom. And if you cannot, then I will not. I do not wish to."

Jack did not bring Maggie to work the following morning, so Ezra and Donald drove Genie to the dress shop where Maggie, William and Arthur were waiting in the back room. Maggie rushed to embrace her, weeping so hard she could barely speak. "Jack says we must go, that it soon will be too dangerous to remain."

"Go where, Maggie?" Genie asked.

"Canada," Maggie whispered, causing Genie to back away from her so she could see her face, and what she saw erased all the good feeling she had shared with Abby the previous night.

"When?"

"Now. Soon."

Genie looked at William. "Can we be citizens in Canada?"

"I don't know," he said, "but they don't have a law that says we can't."

"Then should we leave, William?"

"I don't know, Genie. I can't say. This is something we must give serious thought to."

She had never seen William so unsure of himself, or so wounded. He had been born free to a mother who had been born a slave, and he had dedicated his life to ending the despicable practice, inspired by the mother who had never shied away from sharing her experiences with him, the mother who had taken in the runaway Genie without a moment's hesitation. He had believed with his entire being that an end to slavery was at hand. Until yesterday's Supreme Court ruling—one that the president

228

of the United States and the justice from Pennsylvania supported. "When will we see a copy of the decision and have it explained?"

"Someone is en route to us with a copy of the decision now, so perhaps late tonight or early tomorrow. Then the lawyers will tell us exactly and precisely what it means."

"Then I will make no decision about leaving until after we have that information," Genie said, hoping she sounded more convinced of the rightness of her words than she felt.

"Then neither shall I," Maggie said.

"But Jack?" Genie said. "If he wants to leave—"

"Then I'll not stand in his way. I fully understand. After what he has just endured—he has endured more than enough and he has stood his ground long enough, but I will fight until it is absolutely clear that there is no hope for success," Maggie said.

"Then I will stand and fight with you," Jack said from the door. He had entered unnoticed. He strode over to his wife and embraced her, whispering words to her that were only for her. Then he looked at the rest of them. "I'm not the only one who has suffered and I'll not be the first to abandon the fight. I wished only to spare my wife and daughter from whatever is to come—"

"But we don't yet know what that might be," Maggie said in a near whisper.

"Well, we know the pro-slavers will see it as giving them license to return us to our rightful place," William said, sounding as deflated as he looked.

"And they won't care how they do it, they won't feel a bit of shame being sneaky and violent," Arthur said, none of the usual growl to his voice. He looked and sounded as deflated as William, a circumstance that infuriated Ezra and Donald. Both men so far had been quiet, listening with great interest. But their respect for William and Arthur was huge and seeing these men bereft of hope was too much.

"It will be dangerous for you to meet violence with the same, but I'll be most happy to go into battle on your behalf," Donald said, taking a fighting stance.

"And we have . . . resources . . . at our disposal," Ezra said, "which we won't hesitate to employ."

"Where is Abby?" Maggie said suddenly.

"She is at home," Ezra said. "Eli is with her and they know not to open the door for anyone, for any reason."

"Eli would lay down his life for her, and take a few in the process," Donald said. "That boy is a man now."

"Is it safe for Maggie and me to travel back and forth?" Genie asked.

"As long as I'm doing the transporting it is," Jack said.

"Then please take me to work, Jack," Maggie said.

"And I will go," Genie said. Then she looked at William. "You'll let us know when we have a copy of the Supreme Court decision, and someone to interpret its meaning?"

"I will," William said gravely.

"I should like to be present," Ezra said, "as I'm sure Abby and Donald would as well."

"We would welcome you, Ezra—all of you—as we always do," William replied. And after several minutes of quiet, intense discussion, they decided to meet at Joe Joseph's restaurant.

"That's good," Arthur said, the growl back in his voice. "We're not the only ones who want to know what that evil law says and what it means."

"Then we will wait to hear from you, William, and take ourselves to our work," Ezra said, and he and Donald left, followed by Maggie and Jack.

"I'll walk you, Genie," William said, and she knew he wanted to talk as much as he wanted to check on Adelaide. They left via the back door as Arthur fired up the forge. "Do you ever think of my mother?" William asked when they were outside.

Genie smiled warmly. "All the time, William," she said, and told him how she had recently shared the story of her escape for the first time since telling his mother eight years ago. "I will always be grateful to her and I will never forget her."

"She liked you immediately! She couldn't believe you were so young and so fearless."

"I was terrified!"

"But you didn't show the fear," William said. "You still don't, and I know you feel it. Ezra said the same thing, you know, about the first time he met you and how fearless you seemed."

"Ezra also thought I was a man," Genie said drily, "so don't put too much weight on what he thinks."

"And that sense of humor that's never too far away," William mused. "Mother always wished Adelaide was more like you."

"Adelaide is fine just as she is," Genie said.

William smiled at that. "I think so, too." Then he got to the real reason for wanting to talk. "I am very concerned for Josephine. Robert and Mary are doing well but Josephine . . . I fear too much damage was done."

"Is she not working well at Peter and Catherine's?"

"Too well!" William exclaimed in confusion. "She wants to live there and not as a free woman with her husband and daughter. And you can just imagine the problems that's causing in the Blanding home! Peter and Catherine don't want a live-in house-keeper and they most certainly don't want a slave! But they sometimes can't get Josephine to leave."

"Robert and Mary can't reason with her?"

"It has done no good. I fear we may have made a huge mistake," William said sadly.

"No!" Genie almost shouted. "The mistake would have been to leave them, William. You see what destruction Montague Wright is capable of on a weak spirit." Genie struggled to control her emotions, especially since she thought the same thing of Josephine.

"What, then, can we do?" William asked.

"Find someone who wants a live-in housekeeper," Genie answered.

Abby looked at her strangely. "You are actually proposing to return that poor woman to servitude?" They sat together in the sitting room of Abby's suite. The fire burned brightly in the grate and the tea in the pot was still hot.

"Being a servant is all she knows, Abby, and she apparently is good at it. But I'm not proposing a return to slavery, and certainly not a return to a monster like Montague Wright." Surely, Genie said, Abby must know someone who wanted a live-in servant.

Abby was quiet and thoughtful for several moments. "I will speak with Auntie Florence. She would be a perfect mistress for someone like Josephine."

"Does she have room in her household?"

"Does Josephine have experience as a lady's maid?" Abby asked.

"Good God no!" Genie exclaimed. "She has experience cleaning, cooking, keeping her eyes and voice lowered, and doing exactly as she's told and nothing more."

"Auntie Florence could help her," Abby said, "and I think she'd like to. I'll go see her tomorrow." Abby then gave her a shrewd look. "And what else is on your beautiful, brilliant mind?"

"You know me too well, Abigail."

"I hardly know you at all, Eugenia, but I certainly am enjoying the learning."

"Will you also ask her if she knows whether we are citizens in Canada?"

The question caught Abby by surprise. "Maggie said everyone had decided to wait—"

Genie nodded quickly. "We did, but we need to know. We can't fly away to Canada only to find ourselves in the same situation."

Abby agreed with her and promised to learn the answer, but her face was wrinkled in a frown. "We would take Eli, wouldn't we? And would Ezra and Donald want to go?"

"We certainly would take Eli. As for Ezra and Donnie, I don't know, Abby," said Genie and told her about all of the conversations she'd had that day.

"Am I invited to Joe Joseph's Restaurant as well?"

"Of course you are! We could never have such an important meeting without you," Genie said. "And wait until you taste the food!"

"I'm looking forward to it. And to meeting Rev. Richard Allen—" She suddenly stopped talking and looked worried. "What will Adelaide say?"

"Welcome to my home, Mistress Read," Adelaide said. "It is a pleasure to meet you."

"The pleasure is mine, Mrs. Tillman," Abby said, taking Adelaide's hands in hers. "I have heard so many wonderful things about you. Genie holds you in very high esteem."

Adelaide was almost won over—but not quite—but good manners required her to greet her other guests. Ezra, handsome and polite as always, was easy. Donald and Eli, however, were like letting two overgrown puppies into the house. Just as Adelaide was feeling overwhelmed by them William came to her rescue, leading the two puppies to the one thing he knew would make them happy: cake. Adelaide returned her attention to Abby just in time to watch the startling blue eyes seek out and find Genie. She did not know what to make of what she saw, and the knock on the door and the arrival of the Junipers deprived her of time to think about it.

"Thank you all for coming," William said, starting the meeting. "We're here because Joe Joseph says there is considerable . . . unrest in his clientele—"

"People is scared and mad and gettin' mean," Arthur growled, interrupting William.

William nodded. "And because of that, he didn't think it wise for us to have a group that included white people. Ezra, Donald, Mistress Read—I am sorry for that."

"We are the ones who are sorry," Ezra said, "and we will leave your home immediately if our presence endangers you."

William raised his hands. "You do not, Ezra—"

Arthur interrupted him again. "You all ain't the people who bring harm and danger to us, Ezra. You and Donald and Mistress Read, you all have showed yourselfs to be good friends."

"And we always will be, Arthur, and that's a promise," Abby said quietly.

"And I know that to be a promise that will be kept," Jack Juniper said, and the words were barely out of his mouth when a knock on the door galvanized them. Jack, a revolver suddenly in his hand, was at the front door in an instant. Genie and Arthur, similarly armed, took up a position at the back door. William stood behind Jack at the front door and inquired who was knocking.

"Peter and Catherine," he said to his guests. Jack backed up a step to allow William to open the door to the watchmaker and his wife, but when the door was closed, he remained there instead of resuming his place beside Maggie, just as Genie and Arthur remained near the back door. Ezra then joined Jack near the front door while Donnie joined Genie and Arthur. Eli stood behind Abby who pretended not to see the revolver in the waist-band of his trousers.

William introduced the only man who was a stranger to them—the lawyer who was there to explain in detail the ramifications of the Dred Scott decision handed down by the Supreme Court barely a week ago. However, even without his scholarly discourse, it was clear that every person in the room understood the gravity of the situation, and the peril their lives were in. The lawyer spoke clearly and quietly, but with great sadness: He, too, was in as much danger as was every Colored person in the room. As was every Colored person in the United States of America. "One of the things this decision does is nullify the Missouri Compromise. That means there no longer is such a thing as Free States and Slave States. We are citizens in no states. We have no rights in any state, in any place in this country." The lawyer held up a sheaf of papers. "This now is the law of the land. We are not citizens. We have no rights."

The silence was frightening in its heaviness. How much did despair and hopelessness weigh? Maggie couldn't see her husband in his position as guardian of the front door but she addressed him anyway. "You were right, Jack. We should leave for Canada immediately."

"Can Colored people be citizens in Canada, sir?" Abby inquired of the lawyer.

"There is no law against it," the lawyer replied. "Nothing like this," he said, holding up the copy of the Scott decision. "And slavery was abolished in Canada more than thirty years ago."

More silence, into which Ezra said, "I have heard much talk of war, sir, as a result of this awful decision. Is war possible?"

The lawyer rubbed his side whiskers then nodded. "The Northern states hate this decision as much as the Southern states love it. Even here in Philadelphia there is a resistance building."

"So . . . should we wait a little while to see if changes are possible?" Maggie asked.

"There are those who think . . ." Abby hesitated, unsure whether to complete the thought. "I have heard it said that war is imminent and inevitable, that it is the only way to resolve the conflict over slavery."

"I, too, have heard as much," Ezra said. "Already some of the southern states talk of withdrawing from the Union."

"How would they do that? Just declare that they no longer belong to the United States?"

"They would go to war against the United States," Ezra said, "and if they won, they could make slavery legal everywhere."

"But they're part of the United States!" William exclaimed.

"They would call themselves something else," Ezra said. "The Southern States of America. Or something like that."

Genie was quiet and thoughtful for a while. Then she said, "Then certainly if there is a war we will go to Canada."

"Will we wait to see who wins?" Abby asked.

Genie shook her head. "That's a chance I would not want to take. If we're on the losing side, then it would be too late."

"If this war happens," Donald said, standing at attention, "I will fight on the side that is fighting slavery." Then he looked at the lawyer. "And I'm not an American citizen, either."

"I am," Ezra said, "and I, too, will fight against slavery."

"As will I!" Jack Juniper exclaimed. "If our side wins, then maybe we'll be citizens."

"Me, too!" Eli said.

William, Peter Blanding and the lawyer stood and went to

shake the hands of the four men who had vowed to fight against slavery—three of them too old to join any army but who would continue to support the cause in any way possible. Arthur, who would not be accepted into any army because of his physical impairment, also shook the hands of the men who would risk their lives if there was war to secure his freedom. He looked from Maggie Juniper to Eugenia Oliver to Abigail Read. Somebody would have to make certain that these women traveled safely to Canada. That, then, would be his task, one he would die for if necessary.

"Wings," Abby said.

"To fly away," Genie said.

ABOUT THE AUTHOR

Penny Mickelbury is a pioneering newspaper, radio and television journalist, a career spent primarily in Washington, D.C. She is a teacher of both children (at a Los Angeles Charter Middle School) and adults (in the Los Angeles Public Library's Adult Literacy Program). And, she is an award-winning playwright and a co-founder of Alchemy: Theatre of Change, a New York-based young people's acting company. She is the recipient of the Audre Lorde Estate Grant, and she was a resident writer at the Hedgebrook Women Writers Retreat.

Penny loves mystery and history in equal measures. She is the author of The Mimi Patterson/Gianna Maglione Mystery Series (twice short-listed for the Lambda Literary Award), the Carole Ann Gibson Mysteries (winner of a Gold Pen Award by the Black Writers Alliance), and the Phil Rodriquez Mysteries. She has also authored the historical fiction novels, *Belle City* and *Two Wings to Fly Away*. Penny has contributed short stories to several mystery collections, including *Spooks, Spies and Private Eyes*, *The Mysterious Naiad*, and *Send My Love and a Molotov Cocktail!*. And, in March 2019, BLF Press published her short story collection, *God's Will and Other Lies*.

The love of history and mystery combine to keep Penny busy at her computer: She is well into Book #6 of The Mimi Patterson/Gianna Maglione Mystery Series, and will follow that with a sequel to *Two Wings to Fly Away.*

ACKNOWLEDGMENTS

Writing a novel is a solitary pursuit, one that is made so much more comfortable, however, when the writer can feel the support at her back. I write knowing that the women of Bywater Books have my back. Thank you Salem West, Marianne K. Martin, Ann McMan, Kelly Smith, Fay Jacobs, Nancy Squires, and Elizabeth Andersen for your constant presence.

At Bywater Books we love good books about lesbians just like you do, and we're committed to bringing the best of contemporary lesbian writing to our avid readers. Our editorial team is dedicated to finding and developing outstanding writers who create books you won't want to put down.

We sponsor the Bywater Prize for Fiction to help with this quest. Each prizewinner receives $1,000 and publication of their novel. We have already discovered amazing writers like Jill Malone, Sally Bellerose, and Hilary Sloin through the Bywater Prize. Which exciting new writer will we find next?

For more information about Bywater Books and the annual Bywater Prize for Fiction, please visit our website.

www.bywaterbooks.com

CPSIA information can be obtained
at www.ICGtesting.com
Printed in the USA
LVHW092148160819
627986LV00003B/3/P